**"It's awful, what that**

"It's all right." Abigail put her glass down on the floor to pat Theo's arm. "Really."

"No, it's not. He ought to be horsewhipped for breaking your heart like that."

"But I'm all right now. Maybe I was deluding myself all along. Or maybe I'm just a terrible judge of character. I thought that Henry was honorable and trustworthy and loyal, but he wasn't. In the end, he wasn't remotely the man that I thought. And how could I truly love a man I didn't know?" She knitted her brows together. "Now I feel like I'm in mourning for everything that could have been as well as for my father."

"Just because he wasn't the man for you doesn't mean that love isn't out there." Theo's voice sounded huskier.

"Maybe it is, but even if I met someone else, how would I know that I wasn't just fooling myself all over again?" She tossed her head. "No. I refuse to believe in love stories and fairy tales anymore. From now on, I intend to rely on myself. Then I know who I can trust."

"That sounds lonely."

"Says the man who has no intention of marrying."

## Author Note

One piece of writing advice I really struggle with is the need to make my characters suffer. I know it's what I'm *supposed* to do because stories need tension and conflict and character arcs, but the problem is that I usually like my characters too much. I want them to live their best lives and be happy, preferably with a dysfunctional family, some cake and a dog. So in this story, I've tried to solve that problem by getting (most of) the suffering over with early. Poor Abigail and Theo are both in miserable situations at the start of the book. She's alone, penniless and jilted, while he's burdened with his irresponsible brother's debts, family drama and mountains of paperwork. Fortunately, things can only get better when he hires her as a secretary/companion/governess, which is the way I like things to be. I'm a big believer in the romance genre as a source of hope and positivity, so I hope this book leaves you with a smile. Thanks for picking it up.

# JENNI FLETCHER

---

Cinderella's Deal
with the Colonel

Recycling programs for this product may not exist in your area.

ISBN-13: 978-1-335-72391-8

Cinderella's Deal with the Colonel

Copyright © 2023 by Jenni Fletcher

For questions and comments about the quality of this book, please contact us at CustomerService@Harlequin.com.

Harlequin Enterprises ULC
22 Adelaide St. West, 41st Floor
Toronto, Ontario M5H 4E3, Canada
www.Harlequin.com

Printed in U.S.A.

**Jenni Fletcher** was born in the north of Scotland and now lives in Yorkshire with her husband and two children. She wanted to be a writer as a child but became distracted by reading instead, finally getting past her first paragraph thirty years later. She's had more jobs than she can remember but has finally found one she loves. She can be contacted on Twitter, @jenniauthor, or via her Facebook author page.

## Books by Jenni Fletcher

### Harlequin Historical

*Tudor Christmas Tidings*
*"Secrets of the Queen's Lady"*
*A Marriage Made in Secret*
*Snow-Kissed Proposals*
*"The Christmas Runaway"*
*Cinderella's Deal with the Colonel*

### Regency Belles of Bath

*An Unconventional Countess*
*Unexpectedly Wed to the Officer*
*The Duke's Runaway Bride*
*The Shopgirl's Forbidden Love*

### Highland Alliances

*The Highlander's Tactical Marriage*

### Sons of Sigurd

*Redeeming Her Viking Warrior*

### Secrets of a Victorian Household

*Miss Amelia's Mistletoe Marquess*

Visit the Author Profile page
at Harlequin.com for more titles.

For Mum

# Chapter One

*Mayfair, London—March 1816*

'There was a letter from the marquess, sir. I'm afraid that her ladyship was rather upset.'

*Upset?*

Colonel Lord Theodore Marshall stood in the second drawing room of Salway House, regarding the ruin of his brother's portrait with a stoical eye. If this was upset, then he didn't want to know what angry looked like, although he suspected that he was about to find out. The large red wine stain over Fitzwilliam's face was dramatic enough, but the jagged gash running all the way from the centre of his chest down to what could only be politely described as his nether regions looked particularly vicious. Not that he personally gave a damn. Frankly, his brother deserved that gash and in that precise area, too.

'You can't say she's not thorough.' He glanced downwards, to where droplets of wine were already soaking into the carpet. 'Just out of interest, what kind of weapon did she use?'

'A poker, sir.' The butler, Possett, crossed his legs.

'A poker?' Theo let out a low whistle. 'I only went out for an hour.'

'Indeed, sir. Unfortunately, the letter arrived just a few minutes after you left. We attempted to restrain her at first, but to be honest, I feared for the footmen's safety. She struck me as somewhat…ah…dangerous.'

A shrill cry followed by a splintering sound from a neighbouring room seconded the butler's opinion. Whatever his sister-in-law was destroying now, Theo reflected, her temper was obviously still in control. He'd never heard a person make so much noise, even on the battlefield. She sounded like some kind of Celtic berserker. Frankly, he could have used more soldiers like her.

'This house has a way of bringing out the worst in people.' He raised his voice over the din. 'I don't suppose you know what was in the letter?'

'I'm afraid not, sir, although it came from Bristol.'

'Bristol?' His heart sank.

'Yes, sir.'

'You're certain?'

'I'm afraid so.'

'Bloody hell.'

'My thoughts exactly, sir.'

Theo rubbed a hand over his forehead, reluctantly allowing the implications to sink in. So that was that. Fitzwilliam hadn't just run away for a week or two, as they'd all initially hoped. He'd actually fled the country, leaving a huge pile of steaming mess in his wake, and there was no one else to clear it up except *him*.

For the time being at least, he was trapped there, bound by honour to stay in a role and a place he detested. So much for a fleeting visit before travelling on to America. He could practically feel the walls of the house closing in around him. All of which meant that the sooner he spoke with his sister-in-law, the better.

At that moment, he was prepared to exchange every single one of his medals for bravery and valour for somebody else to do it.

'Do you know, Possett...?' He gestured towards the painting, attempting to delay the inevitable. 'I think I actually met the artist. He was struggling to get his easel out of a cab as I went down the front steps one morning.'

'You have an excellent memory, sir. That must be ten years ago now.'

'Nine years and eight months, the same day I left to join my regiment. Still, he did a decent job, even if the results have ultimately been wasted. It's a good like-ness.'

'Indeed, sir. Although, if you'll permit me to say so, I always thought it looked rather more like you.'

'Me?' Theo turned his head in surprise. For most of his youth, various family members had taken delight in commenting upon the many differences between him-self and his older brother. Whereas Fitzwilliam had been tall, dark and handsome from a young age, with eye-catching features and a charismatic, risk-taking per-sonality, he'd been the polar opposite—small, shy and cautious, with average features, sandy-coloured hair, overly intense blue eyes and a tendency to blend into the background. Definitely not, as his father would tell anyone who cared to listen, marquess material—thank goodness that Fitzwilliam had been born first, et cetera.

Unexpectedly for everyone, himself included, how-

ever, a few things had changed since his sixteenth birthday, that event appearing to have triggered some kind of
delayed growth spurt. Almost overnight, he'd stretched
and broadened and eventually *out*grown his brother,
much to said brother's chagrin and, after an admittedly
rough start, his years in the army had given him a new-
found independence and confidence, too. Still, in most
outward respects, he was exactly the same as he'd always been, give or take a scar or two. If Possett thought
otherwise, then he was in dire need of spectacles.

'It's in the expression, sir.' The butler appeared non-
plussed. 'It's rather noble. Nothing remotely like his
lordship.'

'Good grief, Possett. That sounds like insubordi-
nation.'

'Does it, sir? My apologies. It was intended as a
compliment.'

'I didn't say I objected. I just didn't know you had
it in you.'

'Neither did I, sir. However, I'm afraid that the canvas may be irreparable. Such a waste. His lordship was
very fond of this portrait.'

'Then he should have taken it with him.' Theo winced
as something shattered close by. 'I really ought to go
and speak with her.'

'I've been hoping you would, sir. I hate to mention
the...ah...financial circumstances, but some of the
items she's destroying are rather valuable.'

'Naturally.' He pinched the bridge of his nose between his thumb and forefinger. 'I'm starting to think
the pair of them are as bad as each other. Just give me
a moment to regroup.'

'Of course, sir. Should I gather a few of the footmen?'

'No, it's probably best if I go alone.'

'Are you certain that's wise?' Possett sounded alarmed. 'She may still have the poker.'

'Ah. On second thoughts, have them wait nearby just in case.'

'Very good, sir.'

'This feels like Waterloo all over again.'

He took a deep breath and spun around, resolving to get the scene with his sister-in-law over with, poker or no poker, then muttered an oath as he almost collided with a young woman standing immediately behind him.

'Evelyn.' He tried to look pleased rather than alarmed by his niece's sudden, spectral appearance. During the ten years of his absence, the sweet little girl he remembered appeared to have given up smiling in favour of a preternatural ability to creep up on people and glare at them. 'What are you doing here?'

'A gentleman shouldn't swear, uncle Theo.' A pair of belligerent hazel-green eyes, framed by a mass of auburn hair, stared up at him reprovingly. 'Especially in front of young ladies.'

'In my defence, I had no idea any were present.' He gritted his teeth. 'I was just going to speak with your mother.'

'She had a letter from papa.'

'So I've just discovered.' He quirked an eyebrow. 'I don't suppose you know what—?'

'Yes. She threw it on the floor for anyone to pick up and read. It says that he's leaving the country, he's not coming back and that we ought to forget him.' Evelyn lifted her shoulders. 'So I already have.'

'I see.' Briefly, Theo considered patting his niece's arm and murmuring something comforting along the lines of 'there, there' before dismissing the idea as too dangerous. The resemblance to her mother at that moment was far too uncanny. He got the impression that she might actually rip his hand off.

'Why is mama breaking things?' A smaller, softer voice asked before he could decide on a safer course of action.

'Florence?'

'I already told you.' Evelyn rolled her eyes. 'Because father's gone. He doesn't want us any more.'

'That's not the reason.' Theo crouched down, waiting until a round face, surrounded by a more coppery shade of red hair, peered out from behind her sister's back. 'I'm afraid that your father's got into some trouble with money. A lot of people are unhappy with him.'

'So he had to go away?'

Theo paused tactfully. His brother hadn't *had* to do anything. He might have found himself on the receiving end of some disapproving scowls and comments from investors at his club. He might even, considering the extent of his financial collapse, have found it expedient to retire to the country for a year or five, but he was still a marquess. In the end, people generally forgave the aristocracy their mistakes, but his brother was a coward and so he'd run away. As plans of action went, he had to admit, it was decidedly tempting. Still, it was kinder sometimes not to tell the whole truth, especially to seven-year-old girls.

'Yes, he had to go away, but it's nothing to do with you, I promise.'

Florence nodded sombrely and then brightened. 'At least Miss Calder will look after him.'

'Who?'

'Miss Calder, our governess.' Evelyn waited until he stood up again before unleashing the full force of her most withering glare. 'She's gone, too. We've been waiting for mama to notice.'

*The governess*... He bit back another oath. And there it was, the final nail in the coffin, the proof, as if he hadn't known it already, that when it came to matrimony, the men in his family were doomed. Actually, no, he corrected himself, it was worse than that. They were like poison, slowly but inevitably destroying the very person they were supposed to love. No wonder his sister-in-law was destroying things. She was just the last in a long line of miserable wives, the newest victim of a Marshall husband. If there had been a bayonet to hand, he would have been sorely tempted to stick it in his brother's portrait himself.

# Chapter Two

*Holborn, London—two weeks later*

It was a curious experience, Abigail Lemon reflected, to be happy, secure and full of hope for the future one month and impoverished, homeless and feeling as if you were plummeting downwards into a never-ending chasm the next.

She closed her eyes, recalling an outing she'd taken with her father to Astley's Amphitheatre the year before. Of all the circus performers, the ones that had stuck in her mind the most had been the tightrope walkers, daring men and women performing their dangerous stunts high above the stage. That was exactly how she felt at that moment, she realised, like a tightrope walker—one who'd spent the past few days teetering precariously on a rope she hadn't even known existed and whose foot had finally slipped.

For a few seconds, she wondered if she was about to faint, but of course she didn't because her practical brain wasn't about to let her off the hook so easily and really, she ought to be grateful to it because if she did faint then some useful person would no doubt thrust a vial of smelling salts under her nose and then she'd only have to wake up and face the whole situation all over again.

No, far better that she stay awake, chewing her already bitten-off fingernails, while her father's long-time solicitor, Mr Adams, explained just how completely and irrevocably her life had collapsed.

'I can't believe it.'

Her Aunt Louisa articulated what everyone was thinking—everyone consisting of Abigail herself, her father's two hard-faced sisters, Louisa and Eugenia, their harder-faced respective husbands, whose names momentarily escaped her, and five cousins, none of whom she'd ever met before, but whose profiles might have been carved from granite. It was like sitting in a room full of black-clad statues, only colder.

'Surely there's been some kind of mistake?' This from an uncle. Peregrine? Phinneas? Patrocles? Definitely something beginning with a P.

'I'm afraid not.' Mr Adams, the obviously reluctant bearer of bad tidings, glanced up from his paperwork and then down again quickly.

'But you summoned us here for the reading of my brother-in-law's will. A message like that implies some kind of inheritance.'

'Pardon me, but I invited my client's surviving relatives to a meeting *regarding* his will. I mentioned nothing about an inheritance.'

'So there's really nothing left?'

'Financially, I'm afraid not. There is, however, a message.'

'What message?' Abigail jerked her head upright, then instantly regretted it as she caught a glimpse of

her reflection in the window behind the desk. The tor-
rential downpour outside made it dark enough for her
to see every haggard detail, from her sunken cheeks
to her bloodless skin that now seemed to merge seam-
lessly into her once-flaxen, now sallow-looking hair.

'It was written a number of years ago.' Mr Adams
looked at her kindly before picking up yet another piece
of paper. 'To my dear sisters Louisa and Eugenia. I
know that our paths have separated over the years, but
I write this letter to throw myself upon your mercy and
goodwill. It has long been my fear that, should anything
happen to me, my poor daughter will be all alone in the
world. Therefore, I beg you to take her in—'

'What?' Aunt Eugenia practically leapt across the
table, wrenching the paper from his hands. 'But this
is preposterous! First he loses all his money and now
he expects us to open our homes to a penniless girl!'

'Penniless woman,' Abigail corrected. 'You forget,
I'm twenty-two.'

'Exactly! And engaged to be married next month!'
Aunt Louisa sounded triumphant. 'Surely your fiancé
will take care of you? There's no need for us to be involved.'

'But naturally the wedding will need to be delayed
while Miss Abigail is in mourning,' Mr Adams objected,
'and she can hardly live with her fiancé in the meantime.'

There was a long silence, punctuated only by the
tapping of rain against the window.

'Perhaps I haven't been clear?' Mr Adams looked
around the room, searching in vain for a friendly face.
'The bank wishes to take possession of the house by
the end of the week.'

'Perhaps her mother's family?' Aunt Eugenia suggested.

'She was an only child, like me.' Abigail stood up, deciding that enough was enough. It was both instructive and humiliating to know exactly where she stood, which was apparently outside on the street on her own. 'However, please don't concern yourselves. The end of the week gives me five days to make alternative arrangements.'

'Well said.' Aunt Louisa swept to her feet so fast that Abigail caught the draught from her skirts. 'Although I must say, I feel quite deceived. We came all the way from Wimbledon for this.'

'But, Mrs Hepworth, your brother—' Mr Adams looked appalled.

'My brother was a fool. What kind of man invests the entire of his fortune in some high-stakes building enterprise without making any contingency plan for if it fails? I'm sorry for the situation, but in my opinion, people ought to clear up their own mistakes and not expect others to do it for them.'

'My father was a good man.' Abigail curled her fingernails into her palms. 'But you're right about one thing. People *should* clear up their own mistakes and since we've just established that your coming here today was one, I suggest that you remedy the situation immediately and leave!'

'I say!' A random cousin stepped forward.

*'Do you?'* Abigail swung towards him. 'Because it seems to me that the rest of you haven't said much at all. You only came here to see what you could get.'

'Well!' Aunt Eugenia tilted her head so far back that

Abigail could see down her nostrils. 'I wish you well, my dear, despite your impertinence.'

'And I hope that your carriage leaks on the journey home. Good day!'

She folded her arms, waiting until the sound of footsteps and indignant muttering had faded away before turning back to face Mr Adams. 'I'm sorry.'

'No need to apologise.' The solicitor's brow furrowed. 'I knew that your father wasn't close to his sisters, but I never expected them to be quite so cold-hearted.'

'He always said that when it came to the milk of human kindness, they only had a few drops between them.'

'If you ask me, they're bone dry. The ironic part is that his will, as written, left them with five thousand pounds each. You would have received the remainder of the estate if...'

'If there had been anything left,' she finished sadly. 'Thank you for coming today. I appreciate it, although I'm afraid it seems I can't pay you.'

'Think nothing of it. This is a terrible situation. I advised your father against the building scheme, but he was insistent.'

'He was always too optimistic for his own good.' She hesitated and then went on. 'Mr Adams, forgive me, but if I ask you a question, will you promise to give me an honest answer?'

'Of course.'

'Thank you.' She clasped her hands together. 'Earlier you said that my father invested in this scheme seventeen months ago, just before I became engaged. Was that *why* he invested? To raise enough money for my dowry?'

'I believe it was a contributing factor, yes. If the scheme had succeeded, the returns would have been considerable.'

'And he knew that Henry's parents would never consent to our marriage without the promise of a sizeable dowry.' She heard her knuckles crack. 'I wondered how he was able to offer so large an amount. I begged him to tell me, but he never would.'

'It's not your fault.'

'But if it hadn't been for my engagement, he wouldn't have risked so much?'

'Probably not.'

'And it was the shock of the scheme's collapse that killed him?'

'We don't know that for certain.'

'Given that they both happened on the same day, I believe that we do. The newspaper was open on the table when I found him. I wondered if it was connected somehow, but I never imagined…'

'You mustn't blame yourself, my dear. No one could have taken better care of your father than you did.' Mr Adams reached for his briefcase. 'I wonder if, given your aunts' reaction, your fiancé's family might be more welcoming?'

'I doubt it. Without a dowry, they might not want to see me again at all.'

'But surely they won't withdraw their consent for your marriage now?' Mr Adams shook his head gravely. 'I wish that your fiancé had been here today so we might have discussed the matter.'

'He had another appointment, but don't worry, Henry will stand by me.' Despite the circumstances, she felt her spirits lift again at the words. Yes, she might be plummeting, but Henry was her safety net. He would catch her.

'Good.' Mr Adams sounded relieved. 'And of course there's your mother's old cottage. As part of her dowry, it came to you directly rather than forming part of your father's estate. Obviously the building itself is uninhabitable, but the land still has value. You could sell it.'

'No.' She didn't hesitate. 'I couldn't.'

'But it hasn't been lived in for years.'

'I know. It's a wreck, but it's all I have left of her.' She glanced pointedly towards the small, oval-shaped painting of a cottage on the mantelpiece.

'I understand. As for today, I truly wish there was more I could do.'

'You've done more than enough as it is. Goodbye, Mr Adams.'

She watched him go, wrapping her arms around her waist for comfort as she stood alone in her father's old office. Everything looked so familiar and yet so alien now. The old walnut desk, scuffed at one corner, the bookcases groaning beneath the combined weight of his beloved Walter Scotts, the Aubusson rug where she'd spent so many hours playing as a child. So many memories, so many objects that now belonged to the bank.

She turned away and went to stand beside the window, gazing out at the rain instead. It was practically blowing sideways now, as if the water was trying to force its way through the glass.

'Where is everyone?' Her father's cook, Mrs Jessop, stuck her head around the door. 'I was just coming to offer tea.'

'Gone.'

'You mean they've left you alone on a day like this? Villains! Heartless villains!'

'I think you might be right.' Abigail laughed weakly. 'They appeared to think the whole thing was a waste of time.'

'Your father didn't leave them any money, then? Good.'

'There was no money to leave.'

'What?'

'Unfortunately, poor father invested all of his savings in some kind of fool-proof building scheme, only, needless to say, it wasn't. So it's all gone. I've no fortune, no family and I need to leave by Friday.'

'No!'

'Yes.' She pulled her shoulders back as her voice cracked. 'I need to go and tell Henry what's happened.'

'In this weather? You'd be better off taking a boat than walking. Send one of the footmen with a note.'

'I can't ask the footmen to do anything, not when I can't pay them, but don't worry, I won't be long.'

'Mind you aren't in this rain.' Mrs Jessop tutted emphatically. 'But if you really must go, tell that man to marry you sooner rather than later! It's what your father would have wanted.'

'Do you really think so?' Abigail stopped halfway across the room. 'Mr Adams said—'

'Mr Adams didn't know your father like I did. All he ever wanted was for you to be safe and happy. So go and marry that handsome fiancé of yours and live happily ever after. You deserve it.'

She ought to have listened to Mrs Jessop, Abigail thought, sheltering beneath a bandstand in an otherwise deserted park. The March sky was bleak, a miserable swathe of grey, and the rain was incessant. Her umbrella was already waterlogged enough to be useless and her damp skirts were plastered to her legs like a second, extremely clammy, skin. The whole situation struck her as horribly ominous. She'd assured Mr Adams and Mrs Jessop that Henry would stand by her, but what if...?

'Abigail!'

She spun around at the sound of his voice, swallowing her doubts as she raced across the bandstand to greet him.

'What's happened? What's the matter?' He folded her into his arms on the top step. 'My doorman said you told him it was urgent.'

'It is.' She pressed her cheek against the collar of his greatcoat. It was scandalous for them to be embracing so closely in public, but there was no one around and honestly, after that morning, she didn't care. His voice was so full of concern, she felt foolish for having doubted him, even for a moment. Everything was going to be all right now. They had each other, they were in love and they'd find a way through this together.

'Abbie?' He moved his hands to her waist. 'Nice as this is, I can hardly bear the suspense.'

'Of course. Sorry...' She took a deep breath. 'You know that it was my father's will-reading this morning?'

'That was today? Darling, I'm so sorry, I completely forgot. I wish I could have been there for you.'

'It's all right. I'm not sure I would have wanted you to meet my aunts anyway.'

'Were they very awful?' He pressed a kiss to her forehead. 'Fortunately, I have some good news.'

'Really? I could use some of that.'

'The horses were just as fine as the man said.'

'Horses?' She blinked. 'What horses?'

'The ones I went to look at. It took some haggling, but I got them in the end.'

'I thought you said you had an important appointment that couldn't be moved?'

'I did. The owner was threatening to sell them to someone else if I didn't go today. I'm sure I told you about it.'

'You didn't.' She took a step backwards. 'Henry, it was my father's will-reading. *That* was important.'

'You just said you were glad that I *didn't* meet your aunts.' He reached for her hands, a note of impatience in his voice. 'Now tell me what all this urgency is about? Whatever it is, it can't be worth us freezing to death in the rain for.'

'My fortune is gone.' She didn't even try to cushion the blow.

'What?' His face blanched.

'Father invested all of his money in some building scheme that collapsed.'

'But when you say all, surely you don't mean—?'

'All? Yes. Ow!' She yelped as his grip on her fingers tightened. 'Henry, you're hurting me.'

'What? Oh.' He released her at once. 'Forgive me, but why on earth would your father do something so reckless?'

'For my dowry.' Guilt stabbed her so hard she could hardly get the words out. 'For us.'

'So you're saying that it's my fault?'

'What? No, of course not.'

'That's what you just implied.'

'But it wasn't what I meant.' She held on to his gaze

as a blast of cold air swept through the bandstand. She'd always loved his eyes. They were so unique, green in the middle, brown around the edges, the first thing she'd noticed about him when they'd met three years before. Kind eyes. Thoughtful eyes. Eyes you could trust...or so she'd always believed.

If life were a romance, it occurred to her that this would be the moment he'd take her face in his hands and tell her that money didn't matter, then summon a carriage to whisk them away to Gretna Green and a future of conjugal bliss. Real life, however, wasn't a romance—a fact that was becoming more and more obvious with every passing second.

'Henry?' she whispered when the silence became unbearable.

'I need to speak with my parents.' His gaze slid away from hers. 'They'll be very distressed.'

'Distressed?' She gave a short laugh. 'How awful for them.'

'It was good of them to give their permission for our marriage in the first place.'

'Given my lack of useful connections and barely adequate fortune? Yes, I know, they've only mentioned those facts a hundred times since we got engaged.'

'Abbie.' His voice turned chiding. 'It's not like you to be shrewish.'

'What do you expect?' She flung her arms out. 'I'm cold and wet and, in case you've forgotten, my father died two weeks ago.'

'Of course I haven't forgotten, but you have to see the situation from their point of view. They only agreed to our marriage on condition of a ten-thousand-pound dowry.'

'What about *our* point of view? Henry, we've proven how much we love each other. It's been three years! Surely they'll appreciate that? And if they don't...' She hesitated before playing her last card. 'Isn't love more important than money?'

'Yes, in principle, but if I go through with our marriage against their wishes, they'll disown me, you know that. We need to be practical.'

'We will! We'll earn our own money if necessary.'

'Earn?' He looked as horrified as if she'd just asked him to strip naked and start running laps of the park. 'I'll be a baronet some day. I can't *work*.'

'I see.' She touched a hand to her head, feeling as if she were falling again. Only this time, there was no safety net. Or if there was, then it had a giant, Henry-shaped hole in the centre.

'I'm sorry, truly. You know how much I love you, but without a dowry...' There was an eloquent pause. 'If only your father hadn't invested in that scheme.'

'Don't you dare blame him!' Abigail picked up her umbrella and pointed the tip accusingly. 'You know, I'm starting to think that you and my aunts have a great deal in common. Now, if you'll excuse me, I'm going home.'

'Wait!' He stepped in front of her as she made to leave. 'About our engagement... Obviously, as a man of honour, I can't end it myself.'

'Meaning you'd like me to do it for you?' She glared at him scornfully before wrenching the glove off her left hand and removing the emerald ring from her second finger. 'I thought it was implied, but just to be clear, consider yourself released.'

'Keep the ring.'

'No!'

'Please. It's the least I can do.'

She hesitated, pressing her lips together tightly. Somehow it had become a day of confrontations. Last time, she'd let her pride win. This time, she had to be practical, no matter how strong the temptation to throw the ring in his face. Beggars couldn't be choosers and he was right—after three years of waiting and loving, it was the least he could do.

'Very well. Goodbye, Henry.'

'Take care of yourself, Abigail. You know I—'

She didn't hear the rest, marching down the band-stand steps and out into the rain.


'Well?' Mrs Jessop turned away from the stove expectantly as Abigail trudged down the back stairs. 'How did it go?'

'Even worse than this morning.' She shook her head wearily. 'Suffice to say, I'm no longer engaged.'

'Don't tell me he broke it off?'

'Oh, no, he was very careful not to impugn his own honour. I did it for him. You know, the funny part is that he still says he loves me. He didn't ask me where I was going to live or what on, but he still says he loves me.'

'Villain!' Mrs Jessop smacked a hand on the table. 'Another villain!'

'I must be a terrible judge of character. I really thought I could trust him.'

'Poor dear.' The cook opened her arms. 'What you need is a good cry.'

'I know. I want to. The tears are all in here, but it's like they're trapped.' She rested her cheek gratefully on the cook's shoulder. 'You know who I'd really like to give a piece of my mind? The Marquess of Salway!'

'Another villain.'

'The worst! If it hadn't been for him, none of this would have happened. You can be sure he hasn't lost *his* house. Do you know, a peer can't even be declared bankrupt. How fair is that?'

'It's not. They're all villains, preying on decent men like your father. The *ton*. I'd like to spit on the whole lot of them.'

'So would I!' Abigail lifted her head again. 'In fact, that's what I'm going to do. Where are the eggs?'

'What?' Mrs Jessop sounded nervous suddenly. 'Why?'

'Because pelting him with them would make me feel a thousand times better.'

'You can't pelt a marquess with eggs!'

'Why not? What can he possibly do to me that hasn't already happened?'

'He could have you arrested.'

'Oh. All right, no eggs, but I'm still going. I refuse to sit here like some heartbroken milksop. All of this is his fault and he ought to make some kind of amends.' She shook her head. 'You know, I hate confrontation, but it's all I seem to be doing today.'

'Maybe you ought to sleep on it?'

'No. I might calm down then.'

'At least change your clothes. The last thing we need on top of everything else is for you to catch a chill.'

'There's no point. I'll only get them wet again.' She stormed towards the back door. 'I'm going to confront the Marquess of Salway and I don't care what he or any other man thinks of me!'

## Chapter Three

'What is it, Possett?' Theo looked up from a ledger filled with his brother's near-indecipherable scrawling as the butler cleared his throat in the doorway.

'My apologies for disturbing you, sir, but there's a person at the door asking to see his lordship.'

'Do you know what about?'

'Unfortunately not. She claims that it's private business.'

'She?' He groaned and slammed the ledger shut impatiently. Women! He was surrounded with them! Well, three anyway—and even if one sister-in-law and two nieces didn't exactly constitute an overwhelming force, they still took a significant amount of adapting to after ten years of almost exclusively male company— and now here was another of the species come to visit his brother on 'private business', whatever the hell that meant. He wasn't certain he wanted to know, but he supposed that he ought to see her, if only to apologise for whatever terrible thing that Fitz had undoubtedly done.

'Very well, Possett. Send her in.'

'Are you sure, sir?'

'I was.' He quirked an eyebrow. 'Why? Don't you think I should see her?'

'Truth be told, sir. I'm afraid that she may not be entirely respectable.'

'Really?' He leaned back in his chair, steepling his fingers beneath his chin. 'Any particular reason?'

'She's come alone, sir, without even a maid.' The butler sniffed. 'And she's making a puddle in the hallway.'

'Good grief, why?'

'It's raining, sir. It has been all day.'

'*All* day?' He frowned, momentarily disoriented, although a puddle of rainwater was infinitely preferable to what had first sprung to mind. 'What time is it, Possett?'

'Four o'clock, sir.'

'Are you telling me that I've been sitting here for eight hours?'

'Indeed, sir.'

'What happened to lunch?'

'You ate it, sir. At your desk.'

'Did I?' He glanced at the empty plate and cup beside him, then at the carriage clock on the mantelpiece and finally at the window, surprised to find the butler right on all three counts. He'd been so engrossed in his work that he'd somehow lost a whole day. In terms of actual progress, however…half a day was probably optimistic.

'And you say that she asked for my brother specifically?'

'She did, sir.'

'Then presumably she must have thought that he'd see her?'

'Yes, but…'

'In which case, unless she intends to go off travelling around the world in search of him, I'll have to do.'

'As you wish, sir.' Posset lowered his voice. 'Although perhaps you'd like me to stay in the room in case it's some kind of scheme? You know, the parson's mousetrap?'

For the first time in two weeks, Theo felt tempted to laugh. 'There isn't a piece of cheese big enough. The men in my family shouldn't be allowed to marry, you know that as well as I do. Anyway, she can hardly accuse me of compromising her when she's the one who came here alone. Send her in. And as for you…' He reached a hand under the desk to ruffle the pile of shaggy brown fur curled up at his feet. 'Stay where you are.'

He stood up and stretched, rubbing a hand over the small of his back to soothe the now-persistent ache there. He spent far too long hunched over a desk these days. If nothing else, he supposed he ought to be grateful to this woman, whoever she was, for the distraction.

Still rolling his shoulders, he moved around to the front of the desk as Possett led a bedraggled-looking woman into the study. Judging by the sodden state of her clothing, she'd walked there and from some distance, too. He was aware of a curvaceous figure that, as a gentleman, he had absolutely no business to notice, but damn it, in clothes that wet and clinging, it was impossible not to.

'Miss Abigail Lemon,' the butler intoned, disapproval evident in every syllable.

'An honour, Miss Lemon.' Theo inclined his head, making a supreme effort to keep his eyes on her face. 'I'm—'

'My lord,' she interrupted, striding across the carpet

before he had a chance to introduce himself. 'I'm here on behalf of my father, Mr Frederick Lemon.'

'I see.' He leaned sideways, looking around her at the butler's horrified expression. 'That will be all, thank you, Possett.'

'But, sir—'

'You may go.'

'But—'

'*Now*, Possett.'

He waited until the door had closed again before propping himself on a corner of the desk, trying to guess the woman's identity. She was standing barely an arm's length away, her pointed chin thrust forward combatively, although the way she was panting suggested a degree of nervousness, too. An angry mistress? No, since she clearly had no idea who he was, or more specifically, *wasn't*. A disgruntled employee? Also no. Her clothes, albeit soaking, were far too good for that. Some kind of business associate? Absolutely not, since his brother had very definite ideas about where women belonged.

Her tired complexion and shadow-ringed eyes made it difficult to guess her age, too. Uncharitable as it sounded, she might have been anywhere between eighteen and forty. In short, she was a mystery. A mystery with the most lusciously well-rounded hips he'd ever seen.

'So...' He wrenched his eyes upwards again. 'Mr Frederick Lemon, you say?'

'Yes!' The woman's eyes flashed fire beneath her bonnet. In contrast to her pale hair and brows, they were dark, he noticed. It made for a striking contrast.

'Then you have me at a disadvantage. I'm afraid I'm not familiar with the name.'

'You're not—?' She surged closer, fists raised as if she wanted to strike him. 'You monster! You beast! You don't even know the names of the people you ruin!'

'Ah.' He rubbed a knuckle across his jaw. 'I believe that I'm beginning to understand the situation. Was your father an investor in the Chelsea building scheme by any chance?'

'The one that collapsed, yes! He lost everything.'

'And he sent you here on his behalf?'

'No.' Her fists fell again abruptly. 'He's dead. He died of a heart attack two weeks ago.'

'Two weeks ago?' he repeated the words softly. 'Then I'm sorry. Truly.'

'What use is that?' Her eyes shot back to his. 'I don't want your sympathy.'

'No, I suppose not, but you have it anyway.' He pushed himself up off the desk. 'Were you close?'

'Extremely.' She seemed surprised by the question.

'And your mother…?'

'Dead. She died when I was a child. I've no brothers or sisters either.'

'I see.' He drew his brows together. 'Miss Lemon, I honestly wish that I could give you your father's money back, but I'm afraid—'

'That's not why I'm here,' she interrupted again. 'My father went into the scheme with his eyes open. I wish he hadn't, but that's how business works and there's nothing I can do about it, I know.'

'Then…forgive me, but why *are* you here?'

'To tell you what I think of you!' She thrust her chin even higher. 'And to ask for—no, to *demand* your help. I'm not asking for charity, but I do believe that you owe me something.' She swallowed as if she were working her way up to something. 'The fact is, over the past week I've lost my father, my fortune and my…never mind, but soon I'll lose my home, too. I've no family I can go to and I can hardly ask my friends to give me a permanent home. In short, I need some kind of occupation or I shall be destitute.'

'Meaning you want me to find you a job?'

'Yes.' She nodded firmly. 'I'm not proud. I'm a fast learner and I'll do anything.'

'I wouldn't advertise that too widely if I were you.'

Her fists clenched again. 'Joke all you like, but I'm not leaving here until you help me.'

Theo clasped his hands behind his back, impressed despite himself. Not many people would march into the house of a marquess, call him a monster and then start issuing ultimatums. She was either mad or extremely brave. Or possibly, considering her waterlogged appearance and what she'd just told him, at the very end of her tether. None the less, he didn't appreciate threats.

'Miss Lemon.' He glanced pointedly towards the door. 'This house contains a veritable army of footmen. If I wanted, I could simply ask one of them to remove you.'

'I'm sure you could.' Her lip curled contemptuously. 'But I'd make a scene. They'd have to drag me out kicking and screaming.'

'Trust me, I'm accustomed to those, especially in this house.'

'Then it would be another mark on your conscience.' She pushed her face up to his. '*If* you have a conscience, that is.'

'I believe it's around here somewhere.' He tapped his

forehead with one finger. 'Out of interest, have you read the newspapers this morning, Miss Lemon?'

'No.' She paused. 'Why?'

'You might be interested, that's all.' He reached behind him and picked up a copy of *The Times*. 'Here.'

She gave him a suspicious look before turning her attention to the front page, her lips falling open as she read.

'The Marquess of Salway…collapsed scheme…left the country—' Her eyes seemed twice as large when she lifted them again. 'But aren't you—?'

'The Marquess of Salway? No.'

'But you said—' Her voice jumped up an octave. 'Didn't you?'

'Actually, no.' He clicked his heels together and bowed. 'Colonel Lord Theodore Marshall, at your service. The marquess is my brother. He left almost three weeks ago, right before the collapse of the Chelsea scheme, but I managed to keep his departure out of the papers until now. Foolishly, I hoped that he might still come back.'

'I see.' She looked stricken, all the fight seeming to drain out of her in a single moment. 'Then I'm the one who owes you an apology.'

'Not at all. It was an easy mistake to make. However, now that we've cleared it up, perhaps you'd like to take a seat by the fire for a few minutes? Your clothes appear somewhat damp.'

'Mmm?' She looked preoccupied. 'Oh…yes. The rain.'

'Would you care for some tea to warm you up?'

'No. No tea, thank you.' She sank into, rather than sat down in, an armchair, looking and sounding so beaten that he almost wished he hadn't told her the truth. An angry Miss Lemon struck him as infinitely preferable to a defeated one.

'Maybe something to eat, then?'

'No.' She looked up again. 'I really am sorry. I was unforgivably rude.'

'Not really.'

'No?' She gave a bitter-sounding laugh. 'Then I can't seem to do anything right today.'

'But you said it with conviction. Here, try again if you like.' He spread his hands out. 'Call me anything you want.'

'I wouldn't do any better. Ladies aren't taught how to insult people properly. The strongest word I know is "damn".' She sniffed. 'Anyway, I can't insult you when you're not the real villain. *Damn* villain, I mean.'

'But my brother is, which is why I'd like to help you, if I can. So tell me, what kind of work are you looking for?'

'I don't know.' She rubbed a hand over her brow. 'I didn't think that far ahead. I've looked after my father's house for the past seven years so I know about housekeeping, but other than that... Maybe a governess?' Her expression turned hopeful. 'I don't suppose you need one of those?'

'Actually...' He considered the idea for a moment before shaking his head. 'No. I'm afraid that governesses aren't very popular in this house at the moment. It could lead to violence.'

'Violence?'

'It's a sordid story.'

'Then maybe I could help you with all these papers?' She gestured around the room. 'You seem to have quite a lot.'

'That's an understatement.' He made a wry face. He was positively drowning in paperwork, none of it in any order that he could fathom. There were stacks of letters and ledgers on every available surface, including large areas of the floor. Frankly, the whole place was becoming dangerously flammable. 'Apparently my brother's secretary walked out in protest a couple of months ago.'

'What about?'

'I believe it would be hard to choose one particular reason.'

'Well then?'

Theo rubbed a hand over his chin, considering. He had his brother's many lawyers to help with the more convoluted legal documents, but he desperately needed some kind of help to keep up with the rest of them. He'd put off advertising for a new secretary, mainly because the whole process of interviewing candidates and then explaining the full horror of the workload to them struck him as something else he didn't have time for, but Miss Lemon was conveniently right there and, thanks to her own unfortunate situation, she already understood how bad things were. There was only one problem.

'I'm sorry.' He sighed heavily. 'Tempting as the idea is, I'm afraid that it's impossible.'

'It's because I'm a lady, isn't it?' Her eyes flashed again. 'But why shouldn't a lady be a secretary? I can read and write and I'm good at arithmetic.'

'I'm not questioning your abilities, but it would involve us spending a great deal of time together. It would compromise your reputation.' He lifted an eyebrow. 'Some people would find us just sitting in this room together compromising, my brother's butler among them apparently. Besides which, I'm a soldier. I'm not accustomed to the company of ladies. I might be uncouth on occasion.'

'I don't care! I'm hardly going to swoon. I might even learn a few insults.' There was an edge of desperation in her voice now. 'As for being compromised, what use is a reputation if it means starving on the streets?'

'Good point, but I also have my sister-in-law and nieces to consider. They've been through enough scandal recently.' He shook his head reluctantly. 'I'm sorry, Miss Lemon, but I can't allow it.'

'So that's it?' She leapt to her feet as if she were about to argue some more and then reconsidered, squeezing her lips together tight and blinking rapidly. Up close, her eyes were a very dark grey rather than brown, he noticed. Cloudy, full of smoke or… Oh, good grief. He felt a stab of panic. Tears.

'There's no need to get upset.' He reached into his pocket for a handkerchief. 'We'll think of something—'

'No, you're right, it was ridiculous of me to ask. Coming here was a dreadful mistake.' She twisted towards the door, her movements frantic suddenly. 'I should go.'

'Wait! I never said it was ridiculous.' He held a hand out, but she was already out of reach. 'Miss Lemon?'

'Thank you for your time.' She kept her head down as she ran headlong out of the room. 'Good day, colonel.'

# Chapter Four

At least she hadn't pelted him with eggs.

Abigail closed the front door wearily behind her and then sank back against the wall, letting her body slide slowly to the floor. This, she supposed, was rock bottom. Not only had she lost her beloved father, but between all the heartbreak and humiliation of the last few hours, it was hard to imagine a way in which her plight could get any worse.

She'd set out that afternoon fuelled by an invigorating sense of righteous indignation and ended up making a complete fool of herself. Again. First by insulting the wrong man and then, just when he'd seemed on the verge of helping her, by shooting herself in the proverbial foot by running away.

In her defence, however, she'd had no choice but to run when she'd been on the verge of bursting into tears like a little girl. The whole experience had been beyond mortifying. After two weeks of *not* crying, her tear ducts had decided to start working again at the worst possible moment and once a crack had appeared in the dam, there had been no way to seal it up again. She'd sobbed all the way home. As if the rain hadn't made her wet enough!

But at least she hadn't pelted him with eggs.

She tipped her head back against the wall with an exhausted sigh. Now that the storm of emotion had passed, she felt utterly drained, as if she could sleep for a week, although she knew she really ought to get up and out of her wet clothes first. Sitting on the floor feeling sorry for herself wasn't going to improve her situation one jot and Mrs Jessop was right, if she wasn't careful she'd catch a chill.

'Good gracious!' As if on cue, the cook emerged from the kitchen stairwell at that moment. 'I thought I heard the front door. What on earth are you doing down there?'

'Recovering. It was a disaster. Another one.'

'He made you cry?' Mrs Jessop took one look at her swollen eyes and stamped her foot angrily. 'The low-life bastard.'

'Bastard!' Abigail clicked her fingers. '*That's* what I ought to have called him.' She hiccupped. 'Except that I would have been wrong. He was very kind, all things considered.'

'The marquess?'

'No, the colonel. His brother.'

'What does his brother have to do with anything?'

'He's the one that I spoke to. The marquess has gone, fled the country. He really *is* a low-life bastard, whereas the colonel…' She paused. How to describe the colonel? She'd been too angry to pay much attention to his appearance at the time, but in retrospect…

Not as classically handsome as Henry, but still attractive in a less obvious, slightly weathered sort of way. Young, in his late twenties probably, with cropped, corn-coloured hair, a lean yet muscular build and, now that she thought of it, surprisingly piercing blue eyes. The left one had had a scar just above it, too, a white line that sliced straight through his eyebrow... As for his character, he'd been surprisingly thoughtful, concerned about her wet clothes even when she'd been burning up with embarrassment. Definitely not a villain, but still the brother of one.

'Never mind who was who.' Mrs Jessop rolled her eyes. 'You can't stay down there on the floor.'

'I know, I was just feeling sorry for myself for a moment. Everything seemed to catch up with me all at once. First father, then Henry...'

'You're still dealing with the shock. Go and put some dry clothes on and I'll make us a nice cup of tea.'

'Thank you. Mrs Jessop. I don't know what I'd do without you.' Abigail smiled wanly and then reached into her pocket, pulling out a leather purse and depositing it on the floor with an audible clunk. 'But at least I can pay you and the rest of the staff what you're owed.'

'What's that?' Mrs Jessop bent down and peered inside. 'Mercy me! How on earth—?'

'I sold my engagement ring.'

'What? But what if he changes his mind?'

'He won't, trust me, and I can't afford to be sentimental.' She clenched her jaw, fighting back another wave of emotion. 'The only reason I might have kept it would have been as a warning—never to trust any man ever again, no matter how much he says he loves me.'

'If you're certain...?'

'Positive!' She nodded firmly, then jerked her head up at the sound of a tap on the door.

'Now who can that be?' Mrs Jessop slid her hands to her hips.

'Somebody wanting money probably. If they've come for the furniture, tell them they can just carry it out past me.'

'I'll do no such thing. Nobody's taking anything from this house until Friday and I'll tell them as much.'

'I'd like to hear that.' Abigail laughed softly and then yawned. She'd never felt so tired in her whole life, but she *really* had to get up, had to summon the energy from somewhere. She had to find a job, a new purpose, somewhere to live… Maybe if she just closed her eyes for ten seconds, it would give her the strength.

*One, two…* She heard the door opening… *Three, four…* Voices in the background… *Five, six…* Familiar but indistinguishable… *Seven, eight…* Was that a man…? *Nine, ten…*

'Is this a bad time?'

She jumped, startled, banging her head on the wall behind as she opened her eyes to find Colonel Marshall crouching down beside her. He was wet, too, but dressed in a long blue greatcoat that looked substantially more practical than her own short pelisse and he was holding his hat in one hand, his expression unreadable, though his eyes looked sympathetic.

Close up, they were really extraordinarily blue, the bluest she'd ever seen, like a summer dawn, with tiny droplets of rain shimmering on the lashes. They were also focused very intently on her own, she realised, *too* intently, as if he were trying to see into her mind.

'Ow! I mean, *you*!' She lifted a hand to rub the back of her head. 'What are you doing here?'

'I came to finish our conversation.' He quirked an eyebrow. 'I was concerned when you ran away earlier.'

'So I'm not dreaming?' She looked up at Mrs Jessop, who shook her head. 'And I really am sitting on the floor in the hallway?' A nod this time. 'Oh, dear.'

'May I?' He held a hand out.

'Wait, how do you know where I live?'

He lifted a shoulder. 'My brother wasn't much of a business man, *obviously*, but even he kept a record of his investors. It's one of the few documents I've been able to find. Your father's name and address was in there. However, if this is a bad time, I'm more than happy to come back.'

'No.' She pretended not to notice his hand, putting her own on the floor and pushing herself back to her feet instead. 'Now is quite acceptable.' She wobbled sideways immediately.

'Perhaps you ought to sit down?' A pair of hands caught her around the waist, propping her upright again. 'In a chair, that is.'

'Right. Yes.' She tensed, her stomach swooping at the unexpected contact. There was a foot of air between them, but his body still seemed alarmingly close, not to mention extremely large next to her own. 'My legs do feel a bit numb. The drawing room is this way.'

'Are you sure you can walk?'

'Absolutely.' Honestly, she wasn't remotely sure of that fact, but her stomach was doing more strange things now, the swooping feeling transforming itself into a ball of warmth, like a kitten curled up in her abdomen. It even seemed to be purring, causing a strange vibrating sensation, a feeling so new and unexpected that she almost fell over again. She had absolutely no idea what was going on, but she was aware of an urgent need to put some distance between herself and the colonel.

'Miss Lemon.' He pulled his hands away finally, although he kept them raised, as if he were braced to catch her again. 'Forgive me for saying so, but you look exhausted.'

'Yes,' she agreed quickly. That sounded much better than purring kittens, with the additional benefit of being true. 'I think that I might be.'

'She's been very busy,' Mrs Jessop interjected. 'She had to arrange her father's funeral all by herself.'

'I'm sorry to hear that.' He looked sombre, as if he genuinely meant it. 'In that case, I won't take up any more of your time, except to say that, on reflection, I've decided you were right. There's absolutely no reason why I shouldn't hire a lady as my secretary.'

'Really?' Abigail's heart leapt. 'You mean, you're giving me a job?'

'Yes, provided that we keep the arrangement a secret between us and…?' He glanced sideways enquiringly.

'Mrs Jessop. The cook. I won't tell a soul.'

'I don't know what to say.' The kitten appeared to be dancing a jig now. 'What made you change your mind?'

'It occurred to me that you've suffered enough at the hands of my family.' He made a face. 'And the blunt truth is that I really do need to hire someone.'

'Thank you!' She started to smile and then froze. 'Although, if it's a secret, how will we explain my visiting your house every day?'

'We won't have to. Officially, I intend to hire you as a companion for my sister-in-law, Lady Salway. You'll be my secretary *un*officially.' He tilted his head towards hers. 'And perhaps, also unofficially, you might help my two nieces with their studies on occasion?'

'Of course.' She nodded eagerly. 'So, just to clarify, you're suggesting that I be an official companion, a secretary in secret *and* an undercover governess?'

'If that doesn't sound like too much?'

'Not at all! You have a deal, colonel. You won't regret it, I promise.'

'I'm certain I won't. As for visiting the house every day…' He cleared his throat. 'Perhaps I haven't been clear. The position comes with bed and board.'

'Oh, thank goodness!' Mrs Jessop pushed herself between them, throwing her arms around Abigail's neck.

'I'll take that as a yes.' His lips curved infinitesimally. 'When can you start?'

'Friday!' Apparently Mrs Jessop was doing all the talking for her now. 'That's when the bank's taking possession of the house.'

'Friday, it is.' He made a formal bow. 'I'll see you then, Miss Lemon. Bright and early.'

'Thank you!' She caught his eye over Mrs Jessop's shoulder. 'Thank you so much!'

'Don't thank me yet.' He put his hat back on in the doorway. 'We have a mountain of work to do. Get some rest, Miss Lemon. You're going to need it.'

## Chapter Five

'Good morning, sir! It's a beautiful one, too, if I might say so. Barely a cloud in the sky.'

'What the hell?' Theo started awake as his bedchamber door flew open and then shut again violently enough to rattle the hinges. 'Damn it, Kitchen! You're worse than a cannon.'

'Am I, sir?'

'Yes!' He heaved himself upright with a groan. 'I didn't think it was possible, but you're actually getting louder.'

'Just keeping you alert, sir. Civilian life weakens the nerves.'

'In case you hadn't noticed, the war's over. We're both civilians these days and you're supposed to be my valet, not a sergeant major any more.'

'I prefer to keep to the old routines, sir. As a wise man once said, that wise man being myself, you can take the man out of the army, but you can't take the army out of the man.'

'I can still try. Feel free to take a morning off occasionally.'

'I couldn't possibly, sir, especially today.'

'Why especially today?'

'Because I've got a lead about Armstrong.' Kitchen tapped the side of his nose confidentially. 'Remember Hammond?'

'Urgh.' Theo made a disgusted sound, rubbing his hands over his face before swinging his legs over the side of the mattress. 'How could I forget? One of the worst soldiers I ever had the misfortune to come across.'

'True enough, but he reckons he knows where Armstrong is.'

'For a fee, I expect?'

'Hammond never did anything out of the kindness of his heart, sir. Five guineas, although you can probably bargain him down to three.'

'Will he tell us the truth, though?'

'Oddly enough, I think that he might, but if he doesn't, I'll make sure you get your money back.'

'If he's lying, I'll get it back myself. Do you know where he lives?'

'I do, sir. More importantly, I know that he's sleeping off a hangover at the Crown and Anchor in Cheapside this morning. Best to go early while he's not feeling too clever.' Kitchen held a tray out. 'I brought coffee.'

'I knew there was a reason I keep you around.' Theo picked up the cup and drained it. 'No one else makes it properly.'

'No else believes a person can drink anything that strong.' Kitchen grinned. 'Although the maids told me an interesting rumour about you this morning.'

'They're lying.' Theo went over to his washstand, splashing water over his face and neck. 'I haven't done anything interesting for weeks.' He dabbed a cloth over his face. 'Enlighten me. What am I supposed to have done?'

'Well, the story is that you asked Mrs Evans—'

'Who?'

'The housekeeper.'

'Right. Go on.'

'That you asked Mrs Evans to prepare a room for a new member of staff. A woman?'

'Oh. *That.*' He paused in the middle of pulling on a pair of breeches. He'd been so busy visiting lawyers, trying to unravel the tangled skein of his brother's business dealings over the past few days, that he'd almost forgotten about Miss Lemon. 'Yes. She starts on Friday.'

'You mean today, sir?'

'Is it? Damn. I should probably be here when she arrives.' He glanced at his pocket watch. 'Never mind.'

'The funny thing is that no one seems to know what exactly she's been employed for.'

'She's my new secretary. *Unofficially.* Officially she's a companion for the marchioness.'

'It would take a bloody brave woman to do that.' Kitchen snorted. 'Does the marchioness know?'

'Not yet.' Theo threw a shirt on before shrugging a jacket on top. 'We'll just have to hope they don't bump into each other before we get back. Although we should probably warn Possett to hide any breakables just in case.'

'Consider it done.' Kitchen heaved the bedchamber door open again. 'I have some other news, too, sir. About Fox this time.'

'What's that? Don't tell me he's lost another job.'

'The opposite. He's settled at the smithy and he's getting married. To the blacksmith's daughter, no less. Got his feet firmly under the table there. So that's another one you don't need to worry about any more.'

'You make me sound like a mother hen, Kitchen. Either that or a busybody.' Theo stopped on the landing halfway down the staircase. 'You'd tell me if I was interfering too much in the men's lives?'

'You know me, sir, I've never kept an opinion to myself in my life. For what it's worth, however, they're all very grateful for your help. Not many officers have looked after their old soldiers the way you have. It's just...'

'Yes?'

'Well, truth be told, sir, they're a bit worried about you.'

'Me? What on earth for?'

'They're worried you do too much for other people and not enough for yourself. It's been six months since we were disbanded. They'd like to see you settled as well.'

'Settled? Good grief, Kitchen, are you saying that my soldiers want me to get married?'

'It's an idea, sir.'

'A bad one. I've told you before, not everyone is a suitable candidate for matrimony. I'm descended from a long and distinguished line of terrible husbands. There hasn't been a happy union in the Marshall family for generations. Since the Battle of Hastings, probably. No, for the sake of all womankind, I'm keeping out of the whole business.'

'But surely if you met the right woman, sir?'

'If I met the right woman, the kindest thing I could do for her would be to leave her alone.' He carried on down the staircase. 'Besides, I have enough on my plate at the moment. The right woman could be standing right in front of me and I'd be far too busy to notice.'

Abigail stepped down from a cab, deposited the three bags containing all of her worldly possessions on the front doorstep of Salway House, drew a handkerchief from her pocket and sneezed.

She'd gone to bed the previous evening feeling perfectly well. More than that, she'd been smugly congratulating herself on escaping her day of repeated drenching unscathed, then woken up that morning with itchy eyes, a runny nose and burning sore throat, all made worse by the knowledge that they were entirely her own fault. And even though Mrs Jessop had refrained from actually saying the words *I told you so* out loud, they'd still been hanging in the air like a giant banner of recrimination as they'd embraced and said a tearful goodbye, then embraced again, before Abigail had walked out of her childhood home for the last time.

On reflection, it was a wonder that she hadn't succumbed sooner. According to Mrs Jessop, some kind of physical collapse had been inevitable. Her emotions had been in a state of upheaval for almost three weeks, while a self-destructive combination of guilt, grief and anger had deprived her of sleep, appetite and peace of mind. Even now, she felt completely overwrought and it wasn't even nine o'clock in the morning. She could only hope a change of scene would be good for her. At the very least she hoped that it would keep her mind off everything else that had happened.

She blew her nose one last time, knocked on the door and then immediately regretted it, wondering if she was still permitted to use the front entrance. For all

she knew, a secretary was supposed to use the trades-
man's door at the rear. Then again, she was technically
a secretary-cum-governess disguised as a companion,
so what did that mean?

'Miss Lemon.' The butler answered before she could
decide what to do, regarding her without any discern-
ible hint of emotion, although whether that meant she
was using the right door or not, she had no idea. The
fact that he wasn't actually closing it again in her face,
however, had to be a good sign.

'Good morning.' She tucked her handkerchief away
quickly and smiled. She'd made a bad first impression
on him the other day, that was undeniable, but she intended to rectify the situation as soon as possible. Or at
least make a start. She had a feeling that it was going to
take a lot more than a smile and a 'good morning' to win
him around, but at least this time she wasn't dripping
rainwater all over the perfectly polished front doorstep.

'Good morning.' He spoke slowly, as if every word
were a trial. 'Come in.'

'Thank you. I wasn't sure which door...'

'Neither were we.'

He stepped aside, allowing her to lift her own bags
over the threshold, which she did with another quickly
muffled sneeze.

Just like the first time, she was briefly overwhelmed
by the size and scale of the hallway. It was octagonal-
shaped and vast, with a high dome ceiling topped with
a glass cupola, all supported by a series of peach-co-
loured marble columns. The walls between were stuc-
coed in white, so that the overall effect was one of light
and brightness, exactly how she might have imagined
a snow palace.

'I am Possett. This is Mrs Evans, the housekeeper.' Possett crooked a finger, summoning a grey-haired and disapproving-looking woman from behind one of the pillars. 'She'll show you to your room.'

'This way, Miss Lemon.'

Like the butler, Mrs Evans appeared to be a person of few words, barely pausing to acknowledge her before marching ahead up a spiralling staircase, across a landing, up a second staircase, and then along a wide corridor towards a door at the far end.

Abigail followed, panting in an effort to keep up, faintly surprised by the coldness of her reception, not to mention the absence of footmen to help with her bags.

'This is your room.' Mrs Evans twisted a handle, pushed open a door, and then took a step backwards, as if her work there was done. 'I trust it will be to your satisfaction.'

'Oh! It's lovely.' Abigail took a few steps into the room and whirled around in delight, taking in the powder-blue wallpaper, flecked with a pattern of tiny goldfinches, the spacious four-poster bed, framed by yellow curtains, and white painted furniture. 'It's almost too much.'

'Mmm.' Apparently her companion agreed with her. 'The colonel insisted that you have one of the guest rooms.'

'That was very kind of him.'

'Indeed. There's a view of the garden, too.'

'Really?' She deposited her bags by the wardrobe and walked over to one of the three windows, peering out over a large square lawn, bordered with flowerbeds filled to bursting with daffodils and crocuses. 'It's beautiful.'

'The colonel's out at present, but he left a message asking for you to meet him in his study at ten o'clock. That's down the stairs, through the hall, under the archway and through the second door on the left. I trust that you can find your own way?'

'I think so, yes. Thank you, Mrs Evans.'

'Good. Then I'll leave you to freshen up.' A curt nod indicated their conversation was over. 'Welcome to the household, Miss Lemon, whatever it is that you're doing here.'

'Oh, I'm a—' Abigail stopped mid-sentence, the words fading in her mouth as the housekeeper closed the door firmly behind her. Which, while rude, was possibly a good thing, she reflected, since she hadn't been entirely sure how to answer. She'd presumed that the colonel would have explained her position to his staff, although perhaps he hadn't yet decided on how best to describe it.

On the other hand, perhaps his staff simply disapproved of a woman working as a secretary. Or perhaps, given their evident disapproval, he hadn't told them anything at all and they'd simply drawn their own lurid conclusions… She felt her cheeks flame with heat at the thought, causing a rush of blood to the head that brought on a fresh bout of sneezing.

She blew her nose for the hundredth time that morning and then sat down on the edge of a firm and yet surprisingly comfortable mattress, rummaging inside one of her bags until she found her two most treasured possessions, her father's old pipe and the watercolour miniature of her mother's cottage. The actual building in the picture was little more than a ruin now, but just gazing at it made her feel better. Maybe one day, if she worked hard enough and for long enough, she'd be able to go back there. Maybe she'd be able to do something with it, too. Rebuild, restore, recover... Maybe.

She sniffed the pipe, filling her nostrils with the familiar, comforting scent, then put it and the picture side by side on her bedside table. *There*, that made it feel a little more like home. The past two weeks had been a nightmare, but at least now she had a safe haven, a *much* nicer room than she'd expected, a job, even if she didn't know quite how to describe herself, and a dream to work towards, one that depended on herself alone. She might not have any money, or know who she was or where she belonged any longer, but she'd find her way and adjust. Because from now on, the only person she was going to trust with her future happiness was herself.

Another violent sneeze overcame her.

She just needed to get rid of this cold first.

## Chapter Six

'I'll write to the magistrate at once.'

Theo threw the words over his shoulder to Kitchen as he charged through the front door, tossing his hat and coat aside on his way to the study. Their early morning visit to the Crown and Anchor had been both a resounding success in one way and an unmitigated disaster in another. Three guineas had told them where Armstrong was, but the answer had been the last one they'd wanted to hear.

'Very good, sir. I presume you'll want me to deliver it straight away?'

'As quickly as possible. Who knows what conditions he's being kept in?'

'Good morning, colonel.'

'Bloody hell!' He swung around halfway across the study, just in time to see a woman in a black dress get up from one of the armchairs by the fireplace.

'My apologies.' She dipped into a curtsy. 'I was told to meet you in here. Should I have waited outside?'

'No.' He shook his head, shooting a death glare towards Kitchen, who was standing, chuckling in the doorway. 'I just…forgot. Sorry about the bloody hell.'

'That's quite all right. You gave me a chance to prove I won't swoon.'

'So I did. In that case, you passed your first test.' He glanced down at her feet, surprised to see a bundle of fur stretched out in front of them, stomach-side up and legs in the air. 'I see you've met Lady.'

'Yes, I've just been introducing myself.' She bent down and rubbed the dog's belly. 'I think we've made friends.'

'That's more than most people manage.' He tipped his head with respect. For a fractious old dog who spent most of her time curled up under his desk, resenting anyone who wasn't himself or Kitchen, Lady appeared blissfully contented. 'I just need to write a letter before we begin.'

'As you wish.'

'You can talk to Kitchen in the meantime.' He sat down at his desk and reached for a quill and some parchment. 'Kitchen, introduce yourself.'

'The name's Kitchen, miss.'

'Miss Lemon. Abigail Lemon. Delighted to make your acquaintance.'

Theo put a hand to his forehead, ignoring the rest of the conversation as he attempted to find the exact right combination of words that would persuade a magistrate to release a newly arrested criminal. They needed to be polite yet authoritative, firm but not pushy, appealing without being intimidating. Well, maybe a little intimidating...

It was a quarter of an hour before he was finally satisfied, throwing his quill down to find his former sergeant major sitting cross-legged on the floor, arranging chess pieces into lines. Curiously, Miss Lemon was kneeling down beside him, a look of intense fascination on her face. Even Lady had stirred herself enough to open one eyelid.

'Kitchen, what on earth are you doing?'

'A demonstration, sir. I'm showing Miss Lemon what happened at Waterloo.'

'Of course you are.'

'I've used a rook for our battalion. I wanted a knight, but it seemed confusing, seeing as we weren't cavalry.'

'A rook is acceptable.' Theo folded the parchment and sealed it with a drop of wax. 'Sorry to interrupt, but—'

'Not a problem when it's for Armstrong, sir.' Kitchen leapt back to his feet. 'Excuse me, Miss Lemon.'

'Make sure you give it to the magistrate himself.' Theo held the letter out.

'Don't you worry, I'm as tenacious as a flea when I set my mind to it.'

'Another reason I keep you around.'

'You also enjoy my company, sir.'

'Thank you for the demonstration, Mr Kitchen.' Miss Lemon started gathering up the chess pieces. 'That was most enlightening.'

'If you have any more questions, miss, I'm your man.'

'Funny, but I could have sworn I was there, too.' Theo gestured towards a chair in front of the desk as Kitchen gave a mocking salute and departed. 'Take a seat, Miss Lemon.'

He watched her as she sat down, narrowing his gaze thoughtfully on her face. She looked different today, a lot less bedraggled, of course—disappointingly, the fabric of her dress barely clung to her hips at all, although their generous proportions were still obvious—but not quite better either.

Her skin struck him as unhealthily pale and if she'd actually slept since the last time he'd seen her then it wasn't obvious. In her dry state, however, he noticed that her hair was lighter than he'd first thought—silvery blonde shot through with strawberry threads, accentuated at that moment by the sunshine pouring in through the study windows. It might have looked quite lovely if the rest of her hadn't looked so wretched.

'I take it that you've been shown to your room already?'

'Yes. It's lovely, thank y—Atishoo!'

'Bless you.' He frowned. 'Are you feeling all right?'

'Perfectly.'

'You're sniffing.' He felt a vague sense of dread. 'And your eyes are red.'

'I'm not crying, I promise. It's just a head cold, but I'm sure it will pass soon.'

'Ah. Then perhaps we ought to postpone your first day.'

'No!' she protested quickly. 'I mean, I'd rather not. I'm here to work and I prefer to keep busy. If you don't object to my sneezing occasionally, that is?'

'Not at all. In that case, first things first.' He leaned forward, rested his forearms on the desk between them. 'About the curtsying…'

'Yes?'

'Don't. It's unnecessary.'

'Understood.'

'I mean, if you would be so kind and all that.'

'Of course.'

'You're not my subordinate.'

'Um…' She looked confused. 'Not to argue, but I am, aren't I? You're my employer and I'm your employee.'

'Officially, you're my sister-in-law's employee. As for me…' He made a face. 'Look, given the situation with my brother and your father, I prefer to think of anything I might pay you as a means of making restitution. A debt repayment, if you like.'

'So I'll get a repayment instead of a salary?'

'Exactly.' He reached into his desk, drew out a note and placed it on the table between them. 'And to show that I'm sincere, here's your first repayment. Five pounds.'

She glanced at the note and then back at him with a quizzical expression. 'But I haven't done anything yet.'

'Because you're not my employee. You're simply volunteering to help me with my paperwork in order to expedite the repayment process.'

'I see… I think.'

'Good. Now, about the work itself.'

'Actually…' She shifted position in her chair, squirming to one side. 'If you don't mind, I have a question first, about your staff and what they think I'm doing here.'

'My staff?' He drew his brows together. 'Truth be told, I haven't told them anything about you yet. It was on my list of things to do, only I forgot what day it was.'

'I see.' Her expression tightened, two streaks of colour burning across her cheekbones suddenly. 'In that case, might I ask whether you intend to describe me as a secretary or a companion?'

'Good question.' He leaned back in his chair, considering. 'I suggest, since it seems wise to be as discreet as possible, that we maintain the pretence of your being a companion. Only Possett and Mrs Evans need know the truth. If that's acceptable to you?'

'Perfectly, except...' another squirm, '...would you mind telling them soon?'

'I'll do it today. Why?'

'Because I think that they may be a little suspicious of me. They may even have leapt to some...unfortunate assumptions.'

'Such as?'

'That you might have hired me for some private purpose.' She gave him a pointed look. 'Not as a secretary. *Or* as a companion.'

'What else would I—? Ah.' He looked down at his desk, swearing under his breath before meeting her gaze again. 'That's unfortunate. How offensive were they?'

She lifted her eyes to the ceiling. 'They weren't overtly offensive, just a little standoffish, although I suppose I can understand why, given that your nieces live under the same roof.'

'Damn it.' He pushed his hands through his hair with exasperation. 'I never had this kind of problem in the army.'

'Just seventy thousand French soldiers to fight, according to Mr Kitchen.'

'Not single-handed. Whereas here...' He clenched his jaw, swallowing another oath. 'Anyway, where were we?'

'You were about to tell me about the work.'

'Oh, yes.' He paused as she sneezed again. 'Are you certain you're well enough?'

'Quite well.'

'And warm?'

'Perfectly.'

'Just let me know if you need anything.'

'I will, thank you.'

'Right…' He drummed the fingers of one hand on the table for several seconds before laying his palm down flat. 'Miss Lemon, before we go any further, I need to know that I can rely on your discretion.'

'Of course.'

'Thank you. In that case, the situation is this. I returned home from France a few months ago. I had certain matters to attend to before I sold my commission, after which I decided to visit my family for a few days. Foolishly, however, I made the mistake of sending a message ahead and my brother, having spent or lost most of his fortune, took the opportunity to make his escape, abandoning his family and responsibilities in the knowledge that I would soon be here to take care of them. He even had the nerve to leave a letter authorising me to act on his behalf.

'I arrived back to a scene of chaos and every day seems to have brought some fresh disaster. Then almost three weeks ago, there was another letter stating that he had no intention of ever returning and was, in fact, gone for good. In short, it's been quite a month. The last thing my sister-in-law needs is more gossip about our family.'

'How awful.' She sounded sombre. 'You can trust me, colonel. I won't tell a soul.'

'Good.' He scrutinised her for a long moment before nodding. 'Because we have a lot of work to do. It appears that after his secretary walked out, my brother let all of his paperwork pile up. I'm working my way through the documentation relating to the building scheme in Chelsea, but it's all mixed up with reports and letters from his estates. Frankly, it's a mess. I need to know what's going on so that I can respond to his stewards accordingly, but I don't have the time to read everything.' He tipped his head. 'Which is where you come in. I need it all organising and then summarising.'

'Well, you've obviously made good progress.' She twisted her head, looking around the room. 'There were a lot more papers the other day.'

'There were, weren't there?' He gave a pained half-smile. 'However, I've only kept the ones referring to the building scheme. I asked Kitchen to move the rest through there.' He stood up and walked towards a door in the far corner, throwing it open to reveal a smaller room with another desk almost completely buried beneath several teetering piles of paperwork. 'You see the scale of the problem? This is your office, by the way.'

'Oh.' She came to stand by his side.

'It looks a bit cramped at the moment, I admit, but it shouldn't be too bad once everything's in order.'

'Did you just say that this was *my* office?' She sounded faintly stunned.

'Yes.'

'Just for me? To work in?'

'Yes. So if you could sort everything into some kind of order, I'll be eternally grateful.' He glanced sideways when she didn't say anything, worried that she was about to turn tail and run. Honestly, he wouldn't entirely blame her. 'Miss Lemon?'

'It's… I mean, it's…' She put one hand on the door-frame as if she were struggling to stand upright. 'I thought my bedroom was lovely, but this… I've never had an office before. It's wonderful.'

'It is?' He quirked an eyebrow in surprise. 'I mean, I'm glad that you like it.'

She swung towards him, businesslike again all of a sudden. 'So how many properties does your brother own?'

'Beside the family seat in Norfolk?' He was aware of a faint, but delicious citrusy scent emanating from her hair. 'Fifteen.'

'Fifteen?'

'Fifteen.'

'I see.' She defied all of his expectations then by smiling. 'In that case, I'd better get started.'

# Chapter Seven

She hadn't expected an office.

A corner of the floor, yes. A table, maybe. But her own office? Never in a thousand years.

Abigail sat down, inwardly delighting in the towering heaps of paperwork surrounding her. She'd had a small writing desk in the parlour of her old home, but *this,* a space where she had a purpose and more than simply correspondence and household accounts to deal with, *this* was completely different. As dear as her father had been, he'd never involved her in any of his business dealings, even though she'd offered to help on countless occasions, yet Colonel Marshall seemed to trust her. For the first time in her life, she felt truly useful. Capable. Independent.

Despite the size of the workload, it was positively thrilling.

She set to work with enthusiasm, dividing the papers into categories, first by place, then date. Aside from the properties in London and Norfolk, there appeared to be smaller estates in Suffolk, Shropshire, the Welsh borders and Scotland, as well as various other properties scattered all over the country. The work wasn't too much of a challenge, although it was hard not to feel alarmed by the increasingly desperate pleas from various stewards. She only hoped that it wasn't too late to do something to help.

'I've told them.'

'Mmm?' She jerked her head up at the sound of Colonel Marshall's voice in the doorway. 'I'm sorry?'

'Possett and Mrs Evans. I've explained what you're doing here.' He looked chagrined. 'It appears that your interpretation of the situation was correct.'

'Oh, dear.'

'They'll both be a lot more welcoming from now on. I believe Mrs Evans is also asking Cook to bake a cake as an apology. I'm the one in their bad books.' He gave her a look that was half-shame-faced, half-solicitous. 'How is it going?'

'I'm making good progress, although some of the reports are rather worrying.'

'I don't doubt it.' He ran a hand over his face. 'How are you feeling now?'

'I haven't sneezed for almost ten minutes.' She lied. Honestly, it was more like four. 'There's really no need to worry about me, colonel.'

'In that case, if you're feeling up to it, I probably ought to introduce you to my sister-in-law.'

'Since I'm her official companion, you mean?' She put down the letter she was reading and stood up. 'I'd be delighted to meet the marchioness.'

'I wouldn't go that far. In fact...' he held an arm out, gesturing for her to precede him out of the study '...you might want to brace yourself.'

She looked around, taken aback by the tension in his voice. 'For what?'

'That's the problem. I have no idea. She hasn't been in a very good temper since my brother left. Actually, according to Possett, she hasn't been in a very good temper for the past ten years, but recently she's become worse. Her moods are quite...volatile.' He stopped briefly on the way out to ruffle Lady's slumbering head. 'The truth is, she may not be particularly pleasant.'

'Oh.' Abigail nodded thoughtfully as they crossed the hall and mounted the spiral staircase. 'I see.'

'She might insult you.'

'I understand.'

'I wouldn't want you to be upset.'

'Then I won't be. Trust me, she can't be any worse than my aunts.'

'Aunts?' He gave her a quizzical look as they reached the top of the staircase. 'I thought you said you didn't have any family?'

'I said I didn't have any I could go to for help.' She lifted a shoulder. 'Which is essentially the same thing.'

His brows snapped together. 'You mean they refused to give you a home after your father died?'

'Not directly. They just suggested that I ought to make alternative arrangements.'

'Then it appears we both have difficult relatives.' He held on to her gaze for a moment before rapping on one of the upstairs doors with his knuckles. 'I apologise in advance for anything my sister-in-law might say.'

'I'm sure that she won't be that bad.'

'I'm afraid that she will.'

'Well then, I—'

'*What?*'

Abigail jumped, startled by the volume of the screech emanating from inside the room. As the colonel had warned, it didn't bode well.

'You should probably wait here while I go and explain.' He reached for the door handle. 'Hopefully, I won't be long.'

'I…yes.' She didn't know what else to say as he closed the door behind him, although as it turned out, there was really no point since the marchioness appeared to have no concept of keeping her voice down. Whatever the colonel was saying—his own voice was more muffled—her response leapt quickly from surprise to indignation to outrage, every word perfectly audible and none of them complimentary.

'Come in, Miss Lemon.' The colonel opened the door again after a few minutes, his expression strained. 'Allow me to present the Marchioness of Salway.'

'Your ladyship.' Abigail stepped into the room and curtsied in the direction of a woman lying on a *chaise longue* in front of a large bay window. Despite her furious expression, she was breathtakingly beautiful, dressed in a fiery red robe with a mass of lustrous auburn hair tumbling loose around her shoulders.

'*This* is my so-called companion?' The woman's voice alone could have soured milk, Abigail thought, never mind her contemptuous expression. The combination could have wrought havoc in a dairy.

'Only in name.' The colonel interjected. 'As I explained, Miss Lemon is my new secretary.'

'She's a woman.'

'I noticed.'

'You know what I mean!' Incredibly, the marchioness's voice got even louder. 'Are you determined to bring even more scandal down on our heads?'

'Not at all. There isn't going to be any scandal because nobody else is going to find out.' A muscle twitched in the colonel's jaw. 'And even if they do, I don't see what's so bloody wrong with hiring a woman anyway.'

'You know perfectly well what people will think!' The marchioness leapt to her feet. 'What exactly is she going to do anyway? What possible experience can she have? I hardly need to remind you of how dire our financial situation is.'

'Believe me, I'm perfectly aware of that fact.'

'You need someone who can offer practical help, not just a pretty face.' A pair of large emerald eyes turned and raked over Abigail appraisingly. 'Although, on second thoughts, I don't suppose you hired her for that either.'

'That's enough, Sabrina.'

'Pah!' The marchioness waved a hand in the air. 'I don't know why you even bothered to tell me. My opinion hardly matters these days.'

'Of course it matters.' The colonel glanced longingly towards the window, as if he were tempted to dive through it and make his escape, muttering something under his breath that sounded a lot like 'I know my feelings don't count any more'.

'I know my feelings don't count any more.'

Abigail lifted a hand to her mouth, attempting to disguise a snort of amusement as a cough, although the marchioness's head still snapped towards her suspiciously.

'Your feelings count.' The colonel's voice was clipped

now. 'However, I'm entitled to hire my own secretary and *she* is entitled not to be insulted. She's suffered enough at the hands of our family and she needs some employment. *That's* why I've hired her. The whole arrangement is perfectly respectable.'

'What do you mean, "suffered at the hands of our family"?' The marchioness's tone shifted suddenly.

'My father invested in the Chelsea building scheme.' Abigail decided to answer for herself this time. 'He— *we*—lost everything.'

A gleam of understanding flitted across the other woman's face. 'In other words, you're another of my husband's poor victims?' She whirled back towards the colonel. 'Well, why didn't you just tell me that at the start?'

'Would it have made a difference?'

'Yes! This changes everything.' The marchioness waved a hand imperiously. 'You may go. Tell Mrs Evans that Miss Lemon and I will have luncheon in here together.'

'I'm not certain—'

'Oh, for goodness sake, there's no need to look so alarmed. I'm not going to hurt her. We're just going to get to know each other.'

'If Miss Lemon has no objections...?' He regarded Abigail doubtfully for a few moments, waiting until she nodded assent before retreating towards the door. 'In that case, I'll see you downstairs later.'

'He looks like a man who's just escaped the gallows.' The marchioness rolled her eyes the moment he was gone. 'He loathes coming up here to visit me.'

'I'm sure that's not the case, my lady.'

'Oh, it is, I assure you. I can't even blame him. When

I discovered that my husband was fleeing the country, I'm afraid my temper rather got the better of me.'

'That's perfectly understandable.' Abigail tilted her head sympathetically. 'I lost my temper with my own family recently.'

'Did you destroy five paintings and two irreplaceable vases?'

'Um…no.'

'Then I believe that I win this particular argument. Look.' The marchioness pointed behind her. 'Here's an example of my handiwork.'

'Oh.' Abigail felt her jaw drop. A slashed and stained portrait, or the tattered remnants of one anyway, hung in pride of place on the opposite wall.

'Meet my husband, the Honourable Marquess of Salway.' The marchioness beamed. 'I keep him there in case I ever forget why I'm so angry. Feel free to insult or attack him in any way you see fit.'

'I…' Abigail felt momentarily lost for words. 'I'm sure I'll think of something.'

'Be sure that you do. It's rather liberating.' The marchioness sighed. 'I really ought to be nicer to the colonel, however. None of this is his fault. In truth, he's just as much a victim as the rest of us. He hates being here altogether, but unlike his brother, he has a sense of duty. Now come over here and sit with me.'

She curled back up on the *chaise longue* and patted the space beside her. 'I apologise for my less-than-hospitable welcome. It's actually rather pleasant to see a new face, although your nose is rather red.' She glanced at the handkerchief in Abigail's hand. 'Are you unwell?'

'It's just a head cold.'

'I'll open the window. You may need some fresh

air.' Her perfectly smooth brow puckered. 'It might do me some good, as well. I don't remember the last time I left this house, but where would I go that people wouldn't stare and make comments?' She twisted her head around sharply. 'I don't suppose you've attended any *ton* events recently?'

'No, my lady.' Abigail stifled a smile at the idea. 'My father was a gentleman, but hardly a member of the *ton*. We lived in Holborn.'

'Holborn?' Judging by the marchioness's expression, she might as well have said a swamp. 'Then you don't know what's being said about us in society circles?'

'I'm afraid not.'

'What a pity.' The marchioness slumped backwards. 'I mean, it's probably best not to know, but I have a morbid curiosity.'

'I could make some enquiries, if you wish?'

'Really?' A slender eyebrow shot upwards. 'How?'

'Well, I may not be a member of the *ton* myself, but I have friends who are. I could ask them, discreetly of course.'

'Mmm.' The marchioness pursed her lips. 'It's not a terrible idea, although if you could keep the part about me breaking vases to yourself, I'd be obliged. I've given people enough to laugh at.'

'Whatever's being said, my lady, I'm sure that no one's laughing at you.'

'Ha! That only proves you're not a member of the *ton*! Those who've lost money to my husband will be busy spreading malicious stories about us and those who haven't will be finding the whole thing highly entertaining. I won't be able to show my face in public again for years.' She tipped her head back and let out a muffled scream. 'If only he'd waited a few more months!'

Abigail resisted the urge to slide further away. 'Would that have helped, my lady?'

'Yes! Our eldest daughter was supposed to make her come-out this Season. If he'd just held everything together until the end of the summer then she could have been married off and safe, but, no, he had to go and ruin himself in the spring. It would be madness to present her now. Who's going to want her after all this?'

'How kind of you to say so, mother.' A new voice spoke up from the doorway.

'Oh, for goodness sake, Evelyn!' The marchioness pressed a hand to her chest, though she sounded more irritated than guilty. 'Stop creeping up on people.'

'Why? Because I might overhear something I don't like?' A younger version of the marchioness swept into the room, her expression furious.

'Yes, actually! Evelyn, this is Miss Lemon. Miss Lemon, my daughter, Lady Evelyn.'

'I'm pleased to meet you, my lady.' Abigail stood up and curtsied.

'I've never seen you before. What are you doing here?'

'Miss Lemon is my new companion,' the marchioness answered haughtily, sounding indignant at her daughter's rudeness, as if she hadn't just behaved in the exact same manner a few minutes earlier. 'And when you remember where you've left your manners, you can say good morning.'

'You've hired a companion?' Miss Evelyn looked outraged. 'What about a new governess for me?'

The marchioness thrust out a hand. '*Don't* say that word!'

'What, governess?'

'Stop it!'

'Governess, governess, governess.' The girl swung towards Abigail. 'The last one ran away with my father, did she tell you?'

'Get out!'

'Why should I? It's not fair! If I can't have a Season, then I should at least get a new governess.'

'I'm not discussing this!'

'Argh! If I'm going to be trapped in this house all day like a prisoner, then I might as well learn something.'

'You've learned enough! Do something else!'

'Oh, good. More hours of piano practice. I can't wait.'

'Draw! Paint! Embroider something!'

'I'm sick of embroidery. I'm eighteen years old, not a child any more!'

'Perhaps we might go out on excursions occasionally?' Abigail piped up. 'For walks to the park or visits to museums maybe? I know it's not as exciting as a Season, but it would be a change of scene.'

There was a heavy silence while mother and daughter glared at each other.

'Or to concerts?' she persisted.

'Occasional excursions would be acceptable,' the marchioness answered at last, pointedly changing her expression from a scowl to a gracious smile as she turned away from her daughter. 'And perhaps you could take Florence, as well. That's my youngest daughter.'

'The favourite,' Evelyn hissed.

'Are you surprised when she doesn't constantly answer back? Oh, Possett, thank goodness.' The marchioness glanced towards the doorway where the butler was standing with two footmen bearing trays. 'You may bring luncheon in now. Lady Evelyn will be returning to the nursery, where she belongs.'

'I hate you! It's no wonder father left!' The younger woman spun on her heel, hurling one last parting shot over her shoulder. *'Governess!'*

'You survived, then?' The colonel's expression was both relieved and faintly sheepish, Abigail thought, when she returned to the study several hours later. She hadn't intended to be gone for so long, but the marchioness had drunk several glasses of wine with her luncheon and become surprisingly loquacious. It had been both extremely informative and almost impossible to get away.

'I did.' She walked up to his desk, pausing briefly to tickle Lady's chin. 'Although your abandonment was noted.'

'In my defence, I've been living under the same roof as Sabrina for almost a month now and I thought somebody else could listen to her rant about my brother for a change.' He put down his quill. 'But if it helps, I did feel guilty about it.'

'Just not enough to come and rescue me?'

'I was going to send an expedition once it got dark.'

'How thoughtful.' Her lips twitched. 'Actually, we had a nice talk.'

*'Nice?'* He lifted an eyebrow sceptically.

'Yes! Well, some of it was. The rest was informative. At least now I understand why you can't hire a new governess.'

Both eyebrows lifted this time. 'She told you about that?'

'Sort of. Your niece, Lady Evelyn...'

'Ah.' He sank back in his chair with a frustrated-sounding groan. 'How bad did it get?'

'Quite bad.'

'Sometimes I can hear them screaming at each other from down here.'

'I feel sorry for both of them, especially Lady Evelyn.'

'Yes, I know, she's missing out on her blasted Season.' He laced his hands behind his head. 'One of these days I'll tell her what real problems are.'

'You shouldn't be too hard on her. Eighteen is a difficult age for a woman.'

'And a man.' He dropped his hands again and stood up abruptly. 'I've had to send eighteen-year-olds into battle before. Men who were little more than boys. I fail to see how missing a few dances compares.'

'It doesn't, but that doesn't mean her feelings aren't important.'

'No, I suppose not.' He looked over her speculatively, so speculatively that she began to feel a pink blush spread up her throat and over her cheeks. 'On the other hand, you can't be much older *and* you've lost a great deal more, but you're not storming about the house, shouting at people.'

'I doubt I'd have a position here for long if I did.' She gave him a pertinent look. 'As for my age, I'm four years older. That's a big difference for a young woman, believe me. One is a debutante, the other is an old maid.'

'I'd hardly call you that.'

'Then you're obviously far more enlightened than

most people.' She sighed. 'However, I do know what it's like to lose my position in the world and be afraid of what the future might hold. Lady Evelyn is probably still coming to terms with the change in her circumstances. I'm sure there's a perfectly lovely girl underneath.'

'Liar!' He gave a bark of laughter. 'With the best will in the world, nobody could call her that.'

'Colonel!' She wrenched her shoulders back, offended on his niece's behalf. 'That's a horrible thing to say!'

'I know, but again, I've had to live with her. She *used* to be nice. When she was eight years old, she was actually quite sweet. I used to carry her around on my shoulders, pretending to be a horse. I hardly recognised her when I came back.'

'Surely you weren't away from home for ten full years?'

'Yes and no. Yes, I was away. I left England a decade ago and I only recently came back.' His expression hardened. 'My father died in the interim, but I was in Spain so there was no point in coming home. He would have been buried long before I got here. However, I was not, as you put it, "away from home". This house has never been that.'

'Then where is?'

'Damned if I know.'

'Oh…' She paused, waiting for more explanation, but none seemed forthcoming. Which was fair enough since it was really none of her business. 'Well…' she turned in the direction of her new office '… I'll get on with those papers. I've almost finished sorting them geographically.'

'Absolutely not.' He took a sideways step, blocking her path. 'You've done enough for today.'

'Oh.' She blinked, brought up short by the width of his chest. 'But it really won't take long.'

'None the less, it can wait until tomorrow. You should go and settle in to your new room.' His voice softened. 'I'm sure this must have been a difficult day for you.'

'Yes.' She swallowed, hit with a sudden wave of homesickness. 'It has.'

'And now I've upset you.' He lowered his brows awkwardly. 'My apologies.'

'No! It's just that when you said it like that, so sympathetically…' She bit the inside of her cheek to distract herself. 'I'm not going to cry again, colonel, I promise.'

'I appreciate that.' He grimaced and then snapped his fingers abruptly. 'Would you care for a bath?'

'I'm sorry?'

'A bath? I'm told that women like those.'

'I…yes, I mean I imagine some men like them, too, but I do. Very much.' Her spirits lifted. The thought of a steaming hot bath to clear her nose and throat sounded extremely appealing at that moment. 'In fact, it sounds like utter bliss.'

'Good. Then I'll ask Mrs Evans to have one prepared.' He looked briefly pleased with himself before drawing his brows together again suspiciously. 'You're not going to go to your room and cry, are you?'

'Maybe a little, but it won't be your fault.' She smiled, touched by his concern. Somehow it made her feel better. 'Good evening, Colonel Marshall.'

'Good evening, Miss Lemon.'

## *Chapter Eight*

Theo scrawled his signature at the bottom of a letter, set it aside to dry and then turned his head to peer through the open door of the small study, something he appeared to be doing on an alarmingly regular basis.

To be fair, he hadn't realised that he'd been doing it for the first couple of days Miss Lemon had been there, assiduously twirling a curl at the nape of her neck as she read letter after letter after letter, her wide forehead creased with concentration. It was only the day before, when she'd looked up and caught his eye, that he'd realised it was becoming a habit, one that he couldn't explain, but needed to break.

On the other hand, perhaps he might call for some coffee instead. It was only early afternoon, but already he was yawning. And then perhaps Miss Lemon would join him since she'd been working since just after breakfast, as well.

Over the past four days, she'd proven herself an extremely hard, punctual and conscientious worker. In fact, he concluded, standing up and stretching his arms above his head, that was probably what he'd just been admiring about her. Her work ethic. Although why that should make his pulse quicken, he had no idea.

'Good news, sir!' Kitchen burst into the study just as he was about to ring for Possett. 'Armstrong's free!'

'Already?' He dropped the bell again. 'Without a trial?'

'Whatever you wrote to that magistrate obviously did the trick. He actually apologised for the time it had taken.'

'All I did was remind him of the debt that this country owes its soldiers.'

'Surely that wasn't all, sir?'

'I might have mentioned our good friend the General, too.'

'Fair play. In any case, Armstrong's free and back in his wife's arms.' Kitchen waggled his eyebrows. 'Probably best not to disturb them for a couple of hours.'

'I wouldn't dream of it.' Theo went over to a sideboard, picked up a decanter and poured out two large glasses of brandy. 'However, this still calls for a celebration. To Armstrong!'

'May he never so much as think about stealing again!' Kitchen downed his drink in one gulp. 'Although if you ask me, one loaf of bread's hardly a hanging offence.'

'He must have been desperate.' Theo took a second mouthful of brandy and frowned. 'You know, the Marquess of Granby helped fund hostelries for some of his former soldiers. I've been thinking that something similar might suit Armstrong.'

'Wouldn't that cost a fair bit, sir?'

'He can pay me back with the profits over time. I might have to start looking for properties.'

'Miss Lemon!' Kitchen's face broke into a welcoming smile. 'You're just in time to celebrate with us.'

Theo turned to find his new secretary standing in the doorway to her office, a hint of a smile playing about her lips. Yes, her work ethic really was admirable, he told himself, especially now that she appeared to have recovered from her head cold.

'I thought you both looked happy.' She walked towards them, slowly enough that he couldn't resist stealing a glance downwards to where parts of her body were swaying in a way that made his pulse speed up all over again. 'What are you celebrating?'

'The colonel's just saved a man's life!' Kitchen waved his glass none too subtly in the air for a refill. 'And not for the first time either.'

'He exaggerates.' Theo shook his head. 'Would you care for a brandy, Miss Lemon?'

'No, thank you, I promised to take your nieces for a walk in Hyde Park this afternoon.'

'You don't have to do that.'

'But I want to. I'd like a break from reading and this way I won't feel like I'm lying when I describe myself as a companion. I can take Lady with us, too, if you like?'

'I appreciate the offer, but Lady considers herself retired from walking.' He chuckled. 'Stretching and eating are the only exercises she appreciates these days.'

'She's an old dog like myself, miss.' Kitchen grinned.

'Really? How old?'

'Honestly, I've no idea.' Theo regarded the hound affectionately. 'She was already grown when I found her. That was eight years ago.'

'*Found* her?'

'In a village in Spain, hiding beneath a cart. I offered her some food and that was that. She decided to adopt me.'

'Followed him everywhere he went, miss. We had to tie her up whenever there was a battle so she wouldn't chase after him. The most loyal dog you're ever likely to meet is that one.'

'Which is why she's earned a comfortable retirement.' Theo lifted his brandy glass.

'She certainly has.' Abigail smiled and then tilted her head to one side, her grey eyes alight with curiosity. 'So whose life have you saved?'

'A former soldier.' Theo settled into an armchair by the fireplace. 'He was arrested for stealing a loaf of bread, but fortunately we were able to persuade the magistrate to release him. Kitchen deserves equal credit.'

'To us!' Kitchen thrust his glass upwards again.

'I'll drink to that later.' She laughed. 'In the meantime, I'll leave you to celebrate.'

'She seems like a pleasant young lady,' Kitchen commented once the door had closed behind her.

'Yes, she is.' Theo lifted his own glass to his lips.

'Intelligent, too.'

'Indeed.'

'Not to mention pretty.'

'I suppose so.'

'And looking a lot better now than when she first arrived. Almost blooming today. What would you say? Twenty-one, twenty-two?'

'Twenty-two.' He glowered. 'Too young for you.'

'I know that, sir. I just wonder if—'

'No!'

'I haven't said anything!'

'But you were about to.' Theo took another mouthful of brandy. 'Miss Lemon is my secretary, that's all.'

'All I was going to say…' Kitchen lifted his chin with an aggrieved air '…is that I wonder if you'll find a way to pay her back some of the money her father lost.'

'Oh.' He slumped down in his chair. 'I don't know. I'm trying. If only these papers weren't in such a damned mess.'

'It's a good thing you've got her to help you then, sir.' Kitchen's expression remained suspiciously innocent. 'Wouldn't you say?'

'I don't *want* to feed any ducks.' Evelyn folded her arms mutinously. 'That kind of thing is for children.'

'Then you can just enjoy the walk.' Abigail smiled placidly before turning her attention to the other, smaller girl standing in the hallway beside her. Judging by her large blue eyes and friendly expression, she took after her father rather than her mother, although her aquiline nose and high cheekbones were also somewhat reminiscent of the colonel.

'You must be Lady Florence.' She held a hand out to shake. 'I'm Miss Lemon, but you can call me Abigail. Would *you* like to feed the ducks with me?'

'Yes please, miss.' The girl beamed.

'Wonderful, and of course we'll have to give them all names, too. What do you think of Bernard? I think that would suit a duck very well.'

'I like Bernard. And Alice for a girl.'

'Perfect. Alice is a beautiful name for a duck.'

'Don't forget the geese.' Evelyn snorted contemptuously. 'You could name them after yourselves.'

'Ignore her.' Florence edged closer, lowering her voice to a whisper. 'She's scared of birds.'

'I am not!'

'You are, *especially* geese.'

'In that case, we'll make a point of avoiding the geese.' Abigail started towards the door before yet another argument could break out. Not a single day had passed since her arrival without raised voices somewhere in the house. 'Now, will you show me the way to the park?'

'You don't know the way?' Evelyn sounded incredulous.

'I'm sure that I could find it if necessary, but I haven't spent a great deal of time in this area of London.'

'I'll show you.' Florence's expression took on an air of importance. 'It's not far.'

'Where are you from?' Evelyn actually sounded interested.

'Holborn.'

'I've never heard of it.'

'None the less, it exists, or do you think the world ends at the edge of Mayfair?' Abigail held a hand out to Florence as they stepped down on to the pavement. 'Now you're in charge.'

'Really?' The little girl threw a look of triumph at her sister before turning left. 'This way.'

As it turned out, the park wasn't far at all, barely two streets away in fact, but as streets went, they were spectacular, filled with imposing and towering town houses, each one designed to reflect the wealth and status of its owner. It struck Abigail as downright bizarre that this area of London was her home now—a home of sorts anyway. Henry might have been the heir to a baronetcy, but this was a whole other world. Never in her wildest dreams had she expected to live in a place like this.

It was too early for the fashionable hour, but Hyde Park was still busy with pedestrians, mostly governesses and maids with their charges. More importantly, there were plenty of hungry-looking ducks on the Serpentine, each one of which turned its beak hopefully towards them as Abigail pulled an old loaf of bread from her bag.

'That one's Alice!' Florence pointed excitedly. 'And that mallard can be Bernard.'

'You can't possibly name all of them.' Evelyn sighed. 'There are hundreds.'

'Yes, I can. Beatrice, Samuel, Eleanor, Annabel, Harriet, Georgianna, Toby…'

'Harriet!' Abigail called out, catching sight of a young, dark-haired woman with a pram standing a little further around the lake.

'Harriet…' Florence agreed. 'That's a nice name. Also Belinda, Henrietta, Sebastian…'

'No, it's a friend of mine.' Abigail reached for her hand again. 'Let's go and say hello, shall we? We'll come back and feed the ducks afterwards, I promise.

'Harriet!' She lifted her other hand to wave as they hurried around the perimeter of the lake. Having grown up on neighbouring streets in Holborn, she'd known Harriet for most of her life, although their paths had separated since her friend's marriage to a wealthy merchant in Soho.

The last time she'd seen her had been at her father's funeral, although they hadn't had a chance to speak properly, and she hadn't felt up to visiting afterwards either, although she'd sent a note to say where she was going when she'd left home. Now that she thought of it, however, she hadn't received any reply. That was odd; Harriet was usually a prolific correspondent.

'Abigail?' Her friend gasped as she looked up and saw her.

'Harriet! What a coincidence! How wonderful to see you.' She came to an abrupt halt at her friend's horrified expression. 'Isn't it?'

'Ye-es.' Harriet's gaze darted sideways towards a group of older women, chatting a few feet away. 'It's just...we heard you'd left town.'

'As if I'd leave without saying goodbye.' Abigail shook her head, smiling with relief. No wonder Harriet was reacting oddly if she'd thought that. 'Didn't you get my note? I'm a companion now.' She gestured towards her two charges. 'Allow me to introduce Lady Evelyn Marshall and Lady Florence Marshall. Evelyn, Florence, this is my friend, Mrs Harriet Callahan, and her son, George. Hello, George.' She waggled her fingers at the baby.

'Marshall?' Harriet's eyes widened. 'But how can you be a companion when—?' She stopped, her whole body tensing as one of the older women came over to join them. 'Abigail, you remember my mother-in-law?'

'Of course.' Abigail curtsied. 'A pleasure to see you again, Mrs Callahan.'

'Miss Lemon, is it not?' The woman's eyes iced over. 'I was under the impression that you'd left town.'

'Yes. Harriet was just saying the same thing.'

'Perhaps you ought to consider doing so now before you cause any more scandal?'

'I'm sorry?' Abigail blinked, startled by the venom

in the other woman's voice. 'What on earth can you mean?'

'It's time for us to go, Harriet.' Mrs Callahan turned her back. 'Good day, *Miss* Lemon. We won't be meeting again. '

'Actually, I think—' Harriet attempted a protest.

'Your association with this person is at an end. Say goodbye, if you must.'

'But I…' Harriet quailed as her mother-in-law clamped a hand firmly around her wrist. 'Goodbye, Abbie.'

Abigail watched them go, her mind whirling and her body trembling with shock. Mrs Callahan had never been particularly pleasant to her, or anyone else for that matter, but the cut direct was too blatant to be ignored. What on earth did she mean by scandal? And why did they both think she'd left London?

'What charming friends you have.' Evelyn stepped forward, blocking her view of Harriet's retreating back with her own smirking face. 'You're obviously a great deal more interesting than I gave you credit for, Miss Lemon.'

## Chapter Nine

Half an hour of feeding ducks, geese and even a couple of swans later, Abigail was no closer to working out
what on earth had happened with Harriet and her mood
had plummeted from shock and confusion to utter de-
spondency. Not even a trip to Gunter's Tea Shop for
strawberry-and-jasmine-flavoured ices had been able
to cheer her up. She'd barely tasted a bite.

'You'd better go up to the nursery.' She dredged up
a smile for Florence as they removed their outdoor garments in the hallway. 'I expect that dinner will be ready
soon.'

'Yes, Miss Lemon.' To her surprise, Florence flung
her arms around her waist and squeezed tight. 'I'm sorry
that your friend was mean to you, but thank you for
the ducks.'

'I enjoyed that part, too.' Her smile became a little
more real. 'Alice was my favourite.'

She waited until they'd gone upstairs before heaving
a sigh and heading back to the study, intending to catch
up on some work. As she opened the door, however, she
had the strangest impression that time had somehow

stopped and she'd simply imagined the past couple of hours. The colonel and Kitchen were sitting in almost the exact same poses as when she'd left them, but for a pair who were supposed to be celebrating, they looked the same way she felt. Thoroughly depressed.

'Is something wrong?' She slipped inside, faintly alarmed.

'Not wrong.' Kitchen raised his glass when he saw her. 'We're just reminis-is-isi...'

'Reminiscing?'

'Aye, that too, although you don't look too happy yourself, if you don't mind me saying so, miss.'

'No. I bumped into an old friend at the park and it was...odd.' She shook her head, unwilling to dwell any more on the memory. 'What are you reminiscing about? The war?'

*'Women!'*

'Oh.' She pulled her spine straighter. 'In that case, perhaps I ought to leave you to it.'

'The ones who broke our hearts!'

*'Ones?'* She couldn't resist asking, 'How many have there been?'

'Dozens.' Kitchen placed a hand over his chest. 'In my case anyway. I fall in love easily.'

'That sounds rather exhausting.'

'It is, miss, it is. Ready for a drink?'

'It's only—' She glanced at the clock and then decided she didn't actually care what the time was. After her encounter with Mrs Callahan, a drink sounded like a perfectly splendid idea. 'Maybe just a small one.'

'A small one, it is.' Kitchen winked as he handed her a tumbler. 'The marquess's finest brandy. He forgot to take it with him.'

'Thank you.' She sat down on a footstool, took a sip and then sneaked a look sideways. After a cursory nod in her direction, the colonel had turned his attention to the fireplace, staring into the flames with a brooding expression. He'd also unfastened his cravat and unbuttoned his waistcoat, she noticed, rolling his sleeves up to reveal surprisingly muscular forearms. *Very* muscular forearms, in fact...

She lifted her gaze hastily, wondering if his silence was because of the subject matter. If it was, then it was absolutely none of her business, only somehow the question was out before she could stop it. 'What about you, colonel? Have you had your heart broken?'

'Not as I recall.' He didn't move.

'Tough nut to crack is our colonel.' Kitchen tapped a finger against his nose confidentially. 'All of the officers' daughters used to flirt with him, but he was having none of it.'

'Why not?'

'I had other things on my mind. We were at war.'

'All the more reason to flirt, if you ask me.' Kitchen chuckled. 'And now that we're home, he still makes excuses. Says he's not the marrying kind.' The valet nudged his seat closer. 'He'd make somebody a decent enough husband, don't you think, miss?'

'I'm sure that he would.'

'But he won't entertain the idea. Just says he'd make any woman miserable.'

'That sounds rather extreme.' She frowned, taken aback. 'Any particular reason?'

'Lots of them.' The colonel turned to look at her finally, his gaze hooded. 'I'll show you the portrait gallery one of these days. Row upon row of bad husbands and unhappy wives. I would never want to make any woman as miserable as my father made my mother. My family has a talent for making disastrous unions.'

'I keep telling him, he just hasn't met the right woman yet, miss.'

'And I keep telling you, you're missing the point. I doubt that any of my ancestors actually started out with the intention of being bad husbands. They just *were*. It's in the blood.'

'Surely you don't mean that.' Abigail stared at him incredulously. 'Blood has nothing to do with it.'

'How do you know?'

'Because people *decide* how they behave, don't they? And even if blood is somehow involved, what about your mother's side?'

'You won't argue him out of it, miss. I've been trying for years.' Kitchen shook his head mournfully. 'He's a hopeless case.'

'Might I point out that you're unmarried, too?' The colonel lifted an eyebrow.

'Ah, but I'm ever hopeful. One of these days the perfect woman will come along and I'll snap her up like that.' Kitchen clicked his fingers emphatically.

'I admire your optimism.'

'What about you, Miss Lemon?' Kitchen clinked the side of his glass against hers as if he were making a toast. 'I reckon a pretty, young woman like yourself must have a beau somewhere. I wouldn't be surprised if they were queuing down the street.'

'*Kitchen*...' The colonel leaned forward, draping his forearms over his knees in a way that drew her attention all over again. They really were extremely muscular...

'I'm not suggesting anything untoward! I'm just wondering why she ain't married, that's all.'

'It's none of our business.'

'But—'

'Actually, I *was* going to be married,' Abigail interrupted. 'Next month, in fact. The thirtieth of April.'

'Never!' Kitchen's mouth dropped open.

'What happened?' The colonel's voice sounded different suddenly. Softer and yet paradoxically, steelier.

'I lost my dowry.' She lifted her shoulders. 'We couldn't marry without it.'

'That's terrible, miss!'

'You should have mentioned it before.' The colonel's expression hardened. 'How much do you need?'

'Need?'

'Yes. I might not be able to find the whole amount straight away, but I might be able to give it to you in instalments. There's no reason to cancel the wedding altogether.'

'That's very kind of you, colonel, but it's too late. I'm no longer engaged.'

'Don't tell me the bast—I mean, the *fellow* called it off?' Kitchen sounded outraged.

'No. I was the one who ended it, but only when it became clear that he wanted me to. He said, quite rightly, that his family would disown him if we didn't end things.' She tightened her grip on the tumbler. 'I expect they were relieved. They never approved of me.'

'Why the hell not?'

'*Kitchen...*'

'Because they wanted someone "better". His father is a baronet, you see, whereas my parents...well, my father was a gentleman and reasonably well off, but my mother was an apothecary's daughter with almost no fortune at all.'

'Were your parents a love match?' The colonel looked interested.

'Oh, yes.' She smiled dreamily. 'They met when he was staying with a friend in her village and fell in love at first sight. His family were outraged by the connection, but he married her anyway.' She swallowed another, larger mouthful of brandy. 'So you see, in Society's terms, my fiancé was a long way above me.'

'Don't say that, miss.' Kitchen put a hand on her shoulder. 'How did you meet this fiancé of yours, if you don't mind me asking?'

'Not at all. It was at an art exhibition three years ago. We were introduced by a mutual acquaintance and he called on me a few days later. It became a regular occurrence, twice, then three times a week. At first, I thought I was just some kind of amusement, but then he told me he loved me and I realised that I felt the same way.' She looked down, swilling the amber liquid around her glass. 'I refused his first proposal because I knew the difference in our family's positions would cause problems. I already knew they called me a social climber and fortune hunter behind my back and I thought that one of us needed to be sensible, but eventually I gave in. I never aspired to be *Lady* Anyone, but I loved him.' She pressed her lips together. 'We waited a year and a half for them to give their approval. Presumably they thought that if they prevaricated for long enough then he'd tire of me, but he didn't. Then, eventually, they agreed to our marriage on condition of a long engagement. Another eighteen months, to be precise. I didn't know it then, but my father promised a much larger dowry than he could afford, one big enough to make up for my lack of connections. That's why he—'

'Invested in the Chelsea scheme,' The colonel finished for her.

'Yes.'

'I'm sorry.'

'So am I. I feel so foolish, too. I should have known that a marriage between us was impossible, but I loved him so much and my parents' story convinced me that love would conquer all. I thought that it could overcome any obstacle, like in some silly fairy tale.' She shook her head. 'But what I really don't understand is why Henry waited so long for me in the first place. Why did he do that if he wasn't prepared to stand by me, no matter what?'

'Because he loved you.' The colonel's eyes locked on to hers.

'Just not enough. He would stand up to his family, but he would never outright defy them.' She clenched her jaw. 'I suppose I can understand that. I just wish that he hadn't persuaded me otherwise. I thought that the fact we waited so long *proved* how much we cared for each other, but when it came to it, love wasn't enough. Not without the money.'

She turned her head sharply at the sound of loud sniffing. She'd been gazing so intently at the colonel that she'd almost forgotten the valet was there, too. 'Kitchen?'

'It's bloody awful, what that man's done to you.'

'It's all right.' She put her glass down on the floor to pat his arm. 'Really.'

'No, it's not. He ought to be horse-whipped for breaking your heart like that.'

'But I'm all right now. Maybe I was deluding myself all along. Or maybe I'm just a terrible judge of character. I thought that Henry was honourable and trustworthy and loyal, but he wasn't. In the end, he wasn't remotely the man that I thought. And how could I truly love a man I didn't know?' She knitted her brows together. 'Now I feel like I'm in mourning for everything that could have been as well as for my father.'

'Just because he wasn't the man for you doesn't mean that love isn't out there.' Theo's voice sounded huskier.

'Maybe it is, but even if I met someone else, how would I know that I wasn't just fooling myself all over again?' She tossed her head. 'No. I refuse to believe in love stories and fairy tales any more. From now on, I intend to rely on myself. Then I *know* who I can trust.'

'That sounds lonely.'

'Says that man who has no intention of marrying.' She gave him a keen look.

'Not you, as well!' Kitchen sounded dismayed. 'You can't let one bad apple put you off love completely. The man's a rotter, pardon my language.'

'No need. I quite agree.'

'What was his name?' The colonel's expression seemed very intense suddenly.

'Why?'

'Curiosity.'

'That's not a good enough reason.'

'Polite interest, then.'

'Politely declined.'

He narrowed his eyes, holding on to hers for a few seconds before tipping his head infinitesimally. 'As you wish.'

'It wouldn't be hard to find out, sir. Just say the word.'

'*Kitchen!*' She spun about indignantly.

'Sorry, miss. Just one word, sir.'

'I'm sitting right next to you!' Abigail rolled her eyes and then sighed heavily. 'The worst part of all is that if it hadn't been for Henry, my father would never have invested in the Chelsea scheme. I'm sure he only took the risk for me, to raise enough money for my dowry.'

'And you feel guilty?' The colonel's voice softened again.

'I do.' Her throat tightened. 'Angry, too. At Henry *and* myself. I just wish that I'd realised what he was like sooner.'

'Did your father tell you he was going to invest in the scheme?'

'Not a word. I would have stopped him.'

'Did he ever try to dissuade you from the match?'

'No. He and Henry got along very well.'

'Then you can't blame yourself.' He spoke authoritatively, as if that were an end to the matter. 'Kitchen's right, the man's a rotter.'

'Thank you.' She smiled, feeling better all of a sudden, then realised that she was staring into his eyes again and quickly drank up the last of her brandy. 'And now I think it's time for me to visit the marchioness. She invited me to dine with her this evening. Enjoy the rest of your celebration, gentlemen.'

'Gentlemen?' Kitchen guffawed. 'I ain't been called that before.'

'I wouldn't get too used to it.' The colonel stood up and reached for her hand, lifting it to his lips and pressing a kiss against her knuckles. 'Good evening, Miss Lemon.'

Abigail caught her breath, surprised both by the gesture and her own unexpected reaction to it, a rush of heat that spread up her arm, into her chest, and then out through her body, causing a warm tingling sensation like a feather tracing the length of her spine, ticklish, but pleasant. There was a fluttery feeling in her chest, too, making her feel unusually light-headed. She had to lick her lips in order to speak again. 'Goodnight, colonel.'

He was making a fool of himself, Theo thought, striding along the second-floor corridor with a cup in one hand. More than that, if anyone saw him, *they'd* think he was making a fool of himself, too. That or offering more than just comfort. Frankly, he didn't understand why he was taking the risk, but he felt compelled to do it and not just because of all the brandy he'd consumed with Kitchen earlier.

The look on Miss Lemon's face when she'd told them about her broken engagement had filled him with a combination of sympathy and something else, something stronger and hotter, something which felt a lot like jealousy, but which couldn't be since he had absolutely no romantic interest in Miss Lemon whatsoever. He had no interest in romance, full stop. Never mind the fact that he didn't find her particularly attractive *and* she was his secretary!

So what the hell was he doing?

He accelerated his steps towards the end of the corridor before he could second-guess himself any further, rapping on her bedroom door with his knuckles.

'I was beginning to think that you'd forgotten—' Miss Lemon appeared after only a few seconds, although it was immediately clear that she was expecting somebody else. For one thing, because she was thrusting a book out at him and, for another, because she was dressed for bed in a white-cotton...a *thin* white-cotton nightdress.

Suddenly the air in the corridor felt a lot thinner.

'Colonel?' She drew the book back and reached for a shawl, pulling it modestly around her shoulders. 'I'm sorry. I thought you were Mrs Evans. She asked to borrow my copy of *Evelina*.'

'My apologies for disturbing you.' He kept his gaze determinedly on her face, though not before he caught a tantalising glimpse of bare feet and slender ankles. 'I just thought you might like this.'

She leaned forward and sniffed, her expression somewhat confused. 'Hot chocolate?'

'Yes. I thought it might make you feel better after our conversation earlier. My mother always had a cup before bed. I used to make it for her when I was a boy.' He frowned, wondering if he'd drunk more brandy than he'd realised. Why else would he have just told her *that*? 'Although please don't feel compelled to drink it if you don't want to.'

'But I'd love to.' She reached for the cup, her fingers brushing lightly against his. 'Thank you, colonel.'

'Theo. I believe that we can dispense with the formalities.'

'Very well, on condition that you call me Abigail.'

'Abigail. That's pretty.' He cleared his throat. 'There was just one other matter. Something I wanted to add to my....' he waved a hand in the air before clasping his hands behind his back '...earlier comments.'

'Yes?'

'He didn't deserve you. Whoever your fiancé was, he wasn't good enough.'

'Oh.' Her eyes widened. 'Thank you.'

'That's all I wanted to say.' He took a step backwards, resisting the urge to take another swift peek at her ankles. 'Enjoy the chocolate.'

'Theo?'

'Yes?' He paused halfway down the corridor, looking back over his shoulder to see her holding the cup in both hands, a slow smile spreading over her face until it reached her eyes and gave her cheeks a warm glow.

'It's delicious.'

## Chapter Ten

'Have you ever heard of the Adelphi project?'

Theo looked up from yet another tedious ledger to find Abigail's face peering around the edge of her office door. Or at least he assumed it was Abigail since the woman before him bore only a passing resemblance to the one he'd first met in his office two weeks before. Her dark eyes were twinkling, her skin had a radiant glow and her hair was a lustrous golden shade that put him in mind of sunflowers. She certainly didn't look forty any more.

'No,' he answered more gruffly than he'd intended, but really, *sunflowers*? What the hell was happening to him? 'Should I have?'

'It's a row of terraces beside the Thames, designed and built by the Adams' brothers almost fifty years ago. The project collapsed due to high costs, but the brothers were saved from bankruptcy by a public lottery.' She took a few steps into his office and spread her hands out. 'To be honest, I have no idea what a public lottery is, but I thought it might be something we might look into?'

'Anything's worth a try. I'll mention it to the lawyers

on my next visit.' He grimaced. 'I'll sure I'll be visiting them again in another hour or two.'

'Actually, your next meeting is the day after tomorrow.' She put her hands on her hips. 'Although if you dislike seeing them so much, they could always come here.'

'No, I prefer to go out. I spend enough of my time behind this desk as it is these days.' He stretched his neck from side to side and lifted a hand to his mouth, stifling a yawn. 'So how did you find out about this Adelphi project?'

'Hatchard's. I asked the manager if he had any books on the subject and he found me an old pamphlet. It was most informative. Here.' She leaned over, placing a tattered piece of paper on the desk in front of him.

'I'm impressed.' He pretended to read, though it was well-nigh impossible when the subtle yet tantalising scent of orange blossom was filling his nostrils, causing his nerve endings to leap in response. The fact that her breasts were on a level with his eye line didn't particularly help either. A wholly inappropriate succession of lurid images were whirling through his brain.

'You look tired.' She seemed oblivious to the effect she was having, smiling down at him. 'Are you thirsty? Because I'm ready for some tea.'

'I could probably manage a cup. Sabrina?' He jerked his head around in surprise as his sister-in-law swept regally into the room. To his knowledge, it was the first time she'd been downstairs in weeks. More significantly, she was properly dressed, in a burgundy-coloured day gown with her long hair piled into an intricate coil at the back of her head. It was definitely progress, although something about the determined set of her shoulders alarmed him, too.

'Good, you're both here.' Sabrina strode imperiously into the centre of the room. 'There's something I want to discuss.'

'Go ahead.' Theo rolled his shoulders, trying to stretch the knots out. 'Just don't be offended if I nap.'

'I most certainly *will* be offended. This is important.' She lifted her chin and fixed him with a determined stare. 'I've decided that Evelyn should have a Season this year, after all.'

'You've decided…what?' He felt a lead weight settle in his stomach.

'I want her to still have a Season. It was the original plan.'

'Not to state the obvious, but that was *before*.'

'Yes, but she shouldn't be held responsible for her father's stupid decisions. Or be punished for them either.'

'I agree, but not everyone will see it that way.'

'Only a few members of the *ton* invested in his scheme. I don't see why we should have to keep hiding ourselves away as though we're ashamed. He's the one in the wrong, not us.'

'I agree, but you—*we*—are still tainted by association. Think of Evelyn's feelings. How will she feel if people deliberately cut her?'

Sabrina's expression faltered. 'I've told her what might happen, but she wants to try anyway.'

'So why not wait another year until the scandal's died down? She's only eighteen.'

'Because eighteen is the perfect age for a Season!'

Theo pushed his chair back and stood up, too exasperated to remain seated. 'So after a month of hiding in your room, refusing to receive any callers and saying that you'll never be able to show your face ever again, suddenly you want to start attending balls?'

'Yes! We've received a few invitations despite what's happened. Of course, everybody expects us to decline, but they can hardly retract them. It's not too late to start accepting. And if Miss Lemon comes with us…?' She threw a look of appeal in Abigail's direction.

'It's not as simple as that.'

*'Please.'* A flash of something like fear passed over Sabrina's face. 'I'm afraid that if I don't bring Evelyn out now then I never will. I might lose my nerve by next year.' Fear turned to anger. 'Either that or Fitzwilliam will find some other new way to shame us.'

Theo clenched his jaw. Much as he hated to admit it, the last part was entirely too possible. There was no telling what his brother might do next. 'Look, I understand what you're saying and I'm glad that you're out of your room, but how do you expect us to pay for a Season?'

'The same way that we'll pay for Evelyn's dowry.' Sabrina's eyes glinted triumphantly. 'We'll sell some property.'

'You mean sell one of Fitz's estates? That's a big step.'

'So was abandoning his family. I've even decided which property you can sell.' She lifted an eyebrow. 'The hunting lodge in Wiltshire. That was always his favourite. It should be the first to go.'

'Sabrina…' Theo pushed a hand through his hair, bracing himself for another argument. 'I can't.'

'Why not? He said that he's not coming back and he gave you permission to take over his business dealings. Surely that includes property?'

'He left a letter saying something to that effect, yes, but it's hardly legally binding. In the eyes of the law, he's still the marquess. If he'd signed his authority over to me properly, then it might be different, but I'd need his permission in order to start selling land.' He came around to the front of the desk. 'And I'd need to find him for that.'

'Then we'll find him! There must be ways.'

'There are and I will, but first, I need to get things under control here. It could be months before I can go and look for him. I'm sorry, Sabrina, but a Season this year is out of the question.'

'So that's it?' Her hands curled into fists. 'Fitz still gets to control our lives even when he's not in the same country?'

'That's the law.'

'The law is an insult!' She whirled about, flinging a hand out and pushing a blue-and-white porcelain vase off a table as she stormed back towards the door. Fortunately, he was expecting some kind of violence, diving forward and catching it just before it shattered on the floor.

'You're quick.' Abigail winced as the door slammed behind the marchioness. She'd kept quiet during the exchange, though her expression was troubled.

'Living with my sister-in-law hones the reflexes.' He went to put the vase back on the table and then reconsidered, placing it on top of a bookcase instead.

'Would a Season really be so expensive?'

'I'm afraid so. Think of a large number and then double it.' He went to stand by the window. 'It's not just the clothes either. It's the subscriptions and tickets and transport, not to mention the fact that Sabrina would probably want us to throw some kind of ball ourselves.'

'Oh, dear.' She came to stand beside him. 'And is it really impossible to sell any property without your brother's permission?'

'Honestly?' He stared out at a flock of starlings in the park opposite. 'I don't know and, unfortunately, neither do any of my lawyers. If we could be absolutely certain that Fitz isn't coming back, then I could probably do what I like, but he's always been unpredictable. There's still a chance that wherever he's gone isn't what he expects. And if he comes back and starts making trouble...' He hung his head. 'That's the most frustrating part of all this. I'm not sure how far my hands are tied.'

'It sounds very complicated. Do you really intend to go and find him when things are more settled?'

'I do, but not just to get his permission to act. I intend to bring him back here. I'll sort out his mess as best I can in the meantime, but he's the marquess and he needs to face his responsibilities. This is his and my father's world, not mine. I've no desire to be a member of the *ton*.'

'But what if he refuses to come back?'

'Then I'll drag him by the roots of his hair if necessary.' He gritted his teeth and then grimaced. 'Unfortunately, that might not be so easy. If I knew where he was, I'd set out tomorrow, but the blunt truth is that he could be anywhere in the world by now.'

'Didn't he leave any clue about where he was going?'

'Nothing at all. That doesn't mean I'm going to give up, however. I'll track him down eventually. In the meantime, I'm stuck here.'

'I see.' She turned around, bracing her hands on the

windowsill and leaning back against it. He couldn't help but notice how delicate her wrists were. He had a sudden, quickly suppressed impulse to reach out and stroke one.

'And then what will you do?'

'Mmm?' He looked up again guiltily.

'What will you do once you're finished here?'

'What I was going to do when I left the army. Go to America and start a new life, away from all of this. I only came back to England to make sure my men were settled. I was almost free to be my own man and make my own decisions. *Finally*. Then I made the mistake of coming back here for a brief family visit. All because I thought it was the right thing to do. And now I'm trapped.' His shoulders sagged. 'You know, I loathe this house with every fibre of my being.'

'This house?' She sounded surprised. 'But it's magnificent.'

'I suppose so, objectively. But subjectively...' He shuddered. 'I didn't visit often as a child, but my father lived here for most of the year, like a spider in the centre of a very large and intricate web. You know, I don't remember him uttering a single kind word. Fortunately, I stayed in Norfolk most of the time with my mother, but on the few occasions we visited...all I remember is a lot of shouting and crying. The only memories I have of this place are bad ones, of this room in particular. His study.'

He looked over his shoulder and narrowed his eyes. 'He told me about my commission in here. It was the morning of my eighteenth birthday and he summoned me in and told me I was going to join my new regiment that afternoon. He didn't ask if it was what I wanted, which it definitely wasn't, he just said that he'd bought a commission and that it would make a man of me.'

He tipped his head towards her. 'I was never enough of one for him, you see. He thought that I was too close to my mother and read too many books. Fitz, on the other hand, was the perfect son, brilliant at all the things my father valued, whereas I was the runt. When he sent me off to the army, it was as though he was trying to find a way to dispose of me.'

'No!' She looked horrified. 'I'm sure no father would do such a thing.'

'That's because you never met mine.'

'Was the army very awful?'

'At first, but I got used to it and made friends. It's not the life I would have chosen for myself, but at least I got Kitchen.' He gave a wry smile.

'What did your mother think of you joining the army?'

'If she'd still been alive then, she would have been horrified.'

'Oh.' Her voice softened. 'I'm sorry.'

'So am I. In any case, when I left, I told myself that no matter what happened, I'd never come back here.'

'And now you've been compelled to.'

'Now I've been compelled to,' he agreed. 'To be fair, there are other properties I could use, but they're all essentially the same thing, all part of my father's web.' He laughed mirthlessly. 'You know, he would have been furious at the situation we're in now. That's my one consolation in all of this mess.'

'You could have refused to stay and help when your brother left.'

'It crossed my mind.'

'I doubt that.' She gave him a sceptical look.

'What do you mean?'

'I doubt that it crossed your mind. You're far too honourable. Possett told me that the marchioness threw a decanter at your head a couple of weeks ago. A lot of men would have called that the last straw.'

'I got used to danger in the army. It helps if you think of her as Napoleon.'

She smiled and put a hand on his shoulder. 'Does it hurt?'

'What?' He stiffened at the contact.

'Your shoulder. You keep stretching your neck from side to side.'

'Oh. The muscles are a little tense, that's all.'

'Here.' She moved to stand behind him, pressing her thumbs into his shoulder blades and rolling them in small circles. 'Is that better?'

'Mmm.' He made a strangled sound in the back of his throat. It was more than better. It was the best. Suddenly his shoulder felt better than it ever had in his entire life. His whole body felt weightless. For some reason, it was making his head spin and dots dance in front of his eyes, too. He had to remind himself to breathe.

'There you go.' She patted his back as if she'd just finished stroking Lady and moved to his side again.

'Thank you.' He coughed, trying to make his voice sound normal.

'Colonel?'

'Yes?'

'Forgive me for saying so, but even if you do succeed in dragging your brother back here, surely, unless he and the marchioness reconcile and have a son, then as the next brother all of this will be yours one day anyway? Then you'll *have* to stay here and be the next marquess.'

'Not necessarily. My brother might outlive me.'

'Then your sons will inherit, if you have them.'

'Which I won't because I've no intention of marrying. I told you, the men in my family have an uncanny ability to make terrible husbands. My mother was desperately unhappy. My grandmother, too, from what I remember. I wouldn't know how to be a good husband, let alone a half-decent father. Who's to say I wouldn't be as bad as my own?'

'Me. *I* can say that.'

He blinked at her decisive tone. 'After two weeks' acquaintance?'

She opened her mouth, closed it again and then frowned. 'You're right. When it comes to men, I'm hardly the best judge of character. Look at how badly I misjudged Henry. Maybe you *would* be a bad husband.'

He laughed aloud. 'Is that meant to be consoling?'

'No, but it's ironic. *You* don't want to marry because you think that you'd be a bad husband and *I* don't want to marry because there's a real danger that I'd choose a bad one. We actually have the same problem, only in reverse.'

'So we're either perfect for each other or a perfect recipe for disaster.'

She gave him a startled look and then smiled, her eyes shimmering with amusement. 'That's true.'

'We should probably agree not to find out which it is.'

'Absolutely.' She nodded firmly.

He let his gaze move over her face, reflecting again on how much she'd changed since her arrival. She looked...damn it, she looked remarkably pretty. Captivatingly so, since he seemed unable to move his eyes away from her. When she smiled, her lips looked wider, fuller and redder and…

'Excuse me, Sir.' Thankfully, a tap on the door distracted him. 'But there's a visitor for Miss Lemon.'

'For me?' Abigail sounded surprised.

'Yes, miss. She didn't want to give her name, but she's waiting in the hall. I asked her to come into the drawing room, but she says that she can only stay for a few minutes.'

'That sounds very mysterious.' She lifted her eyebrows at Theo. 'I'd better go and see who it is.'

He turned around, leaning back against the window sill beside her. 'You know, whenever my soldiers wanted to be dismissed, they generally asked my permission.'

'Did they?' She sighed plaintively. 'I always suspected I'd make a very bad soldier.'

'I'd better get back to work anyway.' He chuckled. 'I apologise for talking so much about myself.'

'There's no need. I asked and, for what it's worth, I think that what you're doing for your family is a good thing. A very good thing.'

'Thank you.' He felt a warm glow, a new and stirring sensation, bloom and then spread inside his chest. 'And thank you for listening.'

'Harriet?' Abigail approached her old friend more cautiously than she had when they'd met in the park. 'I thought you weren't allowed to speak with me any more?'

'I know. I'm so sorry about the other day.' Harriet was standing in the middle of the hallway, her expression anguished. 'It was horrible. My mother-in-law was unforgivably rude.'

'But why? I know that I'm working for a living now, but I still thought—'

'It's not because of that. It's because of…' Harriet's eyes dipped pointedly down to her stomach. 'You *know*.'

'No.' Abigail dropped her gaze too, wondering if there was something wrong with the front of her dress. 'I don't.'

'The *baby*.'

'The what?'

'Your baby. We assumed that you'd moved to the country so you could have it in secret.'

Abigail opened and closed her mouth a few times, trying to understand, but her mind seemed to have a problem comprehending the words. She knew what they all meant individually, but together they made no sense at all. 'Harriet, surely you don't think that I'm having a baby?'

'Yes! I have to say, it's not showing yet, but…' Harriet's brow wrinkled '…aren't you?'

'No!'

'But Lady Raven said—'

'Lady Raven?' Her heart slammed to a halt. 'Henry's *aunt*, Lady Raven?'

'Um… Ye-es.'

'You mean, Henry's aunt is going around telling everyone that I'm expecting a child?'

'Not everyone, but she and my mother-in-law are friends so—'

'Wait!' Abigail pressed her fingertips to her forehead. Blood seemed to be rushing in and out of her face in a feverish torrent. 'I don't understand. If Henry's aunt thinks that he and I are having a baby in secret, why on earth is she telling people? It hardly reflects well on him, considering that our engagement is over.'

'Because…' Harriet bit down on her bottom lip, mumbling something incoherently.

'Pardon?'

'Because…' Another mumble.

'Harriet?'

'She says that it's not his.'

'What?' Abigail stared at her friend, aghast. She felt winded, as if she'd just taken a blow to the stomach. Not an accidental blow either, but a full-blown punch. Bile rose in her throat and there seemed to be a weight pressing down on her chest, making her already pounding heartbeat pound even harder. She couldn't seem to take in enough air. 'Then who…' she gasped '…is the father supposed to be?'

'I don't know. She said that she didn't either. Abigail, I'm so sorry. I should never have listened to gossip, but she was so definite and then, when you left so abruptly—'

'I sent you a note!'

'Did you?' Harriet clenched her fists. 'My mother-in-law goes through our correspondence. She probably destroyed it, the interfering old harridan—Oh.' She quickly unclenched and dipped into a curtsy as the colonel strode into the hall at that moment. 'Good afternoon, my lord.'

'Good afternoon. Please forgive the interruption. I just have one quick question for Miss Lemon.' He made a cursory bow before turning to Abigail. 'Do you have any idea where—?' He took one look at her stricken face and stopped. 'What's happened? What's the matter?'

She stared at him, wide-eyed, for a few seconds, unable to find the right words so settling for the first ones that came to mind instead. 'I'm having a baby. Apparently.'

'You're…' His eyes flickered with some emotion she couldn't identify. 'What?'

'That's what people are saying. That I'm having a baby and no one knows who the father is.'

'Who's saying this?'

She blinked at the sudden change in his voice. It sounded hard and cold and intimidating, although the words weren't directed at her, she realised. He was speaking to Harriet, his brows lowered and his jaw set like granite. Suddenly he looked every inch the formidable army colonel, demanding answers from some unfortunate soldier.

'I…um…' Harriet quailed visibly. 'Lady Raven.'

'And what made *her* think such a thing? Who started such a vile rumour?'

'Maybe I misunderstood.' Harriet looked panicked. 'Or I misheard.'

'*Who?*'

'It was Henry's mother, wasn't it?' Abigail put her hands on her hips, shock giving way to anger. 'She never liked me.'

'No.' Harriet shook her head miserably. 'It wasn't her. Or at least, she's not the one Lady Raven mentioned.'

'Then who—? No!' She lifted a hand to her throat, seized with a wave of nausea as the truth finally gripped her. 'He wouldn't.'

'I'm sorry, Abbie.'

'But it doesn't make any sense. Why would he say such a thing?'

'I don't know. I can't believe it either.'

'Does he think that it's true?' She staggered backwards, racking her brains for anything that might have given Henry cause to think she'd betrayed him, but there was nothing. She'd never as much as flirted with another man. And surely, if he'd had suspicions then he would have mentioned them when he'd asked her to end their engagement... But why else would he deliberately slander her reputation?

'Abigail?' The colonel stepped in front of her, eyes glittering with anger. 'Who?'

'My fiancé. *Former* fiancé.' She gulped, her skin prickling as surges of different emotions coursed beneath it like waves. 'But I don't understand why he would do such a thing.'

'What's his name?'

'It doesn't matter.' She moistened her lips with her tongue. 'I need time to think.'

'Henry Quinnell.' Harriet interjected. 'His father is Sir William Quinnell. You'll probably find him at his parents' house in Portman Square at this time of day.'

'Quinnell. Portman Square. Thank you.' Theo spun on his heel.

'Wait!' Abigail caught at his arm. 'What do you think you're doing?'

'First, I'm going to demand an apology. Second, I'm going to knock his teeth down the back of his throat.'

'No!' She tightened her grip. '*No* violence and if anyone's going to demand an apology, then it ought to be me.'

'But surely he deserves to lose at least one tooth?' Harriet sounded positively bloodthirsty. 'How dare he say such things about you! He must have known the rumours would get back to your friends.'

'There's still no call for violence.' She lifted her chin primly and then relented. 'Unless he refuses to apologise, that is. *Then* you can hit him.'

'I'll give him five seconds.'

'Ten! And *I'm* doing the talking. This is about me, not you.'

'Eight.' He gave a curt nod. 'But I'm coming with you.'

'Deal.'

'You won't tell anyone that I told you, will you?' Harriet sounded anxious again. 'Only if my mother-in-law found out…'

'Not a soul, I promise.' Abigail let go of Theo long enough to give her friend a swift hug. 'Thank you for coming. Even if you're not allowed to visit again, I hope we can still remain friends.'

'Of course we can.' Harriet's expression wavered before settling on a look of resolve. 'I'll find a way!'

# Chapter Eleven

'Slow down!'

Theo looked over his shoulder, scowling ferociously, as Abigail ran along the pavement after him. Not that he was scowling at her; he just couldn't seem to arrange his face in any other way. Frankly, he was taken aback by the extent of his own fury. All throughout his army career, he'd prided himself on keeping an even temper and never acting out of anger, but at that moment he wanted to wrap his hands around her former fiancé's neck and squeeze. If the man had insulted him personally, he couldn't imagine being any more livid.

'I can't slow down. I'm too angry.'

'*You're* angry?' She grabbed hold of his arm again, panting. '*I'm* the one who's been insulted!'

'Yes, but—'

'*I'm* the one whose friends think she's been abandoned by her fiancé because she's having a baby with another man!'

'All right—'

'*And* my legs are shorter than yours!' She dug her feet in and pulled him to a halt. 'The least you can do is walk at my pace. I absolutely forbid you from going ahead and confronting him first!'

'You're right.' He forced himself to take a deep breath. 'My apologies, but what the hell kind of a man does something like this?'

'I don't know, but I intend to find out.' She leaned forward slightly to get her breath back, her breasts brushing lightly against his arm before she started walking again. 'I just keep thinking it must be some kind of misunderstanding.'

'Your friend didn't think so.'

'No, but the Henry I knew would never have spread such underhand rumours. He wasn't cruel.'

'He's not the man you thought he was.' He took a strange satisfaction in the words. 'You said so yourself the other night.'

'But this would mean I didn't know him at all! And what would that say about me and my judgement?' She stopped outside a five-storey grey-brick house and shuddered. 'Here we are. I think I loathe this place almost as much as you loathe Salway House. Henry's family were always so horrible to me. I never told my father, but there were several times I almost ended our engagement because of it. Now I wish that I'd listened to my instincts.'

'What did they do exactly?'

'Nothing overt, just looks and disparaging comments. They certainly never made me feel welcome.' She clenched her jaw. 'I wonder if they'll even let me in today.'

'I'll barge the bloody door down if they don't.' He marched up the front steps and rammed his fist against it.

'Good afternoon.' A butler appeared after only a few

seconds, the faintly mocking expression that passed over his face at the sight of Abigail making Theo ten times more furious. At this rate, he was going to combust.

'We're here to see Mr Henry Quinnell.' He pushed past him into the vestibule. 'And we don't give a damn whether this is a convenient time or not.'

'You can't just—' The butler reconsidered as Theo glared at him. 'Might I take your name, sir?'

'Colonel Lord Theodore Marshall.' He lifted an eyebrow. 'I presume that you already know my companion? Given that she was engaged to your employer's son for the past year and a half?'

'Indeed.' The butler looked down at his toes. 'Good afternoon, Miss Lemon.'

'On second thoughts...' Theo jerked his head around at the sound of voices and laughter coming from behind a set of closed double doors. 'Is that the family?'

'You can't just go in!'

'Try to stop me.'

He grabbed hold of Abigail's hand and charged ahead, pushing the doors open to reveal half-a-dozen people gathered around the fireplace, drinking tea.

'Henry Quinnell?' He narrowed his eyes, looking for the man most likely to be Abigail's ex-fiancé. There were only three possibilities, one of whom appeared to be in his sixties, leaving one man with blond hair, not unlike his own, and another darker-haired man with a square jaw and perfectly symmetrical features...

'Who are you?' Annoyingly, it was the handsome man who stood up, his eyes darting between them before finally settling on their joined hands. *Good!*

'I'm sorry, sir.' The butler ran, panting, into the room behind him. 'I tried to stop them.'

'Not your fault, Wilkins.' The man came around the sofa, squaring up to Theo. 'Now, perhaps you might explain your presence here.'

'No.' Abigail's voice was surprisingly calm and steady. 'He doesn't have to explain anything. *We're* not the ones with explaining to do. *You* are.' She let go of Theo's hand to poke a finger against the other man's chest. 'And you can start by telling me why you're spreading rumours about me.'

'I don't know what you mean.'

It was fortunate for the man, Theo reflected, flexing his knuckles, that Abigail had just positioned herself between them. He might as well have been wearing a large guilty sign around his neck.

'Oh, really? Then why is it that people appear to think I'm with child?' She jabbed his chest again, harder this time. 'And who, do tell, is supposed to be the father?'

'This is preposterous.' A woman with white hair and a sour expression stood up from one of the armchairs. 'Miss Lemon, I wish I could say that I was surprised by your appalling behaviour, but I'm not. I insist that you leave my house at once!'

'With pleasure.' Abigail didn't as much as glance in her direction. 'Just as soon as Henry explains himself!'

'It's all a mistake.' The man's ears began to turn a bright purple colour. 'My words were misinterpreted.'

'*What* words?'

'I simply made a few comments regarding the end of our engagement, but it was nothing incriminating.

It's not my fault if people took them to imply something else.'

'I think I can guess what happened.' Theo moved to stand beside her again. '*I* think that people were making insinuations about your broken engagement. Maybe a few even speculated about the kind of man who would abandon the woman he professed to love, knowing that she'd be penniless and homeless, not to mention completely alone in the world, a mere month before their wedding? Maybe some actually had the temerity to suggest that it was dishonourable. So he started a rumour to make himself look like the injured party.'

'Henry?' Abigail's lips had turned very pale. 'Is this true?'

'He did her enough of an honour by asking for her hand in the first place!' The white-haired woman stormed towards them. 'How could anyone expect him to marry her with no fortune at all?'

'Be quiet, Mama!' The man flung the words over his shoulder, visibly sweating now. 'I'm sorry, Abigail. It wasn't intentional, I swear. I don't know how it happened. I never *specifically* said that you were with child.'

'You just said enough to let people imagine the worst?'

'I assumed that you'd moved to Wimbledon to live with your aunts.'

'So you thought it was safe to spread rumours about me?' Her eyes flashed. 'How could you? Wasn't it enough that I lost everything else, but you had to destroy my reputation and make sure that all my old friends would turn their backs on me, too?'

'I'm sorry, Abigail.'

'Like you were sorry about the end of our engagement?' She looked him up and down scathingly. 'How can I believe a single word you say?'

'Because I mean it. Truly.'

'Not good enough.' Theo pushed his face to within an inch of the other man's. 'You're going to make sure that all of Miss Lemon's friends know you were mistaken. Go from house to house, print a pamphlet, put an apology in the newspaper if necessary, but make sure they know.'

'I'll do no such thing. Who do you think you are?'

'Oh, didn't I mention?' Abigail smiled sweetly. 'Allow me to present Colonel Lord Theodore Marshall, hero of Waterloo and good friend of the Duke of Wellington.'

'Wellington?'

'*Very* good friend,' Theo agreed. 'Miss Lemon here has recently joined my household in the capacity of companion to my sister-in-law, the Marchioness of Salway. On top of which, I've asked her to chaperon my niece, Lady Evelyn Marshall, about town during the Season so you see, any stain upon her reputation is a personal insult to my family.' He paused. 'And I don't take kindly to those.'

'No…of course.'

'I'll give you one week to put this right or I'll be back.'

'*We* will be.' Abigail jabbed him in the ribs with her elbow.

'My apologies.' He tipped his head towards her. 'We will be. And next time, we won't be so nice.'

'Are you all right?' Theo crooked his elbow as they descended the front steps a mere ten minutes after their arrival.

'No.' Abigail hooked her hand through his arm, her knees trembling beneath her. Now that the encounter with Henry was over, she felt stunned and sickened and more furious than she'd ever been in her life. She would never have believed him capable of anything so base if he hadn't admitted the truth himself. Part of her still couldn't believe it. How could she have been so wrong about a person she'd thought that she'd loved? Now she felt red hot all over and she didn't know which was worse, that or her whirling head or roiling stomach. She put her foot on the bottom step and stumbled.

'Look out.' Theo lifted his other arm, catching her neatly around the waist.

'I think I need to sit down.'

'Of course.' He kept an arm around her as they walked across the road to a park in the centre of the square. 'Over here.'

He gestured towards a narrow, wooden bench and she sank down gratefully, wrapping her arms around her stomach and curling inwards. If she hadn't known better, she would have thought there was a grey cloud over her head, casting a shadow over her very soul. Even her vision seemed darker.

'Try to breathe through your nose.' He sat down beside her, rubbing a hand over her back.

'I will.' Instinctively, she swayed towards him for comfort. 'Thank you for not hitting him.'

'It wasn't easy.'

'I know.' She laughed bitterly. 'I actually found myself wondering about the etiquette of challenging a man to a duel.'

'Swords or pistols?'

'Pistols. I've never used a sword. *Or* a pistol for that

matter, but it seems like I'd have a better chance of winning.'

'If you're serious about duelling—'

'I'm not. And if you're about to suggest what I think you're about to suggest, then don't. I appreciate the support, but I can fight my own battles.' She twisted her head sharply. 'Just to be clear, I'd be furious at anyone who tried to fight them for me.'

'Understood.'

'At least this way I keep the moral high ground.'

'You don't find that a little overrated?'

'*Very* at the moment, but one day, I'll feel better, knowing that I kept it.' She sat up again, tipping her head back and looking up at the sky. 'More than anything, I just feel so stupid. How could I ever have trusted a man like that?'

'You're not stupid. Everyone makes mistakes.'

'For three years?'

'People change. I'm sure he was charming.'

'He was.'

'Good looking, too.'

'So I'm shallow as well as stupid?'

'No, I didn't mean—'

'I know.' She put a hand on his arm. 'But the truth is, maybe I *was* a little shallow. Everyone used to comment on how handsome he was. I suppose I was flattered that he liked me, yet the funny thing is that looking at him now, I can't see it at all. He just looks…weak, whereas you—' She bit her tongue quickly.

She'd been about to say that with him, the reverse was happening. Theo's less conventionally striking features seemed to be growing more and more handsome. Not that she ought to say anything like that out loud.

'I'm not sorry that it's over, not now I know who he really is. I'm just sorry for everything I've lost. Marriage, children, the future I thought I was going to have...'

'You're still young.'

'No.' She shook her head fiercely. 'I told you, I'm putting all of that behind me and looking after myself from now on. I'm certainly not giving any man a chance to deceive me again.' She laughed suddenly. 'Did you see the looks on their faces when I mentioned the Duke of Wellington, though?'

'I did.' His lips twitched. 'But surely you mean, my *good* friend, the Duke?'

'Oh...' She looked momentarily shamefaced. 'Sorry about that. I might have got a little carried away.'

'Actually, I've met him a few times. I can't say that I know him very well, but enough to know that, under the circumstances, he'd forgive a little exaggeration.' He lifted an eyebrow. 'Now shall we get away from this Square and walk a little? It might help you feel better.'

'Good idea.' She stood up and took his proffered arm, her vision brightening a little. 'Do you think that Henry will really tell people the truth?'

'Yes, unless he wants to be the target of some interesting gossip himself.'

'What kind of gossip?'

'I don't know yet, but I'll ask Kitchen. He has an extremely vivid imagination.'

'In that case, I'm not sure I want to know, but thank you for defending me.' She squeezed his arm, vaguely surprised by how comfortable she felt with him after such a short acquaintance. 'The part about me chaperoning Evelyn for the Season was genius, although I'm sure they'll find out the truth soon enough.'

'Then we should make it the truth.'

She twisted towards him in surprise. 'What do you mean?'

'That you *should* chaperon Evelyn for the Season. Nobody could suspect you were having a baby then.'

'But I thought you said—?'

'I've changed my mind.'

'Colonel—*Theo*—you don't have to do that for me.'

'I'm not. It's also because of what Sabrina said about losing her nerve. She might have a point. I'm not saying that it will be easy, but if she thinks it's the right thing to do for Evelyn, then who am I to stand in the way? She's her mother, after all.'

'What about the cost?'

He shrugged. 'I'll take Sabrina's advice and sell some property. She's right, my brother has abnegated his right to make decisions, morally if not legally. If he comes back and objects, then I'll deal with that when it happens.' He stopped walking again. 'So that's my plan, if you think it's a good one, that is?'

'Does it matter what I think?'

'Yes. I value your opinion.' He made a face. 'I also know very little about young women and what they want. Evelyn still seems very young to me.'

'She's eighteen. A lot of girls are married by that age. Sabrina says she married your brother at sixteen.'

'And look how that worked out.'

'True.' She tipped her head to one side. 'Were they never happy?'

'To be honest, I don't know. I was only eight years old when they got married. I remember a lot of arguing. It was just like my own parents, except that Sabrina argued back. As I got older, I actually wondered if they enjoyed it. All the shouting and then reconciling afterwards. It was as though they loved and hated each other in equal measure. I suppose eventually the balance tipped.' He furrowed his brow. 'You'd think that Sabrina would want to give Evelyn a little longer before she joins the Marriage Mart.'

'On the other hand, maybe it's possible to be too cautious.' Abigail scrunched her mouth up thoughtfully. 'I thought that I was sensible, waiting for the right man to come along, then when I thought that he had, I waited some more, and look what happened to me.'

'So there's no right answer?'

'Or we just don't know it.'

'That's definitely true.' He looked out over the park. 'I just want to do the right thing by Evelyn. I might not be her father, but I feel responsible. I'd hate for her to make a mistake she might come to regret.' He quirked an eyebrow as she started laughing. 'What?'

'You! How can you honestly think that you'd be a bad husband when all the evidence is to the contrary? You're *always* trying to do the right thing by everyone. By your family, by your former soldiers, even by me.'

'I just try to be aware of my faults.' He smiled sheepishly. 'So, what do you say to a Season for Evelyn? Would you be prepared to accompany her about town? I get the feeling that Sabrina will need some moral support. Bear in mind, however, that you're under absolutely no obligation to say yes. I know that you're still in mourning for your father.'

'My father used to say that life was for living. I don't think he'd approve of my staying in mourning for the full year.' She paused, considering. 'I'd be happy to help although, honestly, I might not be the right person. I'm not a member of the *ton* and I've never had a Season. I wouldn't know how to behave.'

'Just behave as you always do. You seem perfect to me.'

'Perfect?' She caught her breath, then caught it again as their eyes met. Suddenly she didn't feel quite so comfortable any more. For a disconcerting moment, she was actually seized with a powerful impulse to move her face closer to his. The tingling sensation she'd felt when he'd kissed her knuckles the other evening was back and making her feel decidedly *un*comfortable, although not in a bad way...

On the contrary, it felt surprisingly good. 'Then I'll do my best.' She touched a hand to her throat, feeling her pulse throb there. 'But what about my work for you? Does this mean I'm not your secretary any more?'

'Hmm.' His brows lowered again. 'I didn't think of that. All right, how about half-days? That way you can choose to work either mornings or afternoons, depending on when Sabrina needs you.'

She nodded slowly. The thought of not working alongside him every day made her feel inexplicably sad, although considering her recent tingles, maybe it was for the best... 'All right, I'll do it.' She tried to perk herself up. 'That way at least two good things came out of today.'

'What's the other? I'm intrigued.'

'That I got you away from your desk for a while. This might not have been a particularly relaxing afternoon, but it's still been a break. That's better than nothing.'

'You're right. I should take more time off.' He clicked his fingers. 'How about a family picnic? Tomorrow? We could visit Chelsea.'

'You mean, go and see the building project?'

'Why not? I should probably make sure nothing's collapsed.'

'I think that sounds like a wonderful idea.' She smiled back at him. 'I'd be very interested to see it. And it might be a nice place to tell Sabrina your decision about giving Evelyn a Season.'

'Actually…' He looked awkward. 'Cowardly as it sounds, I was rather hoping you might do that.'

'You don't want to tell them yourself?'

'Absolutely not.' He shook his head adamantly. 'There'll be even more noise. Squealing probably. In fact, the one proviso I put on this whole project is that I don't have to be involved. Honestly, I'd like them to enjoy themselves without telling me a single word about it.'

## Chapter Twelve

The building site was bigger than Abigail had expected, the size of several cricket pitches. It looked surprisingly well organised, too. Some of the houses seemed almost close to completion, some were little more than foundations, most were roofless shells. There were piles of bricks and sand, but no workmen in sight, giving the place an eerie, abandoned look.

'I didn't realise the scheme was so ambitious.' She stepped down from the open carriage, looking around with interest. 'What a shame. It would have been spectacular.'

'There would have been nice views of the river, I suppose.' Sabrina remained seated, as if she were keen to get away.

'What went wrong?' Abigail turned towards Theo.

'A lot of things.' He rubbed a hand over his jaw. 'Fitz overspent on building materials. He always had to have the best of everything. Unfortunately, he didn't have the same philosophy when it came to labour. A lot of the work had to be redone several times.'

'Is there no way you could finish it? A loan from the bank, maybe?'

He shook his head. 'He was already up to his eye-balls in loans. The bank won't lend any more, especially not for this project.'

'But it seems like such a waste to leave it like this.'

'It does,' he agreed. 'Honestly, if somebody else wants to take over, I'd be happy to give them the deeds at this point.'

'Ahem.' Sabrina coughed loudly. 'There's a meadow over there by the river. It looks like a charming spot for a picnic.'

'I was thinking of the hill.' Theo gestured in the opposite direction.

'But the flowers look so pretty. What do you think, Abigail?' Sabrina pouted. 'Pretty meadow or steep-looking hill?'

'I vote for the meadow.' Abigail threw Theo an apologetic smile before winking at Florence, sitting in the second carriage with Evelyn. 'We can make you a crown of flowers.'

'As you wish.' To her surprise, Theo's voice sounded leaden, though when she looked around, his expression was oddly blank.

They climbed back into the carriage and made their way the short distance to the meadow. It looked idyllic, filled with a bright and sweet-smelling mixture of cowslips, primroses, daisies and even a few isolated bluebells.

'Well, this is charming.' Sabrina sat down on the blanket a footman spread out for her and peered inside one of the picnic baskets. 'I hope that everyone's hungry. Cook appeared to think we were going on an Arctic expedition.'

'I'm not hungry at all.' Evelyn flung herself down heavily.

'Never mind. More for us.' Sabrina rolled her eyes before looking up at Theo. 'Do you know, this is the first time we've eaten together in ten years.'

'Is it?' Theo looked around, still wearing the same oddly blank expression.

'Yes. You're always eating at your desk and I'm always in my sitting room with Miss Lemon.'

'Then we should make a point of all eating together from now on. What's the point of having a dining room if none of us is using it?'

'What about me?' Evelyn sat up again. 'Or do I still have to eat in the nursery?'

'You're welcome to join us. Florence, too.'

*'What?'*

'Perfect.' Sabrina twirled her parasol lazily above her head.

'Can I go and play with Lady before we eat?' Florence rubbed a hand over the dog's head. 'She slept the whole way here in the carriage. I've brought a ball to throw for her.'

'You can try.' Theo looked dubious. 'Although whether she'll run for it is another matter.'

'Let's give it a go, shall we?' Abigail picked up the ball and hurled it into the distance. As Theo had predicted, Lady watched its progress before looking back at her with a half-accusatory, half-baleful expression.

'Oh, dear.' Florence's face fell and then brightened again. 'Never mind. I brought quoits, too.' She dived back into the carriage, remerging with a set of posts and half-a-dozen rings. 'Here you are.' She passed half of them to Abigail.

'Oh, leave Miss Lemon alone.' Sabrina waved a hand. 'Play with Evelyn.'

'I am *not* playing a children's game.'

'I'm happy to play for a while.' Abigail smiled and started walking. 'Come on, let's go over here so we don't accidentally hit anyone. There, that's better.' She laid the posts down on a flat area beside the river. 'Now, you go first.'

'Maybe over there might be better?' Theo, following them at a short distance, was frowning again. 'You're a little close to the water.'

'It doesn't look deep.' She threw a quick glance over her shoulder. 'And I'm sure that you'll rescue us if we fall in.'

'None the less...'

She held on to his gaze for a long moment. There was something conflicted about his expression, as if he wanted to say something else, but didn't know how. 'Very well.' She picked up the posts again and moved them to a spot a few feet away. 'Is this better?'

'Thank you.' He inclined his head, a moment before Florence gave a whoop and a jump. 'Ha! I got a six.'

'Well done.' Abigail threw one of her own rings, still watching Theo out of the corner of her eye. 'Oh, bother. I only scored two.'

Ten minutes later and Abigail had to admit, she was quite comprehensively beaten. The combination of sunshine and fresh riverside air was making her sleepy, too. By the time she went back to sit with Sabrina, Evelyn having sulkily agreed to take her place in quoits, she was finding it hard to stay awake.

'I do wish they'd hurry up.' Sabrina sighed. 'I'm quite famished.'

'I'm sure no one will mind if you steal a slice of pie.'

'I already have.' The marchioness smiled mischievously. '*And* a piece of ginger cake.'

'Good for you.' Abigail lay back on her elbows. 'Do you think the colonel's all right?' She couldn't help but notice that Theo was still standing beside the game of quoits, hands clasped behind his back and brow firmly clenched. 'He seemed perfectly at ease this morning, but now he looks thoroughly uncomfortable. I don't know what happened.'

'It's probably being so close to the water.' Sabrina sighed. 'I ought to have remembered about that.'

'What's wrong with the water?'

'His mother drowned, didn't you know?' She made a face. 'No, I don't suppose you would. It was a long time ago. I'd only been married to Fitz for a few years when it happened. Evelyn was still a baby.'

'How tragic.'

'Yes.' The marchioness gave her a sidelong look before lowering her voice. 'Of course, nobody believed it was an accident.'

'What?' Abigail opened her eyes wide in horror. 'Surely you don't mean…?'

'Then again, I suppose it might have been.' Sabrina sucked air between her teeth. 'Who knows? But she was so unhappy. The only person who ever made her smile was him.' She tipped her head towards Theo. 'He always tried so hard to please her, as though he was trying to make up for his father's behaviour even then. He would write poems and play pieces on the piano for her. It was quite heartbreaking to see. Then he was sent off to school and… Well, that's when it happened. Probably because he wasn't there to make her happy any more.'

'That's awful.' Abigail pressed her lips together tightly, suddenly wishing she'd voted for the hill instead of the meadow.

'It was.' Sabrina agreed. 'Fitz was upset, of course, but Theo was inconsolable. When he came home for the funeral, he looked like a wraith. I don't think he's ever been the same since.'

'Is that why he's so against marriage? He said something about never wanting to make any woman as unhappy as his father made his mother…'

'He said that?' The marchioness twisted towards her in surprise.

'Yes, and something about the men in his family making bad husbands, as if it were some kind of inevitability.'

'It was for Fitz.' Sabrina snorted. 'It makes sense, I suppose. He can't have seen many good examples of marriage.'

'How sad.'

'Either that or a lucky escape.' She twirled her parasol again. 'Anyway, what about you, Miss Lemon? What are your views on the subject of matrimony?'

'Me?' Abigail shook her head quickly. 'Oh, it's not for me either.'

'That seems rather a severe stance for someone so young. At least Theo has a valid reason.' The marchioness's gaze sharpened. 'Or *is* there a reason?'

'Just that I'm not a very good judge of character where men are concerned.'

'Now that *is* intriguing. Do tell.'

'It's nothing so interesting, my lady. I simply waited three years to marry the man I thought I loved, only to find he didn't want me any more when I lost my fortune.' She reached into the picnic basket for a biscuit. 'Afterwards, I decided that I'd only rely on myself from now on.'

'That sounds very wise. I'd promise the same, but fortunately I have Theo.'

'There. I've played with Florence.' Evelyn came to fling herself down beside them again. 'Happy now?'

'And so graciously done.' Sabrina made a scoffing sound.

'I don't want to be here at all. If it hadn't been for that place…' Evelyn glared in the direction of the building site '…then our lives wouldn't have been ruined.'

'Maybe not quite as ruined as you think.' Abigail gave a secretive smile. 'There's something I've been instructed to tell you.'

'What?'

'Oh, nothing in particular, just that you can have a Season, after all.'

'What?' Evelyn leapt forward, gripping her mother's arm. 'Do you mean it?'

'If you're certain it's what you want?'

'Of course it is!'

'There's only one proviso.' Abigail looked from side to side, putting on her most serious expression. 'You're not allowed to make any fuss about it. Or to say thank you to your uncle. Or to mention it at all, I think.'

'But—' Evelyn squealed and then took a deep breath. 'Yes, I can do that. If I have to.'

'I suppose the word "fuss" is a dig at me.' Sabrina smiled. 'But I'll let it go since it's good news. What made him change his mind?'

'I think it was because of what you said, about losing your nerve.'

Except that that wasn't the real reason, she thought, looking over to where Theo was still standing guard over Florence, his sandy hair blowing across his face in the breeze, Lady sitting contentedly at his side. The real, fundamental reason was that he was a good man, someone who genuinely cared about other people, who could be relied on to do the right thing, the kind of man she wished she'd met three years ago instead of Henry... Her heart stuttered at the thought.

'We need to start planning!' Sabrina clapped her hands together, jolting her thoughts back to the present. 'Now I wish I hadn't eaten that cake. There's so much to do!'

## Chapter Thirteen

'I don't know how I let you talk me into this.' Theo was pacing up and down the hallway, his expression brooding, as Abigail came down the staircase precisely two weeks and three days later. 'When I said that Evelyn could have a Season, I explicitly stated that I *didn't* want to be involved.'

'I remember.' She stopped on the bottom step and tipped her head to one side, admiring the snug fit of his black dinner jacket across his broad shoulders. He looked both extremely handsome and extremely grumpy. Oddly enough, the two attributes seemed to complement each other.

'Bad enough that the whole house has been in uproar for days!' He stalked up to her, brows drawn tight.

'It's been bit chaotic, I agree.'

'And I've hardly seen you at all over the past week.'

'Don't tell me you've missed me?' She lifted an eyebrow teasingly.

'Yes, actually!' He blinked, seemingly taken aback by his own admission. 'My office is far too quiet these days.'

'Then you should enjoy going out for an evening.'

'I have better things to do than go to a dance!'

'I'm sure that you do.'

He glowered one last time before relenting. 'And I'm acting like a petulant child, aren't I?'

'I didn't want to say it.' She smiled sympathetically. 'But it's just one ball, Evelyn's *first*. She's nervous and she needs you. So does Sabrina, no matter how much she pretends that she doesn't care. You're a family and you need to show a united front. Just think of it as a military campaign.'

'There are *actual* battles I've looked forward to more than this.'

'You don't mean that.'

'No.' He sighed. 'I don't, but I intended to spend the evening—'

'Sitting at your desk, muttering oaths, trying to decipher your brother's handwriting?' She lifted a hand to his cravat. 'Don't move. This is crooked.'

'Kitchen's not much of a valet.' He went very still. '*Do* I mutter oaths at my desk?'

'Occasionally. I've learnt a lot of new words.'

'Bollocks.'

'That's one of them. There.' She pressed her fingers lightly against the newly adjusted cravat. 'That's much better.'

'You make me sound very dull.' His brow tightened again. 'It's not that I *like* sitting at that bloody desk.'

'I know and I'm sure that there are plenty of other ways you'd rather spend your evening, but you might actually enjoy yourself.' She resisted the urge to slide her fingers through his hair next. It had grown since their first meeting so that now it looked eminently touchable.

'I doubt it.'

'Well, it might cheer you up to know that I received another letter today.'

'Another?'

'That makes four. From one of our old neighbours this time. So Henry's kept his promise.' She felt a muscle leap in her jaw at the mention of her former fiancé's name. The memory of what he'd done was still too fresh in her mind and, as curious as she was about attending a *ton* ball, there was the small, but horrifying possibility that he might also be in attendance.

'I'm glad to hear it.'

'So now we can go and enjoy ourselves.' She pushed all thoughts of Henry firmly out of her mind. 'I'm sure that you're an excellent dancer.'

'I don't dance.'

'Never?'

'Not any more. You have no idea how many officers' balls I've been forced to attend over the past decade. They were interminable.'

'Wait.' She feigned surprise. 'Are you honestly telling me that you *didn't* enjoy having lots of young ladies fawning over you, telling you how brave you were?'

'Some men enjoy that. I don't.'

'So you don't want *me* to tell you how brave I think you were then?'

His gaze skimmed over hers before fixing on a point in mid-air. 'You're different. You're not some seventeen-year-old daughter of a general.'

'I never thought that my advanced age and lack of connections would count in my favour, but it just proves there's a first time for everything.' She laughed. 'In that case, I think you were extremely brave.'

'Thank you.' He inclined his head. 'For what it's worth, I thought you were, too, coming here that first day to shout at me. Not many people would have had the nerve to call a marquess a monster to his face.'

'Ah, but I didn't. You're not a marquess.'

'I meant in principle.' One side of his mouth curved upwards. 'But if you're going to be pedantic, then I take it all back. You're not brave at all.' His gaze shifted, dropping down to her toes before lifting slowly upwards again. 'You *do* look very pretty, however. It's good to see you out of black. Blue suits you.'

'Thank you.' She smoothed her hands over the bodice of her gown. It wasn't hopelessly out of date, but it was hardly the height of fashion either. 'It's from a couple of years ago, but I thought it was still serviceable. I haven't had much occasion for ballgowns recently.'

His brow furrowed. 'Why didn't you tell me you needed a new dress?'

'Because I don't. I'm only going to be sitting on a chair with the chaperons all evening.'

'You don't intend to dance?'

'I doubt I'll have a choice. I'm hardly a debutante. Who's going to ask me?'

'Me. I will.'

'But you just said—'

'I know.' He looked slightly confused himself. 'But as I said, you're the exception. If you wish to dance, that is?'

'I'd be delighted.'

'Good. Then we'll dance. On condition that you visit the dressmaker tomorrow and order half-a-dozen new gowns.'

'Half a dozen? Don't be absurd.'

'I'm not.' He lifted his chin. 'I've never sent a soldier into battle without the right equipment and I'm not about to start now. If you're chaperoning my niece around town, then the least I can do is make sure you're properly prepared. I should have thought of it before.'

'Theo.' She put her hands on her hips. 'I believe that we've already established I wouldn't make a very good soldier. Two dresses will be quite sufficient.'

'Five.'

'Three.'

'Four and a pelisse. A blue one. Final offer. I insist.'

'Oh, very well.' She lifted her eyes to the ceiling. 'But in that case, I want to get you something in return as a thank-you gift.'

'Unnecessary. There's nothing I require.'

'But *I* insist. I don't like being indebted.'

'Are young ladies allowed to buy presents for gentlemen without causing a scandal?'

'Probably not. No more than gentlemen are allowed to buy dresses for their secretaries anyway.'

'I'd rather that you saved your money.'

'And that…' she pushed her face towards his '…is patronising.'

'You're right.' His gaze seemed strangely unfocused suddenly. 'My apologies.'

'Accepted. Now, there must be *something* I can offer you?'

She started as the words emerged from her own mouth. The way she'd just spoken—and why on earth *had* she lowered her voice like that?—had made it sound like an invitation, as if she were offering herself to him instead of a present.

'I mean…' She dipped her head quickly, horribly

aware of the cherry-red flush spreading up from her throat over her cheeks. 'Maybe a cravat pin or—'

'Abigail…'

She stopped, her senses scattering in a thousand directions at once as a hand closed gently around one of her wrists. Swallowing, she lifted her head to find Theo staring down at her, his expression a mirror image of the confusion she was experiencing herself.

She had the definite impression that until the moment he'd touched her, he'd had absolutely no intention of doing so and yet his fingers were still there, as if he didn't want to, or couldn't, let go. She didn't want him to let go either, she realised, although it would be easy enough to pull away. A single tug ought to do it…

As if he sensed the thought, his grip tightened infinitesimally, his other hand coming up to stroke the side of her neck, his forefinger trailing a path slowly from her ear to her collarbone, as if he were trying to stroke the blush away, although if that was his intention then he was having the opposite effect. She felt as though she were sitting next to a roaring fire.

'Abigail?' He murmured her name again as his finger moved down to her chin, tilting it upwards until their lips were mere inches apart.

She sucked in a breath, her mouth turning dry as the whole world seemed to sway and then shift on its axis. The irises of his eyes looked very dark against the blue suddenly, holding her own captive. Only a few moments ago, everything had been perfectly normal between them, yet now it felt as though there was a lightning storm above their heads, gathering energy to strike. All of her senses seemed heightened. She felt more aware of Theo than she'd ever been aware of anyone else in her life, as if nothing and no one else existed, as if the very tips of his fingers against her skin were melding them together in some deeply primal way.

A thrill of pleasure coursed through her, right to the very centre of her body, to places she'd never felt pleasure before, even with Henry. It felt new and exciting and alarming in equal measure. Her heart was beating so hard, it felt in danger of crushing her ribcage, and his was doing the same. She couldn't feel it, but somehow she knew. She felt as if she knew *everything* about him. Except that she didn't want to…did she? She didn't want to feel this kind of connection with a man—*any* man. She'd vowed to be alone and take care of herself from now on and yet the intensity in Theo's gaze made her knees tremble beneath her.

It was strange, but she'd always thought that that was just a phrase, but they really were. Her pulse was racing, her breathing was shallow, there were goose pimples all over her skin despite the fact that she was red hot all over and, if she didn't grab hold of something soon, she had a feeling that she might actually fall.

'I'm ready!' Sabrina's voice, echoing from the corridor above, acted like a bucket of cold water over their heads. 'Where is everyone?'

'Down here.' Theo took a step backwards a scant second before the marchioness appeared at the top of the staircase, resplendent in a crimson-silk gown, trimmed with black lace and ornamented by a large ruby necklace and earrings.

'Sabrina, you look magnificent.' Abigail curled her fingers around the banister, fixing a smile on to her face. It was the most she could manage when her heart was still pounding as though she were in the midst of a race. She wasn't sure what had just happened, but *something* definitely had. One glance at Theo's face told her he was as shaken as she was.

'Do I?' The marchioness looked relieved as she slowly descended the staircase. 'I was going to dress demurely, but then I thought, why should I? I've nothing to apologise for and if people have something to say then they can say it to my face. The *ton* should know that we're still a family to be reckoned with.'

'I couldn't have put it better myself.' Theo's voice was uncharacteristically husky. 'Incidentally, whose ball are we going to again?'

'The Earl and Countess of Gaddesby. She's been a good friend for years.'

'Then at least we know we won't be turned away. All we need now is our debutante.'

'I'm here, uncle.' Evelyn appeared at the top of the staircase next, clad in a plain white gown that made a stark contrast with her mother's. With her auburn hair pinned up in curls at the back of her head, she looked a lot like a woodland nymph, albeit an extremely nervous one. 'What do you think?'

'What do I think?' Theo bowed. 'I think that you're going to put all the other young ladies to shame.'

'Really?' Her eyes darted between them. 'Because I know I said that this was what I wanted, but suddenly I'm terrified. What if people shun us?'

'Then I'll deal with them. If anyone breathes as much as a word about your father, come and tell me.'

'Or me.' Sabrina tossed her head defiantly. 'I'll have something to say about it, too.'

'Thank you.'

'Now, I believe that our carriage is waiting.' Theo

gestured towards the front door, waiting until Sabrina and Evelyn had gone ahead before falling into step beside Abigail, his fingertips brushing lightly against hers as they made their way outside. 'The sooner we go, the sooner we'll find out what our reception is going to be.'

'Colonel Lord Marshall, Lady Salway, Lady Marshall and Miss…ah… Lemon.'

For a moment, it seemed to Abigail that their reception wavered on a knife-edge. There was a telling pause after their names were announced, probably no longer than a couple of seconds although it felt like an eternity, when it seemed as if the *ton* was considering, en masse, whether or not to turn their backs on them or to carry on as if everything was perfectly normal. Fortunately, the latter instinct won out.

'That was close.' Theo murmured as they descended the steps into the ballroom.

'Too close.' Sabrina, flanking Evelyn on his other side, shuddered and let out a heavy breath. 'Another second and I would have turned tail and fled.'

'Does this mean that everything's going to be all right?' Evelyn still sounded petrified.

'I believe so, my dear. Just keep your chin up and don't let them see any fear.' The marchioness took hold of her daughter's arm. 'Now come along. I want to introduce you to a few people.'

'I feel as though my heart just stopped.' Left alone with Theo, Abigail put a hand to her chest, reassuring herself that the organ had, in fact, started again. Heartwise, it was proving to be an eventful evening. Her nerves had been taut enough after what had happened at the bottom of the staircase, but confronting the *ton* had been a whole different kind of ordeal, and there was still the threat of bumping into Henry… 'I've never had so many people staring in my direction before.'

'You looked perfectly composed.' He inclined his head encouragingly.

'I didn't feel it. I feel like such an interloper.'

'Well, you're not. You're a member of our party.' He offered his arm. 'Now, shall we take a turn of the room? I believe that's what we're supposed to do at events like this.'

'I'd be delighted.' She hesitated briefly before placing her hand on his bicep, willing her body to behave normally, but it was no use. The moment earlier had changed everything. She still felt too alert somehow, as if all her nerves were strung tight. 'Although I'm supposed to be keeping an eye on Evelyn.'

'That shouldn't be too hard. She's already dancing.'

'Already?'

'Already. Say what you like about Sabrina, but when she makes her mind up about something, she's a force to be reckoned with.'

'I think you're right.' She let her gaze sweep the ballroom. There was no sign of Henry…

'I'll let you know if I see him.'

'What?' She jerked her head around. 'Who?'

'Mr Quinnell.' Theo's voice sounded overly casual. 'I presume that's who you're looking for?'

She lifted her eyes to his, feeling guilty all of a sudden. 'Yes, but not because I *want* to see him. I just don't want to be surprised if I *do* see him, if that makes sense.'

'Completely. Strategically speaking, it's important to know where the enemy is.'

'The enemy...' She repeatedly the word soberly. 'I hate to think of him that way.'

'Despite the rumours he spread about you?'

'Even despite those.' She sighed. 'A mistake. From now on, that's how I'm going to think of him, as a terrible mistake.'

'I'm glad to hear it.' His arm tightened subtly against hers. 'Now, shall we walk?'

One turn of the room later and Abigail was beginning to wonder what exactly was going on. Theo had stopped to talk with various acquaintances on their circuit of the room, always introducing her as if she were a member of the *ton*, too, but for the most part he'd stayed by her side, behaving like a perfect gentleman. It was both flattering and, considering their moment of madness earlier, extremely confusing. As much as she wanted to discuss it, however, now wasn't the time or the place.

She only wished that she knew what he was thinking. Had it meant anything to him? Or had she—*horrible thought*—simply imagined more than there had actually been? After all, it had been so brief, over almost before it had begun, and it wasn't as though they'd actually kissed, although surely she hadn't imagined the way he'd touched her face?

'Here you are.' He handed her a glass of champagne when they finally stopped walking. 'To cool down.'

'Thank you.' She took a few sips eagerly. 'It's as hot as Hades in here.'

'I'd suggest moving to the terrace, but I see that you're taking your duties as chaperon seriously.'

'That's why I'm here, isn't it?' She lifted her chin

indignantly. Maybe she *had* been staring at Evelyn a little too hard, but it seemed safer than getting caught in another stare with him. 'Although I have to admit, she's behaving perfectly well on her own. She's had partners for the past four dances.'

'I noticed. You do realise she's going to be insufferable from now on, don't you?'

'Probably, but it's nice to see her looking so happy.' She risked a swift glance at his face. 'Although she's not the only one attracting attention. You're getting a number of looks yourself.'

'Me?' He sounded surprised.

'Yes. There are several young ladies who've barely taken their eyes off you since you arrived.' She lifted her shoulders, attempting to re-establish some kind of professional employer—employee relationship. 'Maybe you should ask to be introduced?'

'Why on earth would I do that?'

'Because I think they'd like to meet you.'

He made a scathing sound. 'My brother's still alive and healthy. Just because I'm currently his heir doesn't mean the vultures can start circling.'

'I'm sure that's not the only reason they're looking at you. You're also a handsome military hero. If you were the marrying kind, you'd be extremely eligible.'

'Handsome?' He lifted an eyebrow.

'Yes.' She took another sip of champagne. 'Surely you know that?'

'No. Fitz was always the handsome one.'

'Surely two brothers can both be handsome?'

'Not in our family. Everyone always said we were the opposites of each other.'

'That doesn't sound very fair, but if it's true then your

brother must have degenerated a great deal recently because you're very handsome.'

*Very?* She glanced accusingly at the champagne in her hand. Obviously it was beginning to have an effect. She'd meant to leave it at handsome, not *very,* even if the latter were true.

'I appreciate the compliment.' He raised his glass. 'However, if I ask to be introduced to anyone now then I'll have to take them in to supper.'

'Would that be so bad?'

'Yes.' He nodded vehemently. 'I'd have to make conversation. For an hour.'

'Again, not the worst thing in the world.'

'I'm no good at conversation. Unless you think any of them are interested in discussing military strategy?'

'You talk to me all the time and, as I recall, we've never discussed military strategy.'

'Never?'

'No. In fact, I believe it was Kitchen who told me about Waterloo.'

'So it was.' He cleared his throat. 'Are you trying to get rid of me, by any chance?'

'No! Of course not.'

'Because I'd be happy to go to the card room if my company is becoming tedious.'

'It's not.' She felt her cheeks darken again. 'All I'm trying to say is that you don't have to stay here and look after me. I know you always feel responsible for everyone and it's kind of you to think of my feelings, but I'm perfectly content with the chaperons.'

'*Kind?*' A frown notched itself between his brows. 'Is that what you think I'm being?'

'No-o, not exactly.'

'Has it never occurred to you that I actually *like* your company?'

'Well…yes. I suppose so. I like yours, too.'

'Because I'm not just standing here out of the goodness of my heart. I'm perfectly aware that you can look after yourself. I'm also aware that several gentlemen have been looking in your direction as well and I don't blame them. You're the most beautiful woman in the room.' He tossed back the last of his champagne. 'So stop telling me to go and talk to other women.'

'All right.' She pursed her lips, hardly knowing whether to be pleased by his words or irritated by his tone. Pleasure won. It seemed like a long time since anyone had called her beautiful… 'The next dance is a waltz anyway. Evelyn might want to come over and talk since she doesn't have permission to dance them yet.'

'Her mother can talk to her.'

'Why?'

'Because you promised me a dance.'

'A waltz?' She blinked, startled.

'If you have no objections?'

'I…no.'

'Well, then?'

She stared at his outstretched fingers, trying to decide how to respond. On the one hand, she still had no idea what exactly had happened between them earlier *or* what it meant, in which case, such an intimate dance was probably a supremely bad idea. On the other hand, the thought of waltzing with him was far too tempting to resist. Slowly she reached her own fingers out, feeling an unwonted yet delicious frisson of excitement as his closed around them.

They walked into the centre of the dance floor and

stood facing each other, both of them completely still for a few seconds, as if they were bracing themselves in the calm before the storm. Then Theo closed the distance between them, pressing his other hand against the small of her back while she let hers hover above and then land, gently, on his shoulder.

Instinctively, she tensed. It felt strange to be standing up with a man who wasn't Henry, but then again, why shouldn't she dance with a handsome military hero? They'd just agreed how much they enjoyed each other's company, and it wasn't as if she was about to get any romantic ideas, no matter how many frissons she felt.

They were both firmly against marriage. They were friends. And friends could find each other attractive, couldn't they? It didn't necessarily mean anything. It didn't have to lead to anything either, not unless they wanted it to…and that thought quite took her breath away.

'Abigail?' Theo leaned forward, bringing his lips close to her ear. 'If you've changed your mind about dancing…?'

'I haven't.' She swallowed as the warmth of his breath made the whole side of her body prickle with goose pimples. 'It's just… I'm not sure I can remember the steps. I might crush your toes.'

'It's been so long since I danced that you're taking the same risk.'

'Oh, dear.' She laughed nervously. 'We could both be black and blue by the end of this.'

He smiled, a slow smile that started off bashful and turned into something impish, making him look almost boyish suddenly. 'Then let's see how much damage we can inflict, shall we?'

The orchestra struck up the waltz and she lifted a foot…the right foot, thankfully, and then they were dancing, twisting and twirling and spinning around the dance floor, and at some point, she stopped concentrating on the steps and let herself relax into the music, surrendering to the feeling of weightlessness, to the rhythmic swing and sway of their bodies and the feeling of his shoulder and arm muscles moving beneath her fingertips.

She let her mind wander, too, into territories she'd never let it wander before. It seemed faintly wicked, but the feeling of his arms around her was…what was the word…? Inspiring. Tension seemed to simmer in the air between them, a low thrum like some other, separate heartbeat as they moved in perfect harmony, while excitement coursed through her body and coalesced like a tight, throbbing knot in her stomach.

She felt more alive than she had for a long time, as if she'd just taken some kind of momentous step forward. She couldn't help but wonder what it would be like to kiss him, to hold him, to lie in his arms, just as friends, just out of curiosity.…

'There. That wasn't so bad, was it?' He bowed over her hand when the music finally stopped.

'No.' She met his gaze directly, every nerve in her body sizzling with feeling. 'It wasn't bad at all.'

## Chapter Fourteen

Theo unravelled his cravat, leaving it to hang loose around his neck as he stepped down from the carriage, then turned to help first his sister-in-law, then his niece and finally Abigail down on to the pavement outside Salway House. He was particularly relieved they descended in that order since the flare of heat that shot up his arm as his fingers connected with Abigail's had an immediately stirring effect on the rest of his body.

He wasn't surprised by it any more. He'd been feeling hot under the collar ever since he'd touched her face and they'd almost—*almost*—kissed earlier, the strength of his attraction to her catching him off guard, so much that he'd found it hard to think about anything else all evening. He'd done his utmost to behave like a gentleman, but he still hadn't been able to stay away from her.

Now, he was acutely aware of every tiny movement she made. Which was completely inappropriate, he reminded himself. No matter how much he liked and admired her, she was his secretary. Or companion. Or governess. Or *something*! The main point was that he was a gentleman and since he had no intention of offering marriage then he ought not to feel anything at all. On the contrary, he ought to apologise.

If only every part of his body wasn't screaming out to touch her again…

He looked up and down the street to distract himself. Dawn wasn't far off. The city would be waking soon, but for now the streets were still swathed in darkness. Despite a wobbly start, the evening had proven to be a triumphant success. Sabrina had somehow convinced most of the *ton* to feel sorry for her and Evelyn had been the belle of the ball. From now on, the house would probably be full of admirers and suitors. It was going to be hell.

'Be careful.' Sabrina called out as her daughter danced up the front steps and into the hallway, humming to herself. 'Or you'll bump into one of the pillars.'

'It won't hurt. Nothing can hurt me this morning.' Evelyn whirled around giddily. 'This has been the most wonderful night of my life.'

'That's all very well, but if you twist your ankle then you won't be able to dance again for weeks.'

'Oh.' The dancing stopped abruptly. 'I didn't think of that.'

'It's time for bed anyway.'

'But how can I possibly sleep now?' Evelyn clutched her hands in front of her. 'I have so much to think about, it's like there are butterflies fluttering around inside my head. I want to relive every single moment of tonight. It was sublime.'

'Then at least go and relive it lying down.' Sabrina rolled her eyes. 'Give your poor uncle some peace or he might change his mind about the rest of the Season.'

'He wouldn't do that. He's the best and kindest uncle in the whole world.'

'Can I have that in writing?' Theo lifted an eyebrow.

'I'll make sure of it.' Sabrina smiled over her daughter's shoulder as they mounted the staircase together. 'I do believe that she's enjoyed herself.'

'Happy to help.' He watched them disappear around the upstairs landing before tilting his head towards Abigail. She was standing beside him, removing her gloves. 'How much champagne did she drink?'

'None at all.' Her lips twitched. 'As far as I could tell, she only drank lemonade all evening. She's just delirious with happiness.'

He blew air from between his teeth. 'I've never been accused of making a woman that before.'

'I find that hard to believe.' She stiffened abruptly. 'That is, I mean…'

'Not at all.' He couldn't repress a smirk. 'I'm more than happy to take the compliment.'

'Anyway…' She stepped, red-faced towards the staircase. 'I think it's time for me to go to bed, as well, before I say something else stupid. Goodnight, colonel.'

'Goodnight. Unless…' He put a hand out before he could stop himself. 'Unless you'd care for a nightcap?'

She paused with one foot on the bottom stair, standing immobile for so long that he was just starting to think she wasn't going to answer when she turned around again. 'Why not?'

'Very well.' He gestured towards the study, his blood temperature rocketing. 'After you.'


'I can still hear Evelyn singing.' He lifted his eyes to the ceiling, smiling as he poured out two glasses of port. 'She'll wake up the entire house if she's not careful.'

'She has a lovely voice.' Abigail smiled back. Somehow it did strange things to his insides.

'She does,' he agreed. 'It's also particularly nice to hear her using it for something other than shouting. All thanks to you.'

'Me?' She looked surprised.

'You've had a good effect on all of us. Sabrina and I would never have gone ahead with Evelyn's Season without your influence. We'd still be avoiding each other.' He handed her one of the glasses. 'I don't know what we'd do without you.'

'In that case, maybe I should ask for a pay rise?'

'Believe me, if I had any spare funds, I'd give it.'

She laughed and sat down on the rug in front of the fire, curling her legs up beneath her. For once there was no sign of Lady. No doubt, she was fast asleep in Kitchen's room.

'To be honest...' Abigail put her glass aside, untouched '...it's nice to feel useful. That's something I've discovered since I came here. I suppose I never felt properly useful before.'

'Really?' He sat down on the floor opposite, leaning back against an armchair and stretching one leg out in front of him. The tension he'd felt for most of the evening was back, vibrating in the air between them, but he knew he had to ignore it. He'd invited her there to apologise...hadn't he?

'Yes. I'm not complaining. My father was a wonderful man, but in some ways, he always treated me like a child. Now I have a purpose.' She caught hold of his eyes and then dropped her own. 'I know you hate it here, but I like my work.'

'I'm glad.' He leaned forward. 'Abigail, about earlier—'

'Why is the fire still so bright?' she interrupted him.

'I'm sorry?'

'The fire. Why is still so well lit at this time of night?'

'Ah.' He sat back again. 'The maids know I often come down and work during the night so they keep it well stoked.'

'Please tell me you're not planning to do some work now.'

'Perhaps. There doesn't seem to be much point in going to bed at this hour.'

'It's not healthy to work all the time.' She shook her head remonstratively. 'You don't sleep well, do you?'

'What makes you think that?'

'Because you're always at that desk. Every morning when I arrive after breakfast and every night when I go to bed.

'I've no choice. The sooner I sort Fitz's mess out, the sooner I can escape.' He rubbed a hand over his face. 'But, no, I don't sleep well either. Not since seventeen ninety-nine.'

'Your mother?' she asked the question softly. 'Sabrina told me.'

'Ah.' He nodded. 'Yes. It was the year she died. Nothing was ever the same again. *You're* sleeping better, however.'

Her brow wrinkled. 'How do you know that?'

'Because you had dark circles around your eyes when you first arrived.'

'Ah. I think I was still in shock back then. I felt the way Evelyn described, as though I had butterflies in my head, only bad ones.'

'And now?'

'Now they've settled down. They're still there, but they're asleep. I'll always be sorry for what happened to my father, but at least now I know it wasn't my fault. I know he wouldn't want me to blame myself either. As for Henry, I don't miss him, although I do miss…' She stopped and reached for her glass, her skin flushing.

'What?'

'The way he made me feel.' A wash of colour spread over her cheeks as she spoke, though whether it was due to embarrassment or port, he couldn't tell. 'That sounds very foolish, I suppose.'

'Not at all. Everyone wants to feel loved, don't they?'

'I thought you were against marriage?'

'I am, but just because I know I'd be a terrible husband doesn't mean that I don't enjoy companionship sometimes.'

'Companionship?' She repeated the word thoughtfully. 'You mean like this?' She waved a hand between them.

'Not quite.' He shifted position, feeling his body stir again, already regretting his choice of words before he said them. 'This is pleasant, but I meant…physical companionship.'

'Oh.' Her eyes widened. 'You mean you have a mistress?'

'No!'

'But you just said—'

'I know.' He frowned, wondering how the hell they'd got on to this subject when he'd been intending to apologise. 'What I meant was that I've had…companions in the past, usually widows who haven't wanted any kind of commitment.'

'I see.' She drew her brows together, staring into her glass for a long moment before lifting her gaze again. 'So *just* for…companionship?'

'I suppose so.' His throat tightened around the words.

'And pleasure. Just because a person doesn't want to get married doesn't mean they have to be all alone.'

'I see.' She sounded pensive. 'In that case, maybe *I* should take a lover.'

'What? No!' He jerked upright, enraged by the very idea. 'That's not what I meant at all.'

'It sounded like it.'

'I don't know what I meant, but I think that we ought to change the subject.'

'*I* think that what you meant was that it's acceptable for *you* to take lovers, but not me.' She narrowed her eyes accusingly. 'Because I'm a woman.'

'I didn't say it was fair.'

'Mmm…' She tossed her head, causing a lock of blonde hair to escape and fall across one eyebrow. 'Maybe I should move to a new town and call myself a widow. Then I'd be allowed to behave any way I liked.'

'*Don't.*'

'What?'

'Don't move away.' He was surprised by how alarmed he was by the idea. 'How would I cope without you?'

'All right then.' She angled her body towards him. 'I won't move away. On one condition. That you tell me what *exactly* you mean by "physical companionship".'

'Physical…?' He heard a strange guttural sound emerge from his own throat. 'Abigail, are you saying that you want me to explain marital relations to you?'

'Yes!' She nodded eagerly. 'I kept hoping that somebody would talk to me about it before my wedding, but nobody ever did. I even tried asking Henry, but he just said it would be easier to show me.'

'It definitely would.' He swallowed. He'd drunk far too much champagne that evening for this subject. For a start, because he might choose his words badly and terrify her. For another, because talking about it would undoubtedly make him want to do it, too, and *that* would be a decidedly bad idea. If he had even a scrap of common sense, he would put an end to this discussion and order her to bed right now. Only the thought of ordering her to bed definitely wasn't helping him think straight...

'And now I'm no longer engaged,' she went on, 'it's like I'm just supposed to bury all those feelings and questions, as if they no longer have anything to do with me. But why *should* unmarried women be so chaste and virtuous when men don't have to be? It's not fair.'

'I agree.'

'So?'

'So?' He looked up again to find her staring back expectantly, eyes bright like an inquisitive bird.

'So are you going to tell me or do I have to move away and find out for myself?'

'Abigail...' He groaned, aware that he'd just been trapped. 'I presume you've been kissed?'

'Oh, yes, a few times.'

'A *few*?' His voice sounded gravelly. It seemed to scrape the inside of his mouth. 'Surely a little more than that over three years?'

'Henry and I were rarely alone.'

'Didn't he try to get you alone?'

'Not as I recall.' She looked disconcerted. 'Why? Should he have?'

'*I* would have.'

'Oh.' Her lips parted. 'You mean you enjoy kissing?'

'Among other things, yes, I enjoy kissing.'

Her gaze flickered as she leaned closer, lowering her voice as if she were about to confide some long-held secret. 'So do I. I always thought that Henry and I never did it enough. Or *for* long enough. He always pulled away just as I was starting to—'

'Abigail.' Theo closed his eyes.

'Yes?'

'If we're going to discuss this, then I need you to stop saying his name.'

'Whose? Henry's?'

'Yes. Stop saying Henry.'

'Why?'

'I don't know.' He opened his eyes again, clearing his throat for what felt like the millionth time. 'It just makes me feel like he's here in the room with us.'

'Oh.' She pursed her lips, making a pretence of looking around before putting her hands on the floor and crawling across the carpet towards him. 'He's not.'

'Do you want to know more or not?' He clenched his jaw, acutely aware of the view down the front of her bodice.

'I do. Please continue.'

'I can't remember where we were.'

'Kissing.' She sat down next to him. 'Actually, I have another question.'

'Oh, good.'

'It's theoretical really. I mean, if it's so scandalous for an unmarried woman to take a lover, then what about *just* kissing instead? Surely it wouldn't be so very bad for her to simply kiss someone, even someone she wasn't in love with? As long as she liked the person, I mean? Just out of curiosity, say?'

'Curiosity?'

'Yes. To see if it felt the same as with Hen—*other* people. It might be...' she paused as if she were searching for an appropriate word '...*interesting* to compare. Educational. Like an experiment.'

Damn it if his throat didn't need clearing again... 'Perhaps.'

'So, what do you think? Would it be very scandalous?'

'I don't think so, no.' He shifted position uncomfortably. 'It might even be useful. To see if you were compatible with that person in other ways.'

'What other ways?'

'We should probably stick to kissing for now.'

'Right. So?' She looked up at him, one eyebrow raised. 'Would be all right for me to kiss you, for example? Or would you think me terribly wanton?'

He had the vague impression that his head was about to split open. With her citrusy scent all around him, he was finding it harder and harder to think straight. Her kissing him would be more than all right, while at the same time being extremely wrong. 'I could never think of you as wanton, but, Abigail, it's late and this conversation... I'm your employer and a gentleman. Supposedly.'

'A gentleman who never intends to marry. And I'm a lady who intends the same, but I still want to know what it is I'm missing. As for being my employer, you said that you were only providing restitution for my father's investment. I don't see how one kiss is going to change anything.'

'I still wouldn't want to take advantage. After the port.'

'I've barely touched it. You've had a lot more.'

'I'm more accustomed to it.'

'Would it help that I wanted to kiss you before I had the port?'

'It might.' He paused. 'When?'

'In the hall earlier, just after I'd straightened this.' She picked up one of the loose ends of his cravat and drew it between her fingers.

'Not when we were dancing?'

'Why?' Her eyes sparked. 'Did *you* want to kiss me then?'

'It crossed my mind.'

'There you go. Both of those occasions were before the port when we were both perfectly clear-headed.'

'That makes sense.'

'I was always so cautious with Hen—that other person…and look where it got me. I wasted three years of my life. I want to be impulsive for once. I want to take risks, even if they turn out to be huge mistakes. At least I'll have done something. I'll know things…' She sighed and started to crawl away again. 'But if you don't want to—'

'Wait.' He caught her around the waist, pulling her backwards so that she fell into his lap.

'Wha—?' She looked surprised. 'That was impressive.'

'I still feel like I'm taking advantage.'

'And now you're patronising me again.' She rolled her eyes. 'If anything, I'll be taking advantage of you. Just curiosity, remember? No commitment.' She lifted a hand to his throat, stroking her fingers gently across his skin. 'But I could kiss you first, if you like? That way, you wouldn't need to feel guilty at all. You don't even have to move. You can just sit there and enjoy it. Maybe.' She grimaced. 'You might not. I can't promise.'

'I'm quietly confident.' He found himself unable to drag his gaze away from her mouth. Slowly, he lifted a hand and touched his thumb to her lips. They were warm and soft and yielding. As he watched, she flicked her tongue out and he heard a roaring sound in his ears.

'So…' She shifted position, looping an arm around his neck. 'Just to be clear, this is only for curiosity and companionship's sake. In the morning, it'll be as though it never happened. We'll forget all about it and continue working together as normal.'

'Understood.'

'Nobody else ever needs to know.'

'Absolutely.'

She leaned closer and brushed her mouth against his, lightly, like a paintbrush skimming across a canvas, tantalisingly there and then gone again. She tasted of port, inflaming his senses, but not providing anywhere near enough satisfaction. She skimmed again and this time, he moved with her, catching her lips with his own and refusing to let go. This time, he clung.

Before he knew what he was doing, he'd closed his arms around her, too, curving his fingers around the nape of her neck and deepening the pressure of the kiss, letting it grow harder and hungrier. She moaned softly and he echoed the sound, using his tongue to tease her lips apart before sliding it inside.

'You taste even better than I imagined.' He broke away from her finally, pressing his forehead against hers.

'Do I?' Her eyes looked heavy. 'You've thought about me?'

'I've thought about this, about holding you in my arms and kissing every last inch of your skin.'

'*Every* inch?'

'If you think that would also be educational?'

'It certainly sounds enlightening.' Her cheeks and eyes darkened together. 'In that case, where would you like to start?'

For a moment, his mind went blank. Kissing her on the mouth was one thing, but kissing her anywhere else…kissing her where he'd *like* to kiss her… He felt his groin swell and tighten. This had to stop. Now. Definitely soon anyway… Only his mind and his body seemed to be pursuing two completely different paths. The feeling of her body in his arms was irresistible. *She* was irresistible.

'Well…' He slid a finger beneath the sleeve of her gown and tugged it gently over her shoulder. 'I suppose that would depend on how curious you are. I thought I could start at the top and work my way down.'

'It sounds like a lot of work.' She sounded breathless. 'Every inch, I mean.'

'Too much?'

'Not if you don't mind?'

'Not at all.' He lowered his head to the side of her neck, trailing feather-light kisses in a slow path over her collarbone and around to the dip in her throat. If this was work, then it was the kind he relished.

'Tell me to stop whenever you want,' he murmured against her skin.

'No.' She shook her head, her breathing ragged. 'Not yet.'

'Good.' He moved his head lower, pressing his lips to the curve of her breasts. After all, there was no harm in just kissing, he told himself, even if he had the strong feeling that he was trying to drive himself mad.

'Wait.'

He froze, holding himself in check, as she lifted a hand suddenly. 'I'm sorry. I'll stop.'

'No, it's not that.' She reached behind her back. 'It's my laces.'

'Ah.' A rush of relief swept through him. 'Here. Let me.' He swept his arms around her, quickly untying the laces holding her dress together, before setting to work on her stays and corset.

'You should get out of this, too.' She unfastened his waistcoat, easing it over his shoulders before doing the same with his shirt, her fingers trailing an exploratory path over his biceps.

'Abigail...' He pushed her down on to the fireside rug as he tossed the pile of clothing aside. He *really* ought to stop, but the thought of her unbound body beneath his was too much of a temptation to resist.

With only her shift remaining, he could feel the points of her nipples, straining upwards against his chest. Greedily, he dipped his head, drawing the material aside so that he could take one in his mouth. Truly, her fiancé must have been mad to resist her for so long...

'Oh...' She dug her fingernails into his shoulders, tipping her head back with a moan. 'That feels...'

'What?' He pulled her shift lower, cupping her breast in one hand as he drew his tongue in slow circles around it.

'I don't know. I've never felt it before. It's...strange.'

'Strange?' He moved to the other breast, trying not to feel too disappointed. As words went, it wasn't the greatest of compliments.

'It's as though I can feel you there and...' she laid a

hand on her stomach '…here, too. Is that supposed to happen?'

'It is.' He grinned, his confidence rising again as he shifted his weight lower, pressing a row of kisses over her stomach while he slipped his other hand beneath the hem of her shift and moved it slowly upwards, over her stockings, her garter, between her thighs… 'How does it feel now?'

'Stronger.' She arched her back, lifting her hips up to his in a way that very nearly unmanned him.

'And now?' He slid his fingers into the curls between her legs. Her shift was bunched around her waist. If she lifted her hips again, then—'Wait!' He stiffened and sat up abruptly.

'What?' She pushed herself up, too, her eyes unfocused. At some point, her pins had come loose so that now her hair tumbled about her shoulders like molten gold in the firelight. It took every ounce of willpower he possessed not to push her back down again.

'You had champagne, too.'

'Champagne?' She sounded confused.

'Yes. You drank champagne as well as port.'

'Ye-es.'

'So you might not be thinking clearly. We need to stop before this goes any further.' He shifted away from her with an effort, willing his body to cool down.

'I… Yes, of course, you're right.' Quickly, she wriggled back into her gown, her face averted. 'I'm sorry.'

'I'm the one who should be saying sorry. Abigail, I—'

'It's late.' She spoke across him. 'I should go to bed.'

'That's probably best. I'd escort you upstairs, but under the circumstances…'

'I completely understand.' She pushed herself to her feet, rearranging her dress around her shoulders with her back turned.

'It's not that I don't want to continue, obviously.'

'Yes, I know.' She turned around again, her chin high. 'In any case, that was very educational. I appreciate your help and…' Her voice faltered as if she wasn't sure what else to say. 'I hope that you sleep better tonight.'

He watched her go incredulously. If there was one thing he was absolutely certain of, it was that he wasn't getting a single wink of sleep that night.

## Chapter Fifteen

'Go away…' Abigail rolled on to her side and groaned at the sound of light tapping on her bedroom door. For a few groggy seconds, she couldn't remember where she was or why it was proving so difficult to drag herself back to wakefulness. One deep breath later and it all came rushing back to her. An almost-kiss in the hallway, the ball, the dance, a glass of port in the study afterwards…an actual kiss…several actual kisses… Oh, no.

'Miss Lemon?' Mrs Evans's voice came from the other side of the door. 'Are you awake?'

'Yes. I'm coming!' Quickly, she swung her legs over the side of the bed and staggered towards it, her sleep-fogged brain making the room feel as if it were swaying around her. It felt like a monumental effort to heave the door open.

'Good morning.' Mrs Evans gave her a quick up-and-down look, the faintest hint of a smirk playing about her lips.

'Is it still morning?' Abigail lifted a hand to her mouth, attempting and failing to stifle a yawn.

'*Just*. It's a quarter of an hour until luncheon. The marchioness asks that you meet her in the dining room for something to eat before you go.'

'Go?' She blinked. 'Go where?'

'On your shopping expedition. Apparently you arranged it on the journey home last night.'

'Oh…' More details came back to her. 'Yes, I remember now. How is she this morning?'

'In a better mood than I've seen her for weeks.' Mrs Evans leaned forward confidentially. 'Of course it's helped that she's had one of Possett's remedies. Between you and me, they're extremely effective. I could have one sent up, if you like?'

'Mmm? Oh, no.' She shook her head. 'I'm perfectly all right, just tired. It was a late night.'

'If you say so.'

Abigail closed the door on another smirk and made her way to the washstand, gripping the wood tightly in her hands as memories continued to assail her, sending waves of guilt prickling along her veins. Had she really kissed Theo? And so soon after Henry, too? She'd barely known him a month! How had it even happened?

She lowered her head on to her arms, trying to remember, then wished that she hadn't as fragments of conversation floated back into her mind, making her groan aloud. Bad enough that she'd asked him to explain marital relations, but how could she have actually asked him to *kiss* her? Wasn't there a phrase about curiosity killing the cat? Well, she wasn't dead, but she must have been mad, carried away by the success of the evening.

And yet, it had felt *so* incredibly good.

She lifted her head and regarded herself in the mirror. Despite what Mrs Evans, and even Theo had seemed to think, she hadn't had *that* much to drink the previous evening. She might have behaved as if she were intoxicated, but in truth she'd been perfectly sober. Her mind had been clear—well, clear enough anyway. She'd known what she'd wanted and…well, Theo was the one who'd invited her for a nightcap.

Why *shouldn't* she have asked him to kiss her? It wasn't as if she'd forced herself on him. She'd explained her request in a calm and logical manner. And if she was mad, then it had certainly been a fun kind of madness.

Hadn't she been sensible for long enough? She'd been good and virtuous for twenty-two years and look where that had got her. Heartbroken, abandoned and penniless. No, she decided, she was *not* going to feel guilty or ashamed. Society's expectations could go to hell. She wasn't going to regret a single moment.

Slowly, she touched her fingertips to her lips and smiled, reliving some of the more *educational* aspects of the evening. At least now she knew some of what she was missing. The way that Theo had kissed her, an almost primitive look on his face as if he couldn't get enough of her, had made her feel powerful and beautiful and desirable in a way that Henry never had. He'd given her exactly what she'd wanted, even if the experience had provoked as many questions as it had answered.

Such as, what happened next? Because she'd had the very strong impression that there was more. He'd said something about not going any further and the aching sensation in her stomach and between her thighs had seemed to be building to something, only she could hardly ask him what it was now… Could she?

Absolutely not! She shook her head quickly. No matter what madness might have possessed her the previous evening, it couldn't happen again. Once had been highly enlightening, but twice would be playing with fire. It was going to be awkward enough seeing Theo again, especially with the memory of his naked chest so vivid in her mind—and what a chest—but they were both adults, and they'd made an agreement. It had been one evening of curiosity, that was all.

She took a deep breath, ardently hoping he saw it the same way. In the cold light of day, she had a horrible feeling that he might feel compelled to do something honourable, despite his feelings about marriage.

Worse, what if he thought that she'd planned the whole thing and was some social climber out to entrap him? The accusation had been painful enough coming from Henry's family, but she didn't think she could bear it if Theo thought so, too. No, if he tried to be honourable, then she'd stop him at once, make it clear that she didn't want or expect anything. She might not believe in love stories any more, but she certainly didn't want a marriage of obligation either.

She pushed her hands through her hair, wishing that she could see him straight away to make sure nothing had changed between them, but first she had to go shopping.

Four dresses and a pelisse. In blue.

'We're looking for modest but pretty.' Sabrina rifled through a book of dress patterns, her beautiful face contorting with either delight or disgust at each new design. 'Nothing too fussy, but not too plain either. Ah, how about this one?' She settled on a picture of a wide-necked day gown with a high waist and short, scalloped sleeves. 'This should suit your figure very nicely, don't you think?'

'Yes, it's very nice.' Abigail peered across while the modiste wound a tape measure around her waist.

'In red, I think.'

'With my hair?'

'With the right shade, it could look very fetching.'

'It's your colour. What about blue?'

'Blue?' Sabrina screwed her mouth up, considering. 'I suppose it could look quite pretty. Lavender, perhaps. Or teal?'

'And a pelisse in royal blue. So that they all match.'

'Good idea, miss.' The modiste nodded approvingly. 'I'll go and fetch some fabrics so you can choose your favourites.'

'Thank you.'

'So…' Sabrina patted the space on the sofa beside her when the modiste had left the room. 'How did you enjoy last night?'

'It was very entertaining.' Abigail sat down cautiously. After a brief luncheon and even briefer carriage ride without any mention of her waltz with Theo, she'd been tentatively hoping the marchioness hadn't noticed. 'Evelyn was a great success.'

'She was, wasn't she?' Sabrina's face burst into a smile. 'I knew that she could be, given a chance, although I admit, I was worried. The *ton* can be cruel when they decide to be.'

'It was certainly nerve-racking at first.'

'Of course, Theo's presence helped. Did you see his face when we were announced? He looked so stern, as though he was ready to do battle with anyone who slighted us.'

'I did.' She smiled at the memory.

'You know, he was only a boy when I married Fitz. Not shy exactly, but sensitive. Reserved. We barely exchanged more than a few sentences whenever he was home from school in the holidays. I could never imagine him as a soldier, even when he joined the army. Fitz always gave the impression of being the brave one. Only as it turns out, I had it the wrong way around. Theo was the real hero. Thank goodness we have him to look after us now.' She sniffed. 'I'm just fortunate that he doesn't want to marry. I was so relieved when I saw him dancing with you last night.'

'Relieved?'

'Yes. He has a good heart. Not that dancing with you was an act of charity, of course, but it was good of him to do it, especially with all those husband-hunting debutantes gawping in his direction. Could you imagine if he'd actually taken a fancy to one of them? The very idea of some eighteen-year-old chit coming to push me out of my own house churns my stomach.'

'But you'd still keep your position even if he did marry, surely?'

'In theory, yes, but in practice, it would be very different. Without Fitz, he's the acting marquess, which would make his wife a kind of acting marchioness. I'd simply be in the way.' She tapped a hand against Abigail's knee. 'So just in case, I think it's wisest if he doesn't accompany us to any more *ton* events from now on. There's no point taking the risk, especially since he doesn't want to be involved in the Season anyway.'

'I suppose so.'

'Then all he has to do is sell the hunting lodge to pay for it.'

Abigail gave a small start, suddenly reminded of something, a half-formed idea that had been flitting around the edge of her consciousness for a few days now…

'And perhaps…' Sabrina continued before she could grasp what the idea was, 'with the two of you working so closely together, you might tell me if he *does* show any interest in anybody?'

'Of course, my lady.' Abigail reached for the book of patterns, her earlier queasiness surging back in a torrent. At least Sabrina didn't suspect that there had been anything more than friendship behind her dance with Theo, but the fact that she apparently couldn't even imagine it hurt a little… Although, of course, there really *was* nothing more to it than friendship. And curiosity. And companionship. The combination of which had been quite—*very*—pleasant.

'Thank you.' Sabrina reached across and patted her arm just as Evelyn swept around the corner. 'There you are, what on earth have you been doing?'

'Sorry, mama.' Evelyn squeezed herself on to the sofa between them. 'I was looking at shoes in the shop next door.'

'Where's your maid?'

'Over there.' Evelyn pointed towards the door. 'Don't worry.'

'Good.' Sabrina nodded approvingly. 'Because I'm sure I don't need to remind you that we can't afford any scandal. Not so much as a whiff. You need to be on your best behaviour at all times from now on.'

'I know, mama. You've only told me a thousand times already.'

'And I'll tell you a thousand more before the Season's

finished. On a cheerier note, however, do you have any favourite suitors after last night?'

'Yes!' Evelyn perked up again, beaming. 'There were some very entertaining gentlemen. Baron Aldershott, for example.'

'Absolutely not!' Sabrina put a hand up immediately. 'He's far too old for you.'

'He's forty-five and extremely charming.'

'He's charming because he's a rake and how do you know he's forty-five?'

'He told me.'

'Oh, good grief.' Sabrina put a hand to her forehead. 'Miss Lemon, please tell my daughter that she can do far better than some middle-aged rake.'

'He may have been a rake in the past…' Evelyn thrust her nose into the air '…but he says he's reformed. He told me that he was looking for a bride this Season.'

'Just because he says something doesn't make it true! And even if he means it, he's still not good enough. Does he really think that after breaking at least a dozen hearts every year for who knows how long, he can just click his fingers now and women will fall over themselves to marry him?' She snorted. 'Yes, of course he does. He's a man.'

'Your mother has a point.' Abigail chimed in. 'You need to find someone you can trust and respect.'

'Exactly!' Sabrina snorted. 'Not a charmer like your father. He claimed to be head over heels with me. When we were courting, I was practically deluged in flowers every day. To reflect my beauty, he said. Then the moment we were married…' She clicked her fingers. 'I'm not sure I received as much as a compliment ever again.'

'Just because father deceived you doesn't mean that all men are liars.'

'Ha! Tell her, Miss Lemon.'

'What does she mean?' Evelyn turned towards her inquisitively. 'What happened to you?'

'Well…' Abigail sighed. She didn't particularly want to talk about Henry, but if it proved instructive… 'I had a fiancé once. Quite recently, in fact. We were engaged for a long time and he said that he would always stand by me no matter what. Only when I lost my fortune, he didn't. He abandoned me right at the moment I needed him most.'

'I'm so sorry.' Evelyn put a hand over hers.

'You see!' Sabrina crowed. 'Most men are liars.'

'*Mama!* If men are so bad, why did you agree to my having a Season at all?'

'Because society doesn't give us any option besides marriage, but I'll be damned before I let you marry a rake like Aldershott.'

'Is he really so bad?'

'He was a friend of your father's.'

'Urgh. He didn't tell me that.' Evelyn shuddered. 'Anyway, it doesn't matter. If you'd let me finish earlier, I'd have told you that my real favourite is Viscount Everly.'

'Everly?' Sabrina looked thoughtful. 'Black hair, blue eyes?'

'And *such* a noble expression. He's very handsome, don't you think?'

'I suppose so, although there are far more important qualities in a man, believe me.'

'You're so bitter.' Evelyn made an impatient sound. 'What about you, Miss Lemon? Did you meet anyone interesting?'

'Me?' Abigail's breath hitched guiltily. 'Of course

not. I've put that kind of thing behind me. I'm perfectly content being a spinster from now on.'

'Good.' For a moment, she thought she saw Sabrina's eyes flicker with satisfaction. 'Because we wouldn't want to lose you.'

## Chapter Sixteen

Shopping. It was the middle of the afternoon before Theo remembered that Abigail and Sabrina had arranged to go shopping. Which, if he'd remembered earlier, would have saved him several hours of looking expectantly towards the door every time he heard so much as the creak of a floorboard outside. He didn't know why he'd even bothered to sit down at his desk that morning. He'd been neglecting his duties, unable to concentrate on a single thing all day.

He leaned back in his chair, absently stroking Lady's ears with one hand, going over, yet again, the decision he'd made in the early hours. It hadn't been a difficult one. As both defendant and judge, he'd known there was only one punishment for his crime. He should never have let last night go so far. He should never have invited Abigail for a nightcap, full stop. After that moment in the hallway before the ball, he should have kept away from her all evening, only he hadn't been able to help himself.

Damn it, he enjoyed her company too much. She affected him in a way no woman ever had before. And when she'd asked about 'companionship'…well, he'd known what they were getting into while she obviously had not. He'd abused his position both as her employer and as a gentleman.

All of which meant that there was only one thing he could do, the one thing he thought he'd never do, the last thing he wanted to do, the *worst* thing for her, but that his honour and conscience demanded. He had to take responsibility and make amends for his actions.

Although marriage might not be the gallows exactly, especially marriage to Abigail, he was still aware of a hollow, hopeless sensation in the pit of his stomach at the prospect. He was going to propose. Just as soon as she came through that door, which, judging by the sound of commotion outside now, wouldn't be long.

He stood up, tugging at the hem of his waistcoat and straightening his cravat. If the shopping party had returned, then Abigail would soon be coming to catch up on some work. No matter how awkward the situation between them might be after last night, he had no doubts regarding her work ethic.

It took, in fact, ten minutes, every one of which felt like another hour.

'Good afternoon.' She gave him a polite nod as she entered, looking so calm and composed that if he hadn't known better he might have thought he'd imagined the whole evening and nothing had ever happened between them.

'Good afternoon.' He inclined his head, also politely. 'How was your excursion? Successful, I hope?'

'Very, thank you.'

'Four dresses and a pelisse?'

'One dress and some new shoes.'

'Just the one?' He lifted an eyebrow enquiringly.

'Which I paid for myself.' She came to stand in front of his desk, her gaze faintly accusing.

'I thought we discussed—'

'We did, only something occurred to me earlier.'

'Earlier?' He felt his body stir at the memory of it.

'Yes. You haven't put the hunting lodge up for sale.'

'I beg your pardon?' All stirring ceased. He wasn't sure what he'd expected her to say, but it definitely hadn't been that.

'Yes. It occurred to me while we were shopping-just before I was about to order those new gowns, incidentally-that you told the marchioness you were selling the hunting lodge in Wiltshire in order to pay for Evelyn's Season, but you haven't put it up for sale yet.'

'*That* was what you were thinking about earlier?'

'Not *early* earlier.' Her skin flushed. 'More recently.'

'Ah.' He needlessly shuffled a few of the papers on his desk. 'Who says that I'm not selling it?'

'I do. If you were, then there would have been some kind of correspondence about it over the past couple of weeks, but there's been nothing about a sale. Nothing about that property *at all*.'

'I'm getting around to it.'

'Is that so?' She folded her arms sceptically. 'Shall I tell you what I think? *I* think that you're paying for Evelyn's Season yourself. Which means that you also intended to pay for my clothes yourself.'

'Would that be so bad?'

'Yes.' She dropped her hands again, moving them to her hips. 'It would mean that you lied.'

'Not maliciously.'

'But it was still a lie.'

'All right.' He rubbed his hands over his face. 'I admit it. I'm not selling the hunting lodge, but I can afford a Season and a few new dresses.'

'I thought you said that a Season was very expensive?'

'It is.'

'Then your brother should be the one paying for it. You shouldn't be using your own money. Unlike your brother, you actually earned it.'

'I still ought to cover your costs. I'm the one who asked you to escort Evelyn about town.'

'That's not the point. You lied when I thought I could trust you.'

'You *can* trust me.' He braced his hands against the desk. As proposals went, this wasn't exactly the best start. 'All right, yes, I shouldn't have lied about the lodge, but I never meant to insult you.' He cleared his throat heavily. 'Anyway, I'm glad that you're here. I thought we should talk. About last night and…this morning and what happened between us.'

'Oh.' Her eyes darted briefly in the direction of her office before focusing on him again. 'Yes, I suppose we should.'

'I want to apologise. After the ball… I behaved dishonourably. Both as a gentleman and your employer, and I—'

'Don't!' She put a hand up abruptly. '*Don't* apologise.'

'I need to.'

'No, you don't.' Her voice was clipped. 'We discussed it at the time and came to a mutual agreement. I was curious about certain aspects of…*companionship* and you helped me to understand. Perhaps we got carried away, but I was hardly an unwilling participant. In case you haven't noticed, I'm also a grown woman and I can make my own decisions.

'We were both perfectly aware of what we were doing and we agreed on no commitment. So while apologising might make you feel better, it's humiliating to me. If there was any dishonour, then we might at least share it.' She lifted her chin. 'In short, don't you dare apologise, unless you place your sense of honour above my opinion.'

'Understood.' He inclined his head. 'However, considering our respective positions, I feel that—'

'It was most educational,' she interrupted as if he hadn't been speaking, 'but it's over. Neither of us has any interest in marriage so it would probably be best if we simply put it behind us and forget the whole thing ever happened. Therefore we ought to carry on working as normal and be completely professional.'

'Abigail, surely you understand that I have to—'.

'No!' Her eyes flashed. 'One more word and I'll walk out that door and never come back.'

'*Abigail...*' He looked from her to the door and then back again.

'So that's that.' She turned her face away as if the matter were completely settled. 'Now I suggest that we both get on with some work.'

'Is that really what you want?'

'It is.'

'Very well.' He watched powerlessly as she stalked across the room to her office, his thoughts spinning so fast that she was almost at her door before he burst out. '*Educational?*'

'I'm sorry?' She looked back over her shoulder.

'*That's* what you thought of it?'

'Well, yes, but not just that.' She ran her tongue along the seam of her lips seemingly unconsciously. 'It was also…nice.'

'*Nice.*' He dropped down into his chair. 'You overwhelm me.'

'How would you like me to describe it? Earth-shattering?'

'That would be an improvement.' He drummed his fingernails on the desk. 'Although it wouldn't need to be the whole earth, just a continent or two.'

'Europe-shattering?'

'That would do.' He lifted an eyebrow. 'What about your comparison? I believe that was your ulterior motive?'

'Oh…yes. It was.' She lifted a hand to her head, toying with the curl at the back of her neck.

'And?'

'And you told me to stop mentioning his name.'

'That was then. Today is a different matter.'

'You can hardly expect me to tell you.' She folded her hands primly. 'It wouldn't be ladylike.'

'So you refuse to let me apologise like a gentleman, yet retain the prerogative of acting like a lady yourself?'

She opened her mouth, closed it and then opened it again. 'Yes.' She looked uncertain. 'Unless you're saying that you think I'm not.'

'Not what?'

'A lady. You might think that my behaviour last night was *un*ladylike, for example.' The muscles in her face looked very taut suddenly.

'I never thought anything of the kind. I told you, I could never think that way about you.'

'Good.' She lowered her chin a fraction. 'Well, that's all right then.'

'Excuse me, my lord?' Possett poked his head around the doorway at that moment. 'But there's a person here to see you, a Mr Sidney Jones.'

'Tell him I'm busy.'

'No.' Abigail spun around. 'Tell him to come in now. We've just finished what we were doing and I have work to catch up on.'

'Sir?' Possett looked between them uncertainly.

Theo ground his teeth. So much for making a proposal. He ought to feel relieved, as if he'd just had a narrow escape, but instead he felt oddly deflated. Disappointed even. Which made absolutely no sense at all.

'Send him in.' He jerked his head at Possett, trying to repress a sinking feeling as a tall, heavyset man came into the room, no doubt to tell him about some new debt of his brother's.

'Mr Jones?' He stood up again and extended a hand. 'What can I do for you?'

'Colonel Marshall.' The man bowed, looking faintly overwhelmed by his surroundings. 'I apologise for calling on you without an appointment.'

'Not at all. Please sit down.' He gestured towards the chair opposite. 'I presume this is business related?'

'Yes, sir, and again, I hope you won't take it remiss that I've come, but the fact is, I have a proposition for you.'

'A proposition?' He tipped his chair backwards, trying to focus on the words and not Abigail as she pushed her office door shut behind her. 'That sounds promising.'

'I hope so. You see, my partners and I, that is, Mr Alfred Tavistock, Mr Blackburn Rawlinson and myself, we own a building company.'

'Indeed?'

'And we're very interested in your Chelsea building project, the one that's…pardon my saying so…run out of funds.'

'Interested in what way?'

'Well, the thing is… I'll get straight to the point… the long and short of it is…we'd like to buy you out.'

'I beg your pardon?' Theo sat forward again with a thud.

'We'd give you a fair price for what's already been built, as well as for the land.' Mr Jones held out a piece of paper with a number scrawled across the top. 'We were thinking of this kind of amount?'

Theo looked down at the paper, thunderstruck. 'You mean, you want to buy the entire enterprise?'

'Every brick.'

'But…*why*?' He shook his head in bewilderment. 'I mean, you obviously know the venture collapsed?'

'We do, but we also think it can be saved.' Mr Jones perched on the edge of his chair. 'I know it might not look like a huge amount, considering what you would get for the finished houses, but I promise you it's fair. We'll give you some time to think about it, of course, but we'd like to get started as soon as possible, what with summer coming.' He got back to his feet and bowed as Abigail emerged from her office, open-mouthed. 'Pardon me, miss.'

'Good afternoon.' Abigail caught Theo's eye, her own suspiciously bright. 'I didn't mean to eavesdrop, but…well, I couldn't help it.'

'Not at all.' He beckoned her closer, holding out the piece of paper. 'Mr Jones here just offered me this for the Chelsea project.'

'I can add another five hundred, but that's as high as we can go.'

'Another five hundred?' Her jaw dropped even further. 'Have you built many houses before, Mr Jones?'

'Lots of them, miss.' The builder looked offended. 'Tavistock, Rawlinson and Jones have built half of Islington and Holborn. You can go and inspect our work if you like. It's good quality.'

'I'm certain it is. I'm from Holborn myself.'

'Which street, miss?'

'Cavendish Lane.'

'Why, that was built by my own father!'

'Then he did a very good job.' She smiled. 'I don't recall ever having a single problem with our house.'

'Then I'll take that as a sign.' Theo came to a decision, not that it was a particularly hard one to make. 'You have a deal, Mr Jones. The Chelsea project is yours.' He held a hand out. 'I hope you make a fortune from it.'

# Chapter Seventeen

Abigail stared at the door as it closed behind Mr Jones, wondering if she'd just hallucinated the whole exchange. It seemed much, *much* too good to be true.

'Did that really just happen?'

Theo turned to face her, evidently thinking the same thing. At some point over the last few minutes, he appeared to have taken hold of her hand. Or she'd taken his. Honestly, she had no idea which one of them had first reached for the other or whether it had been a mutual impulse, but either way, their fingers were tightly entwined.

'It did.' She felt the corners of her mouth curve irresistibly upwards. 'It really did.'

'He wants to buy the whole project?'

'Every single brick. As soon as possible.'

He was silent for a few seconds, as if he were still struggling to take the words in, then let go of her hand to catch hold of her waist instead, swinging her around in a circle with a loud whoop.

'Careful!' She laughed as a pile of ledgers went flying from the desk and scattered all over the floor.

'No! No more being careful! He wants to buy the whole damned lot!' He kept on swinging. 'Every brick!'

'Yes!' She couldn't stop smiling.

'No more sitting at that desk.'

'No more.'

'Or acting for the marquess.'

'Exactly!

'I'll be able to pay back the people Fitz owes.' He lowered her back to the floor, though he didn't remove his hands from her waist. 'Including you.'

'Including me.'

'I feel like I've just escaped from prison.'

'Not escaped. Been released.'

'I want to buy you those shoes.'

'Absolutely not.'

'Please.'

'No.'

'Abigail…' A muscle leapt in his jaw as the mood shifted, attraction fizzling in the air between them suddenly. She felt seized with a powerful urge to kiss him again. It wasn't curiosity this time, it was desire, pure and simple. Now that she knew how it felt to kiss him, she wanted to do it again. And again. And several more times for good measure.

She swallowed, trying to regain some control over her own errant thoughts, and let her gaze drop to his chest. Which was a mistake as it only reminded her of their evening together. She knew what he looked like beneath his shirt, knew that there was a dusting of sandy-coloured hair across his torso, knew that the muscles of his stomach were hard and yet smooth to the touch.

Her whole body seemed to be straining towards him,

but in the cold light of day, she knew she had to be strong. If they kissed again, then it would make their situation even more complicated. Only her blood was surging, her thoughts had scattered in a hundred separate directions at once and it seemed completely impossible to move away.

'You were better.' The words were past her lips before she could stop them.

'Better?' His voice sounded hoarse.

'At kissing. Than...*him*.'

'More than educational?'

'Much more than that.'

'Like this?' His eyes glittered as he lowered his head, moving slowly, closer and closer, touching her lips just in time to be interrupted by another knock on the door.

'Bloody hell.' He took a step backwards, looking as if he wanted to throw something. 'What the thundering blazes is it now?'

'Another visitor, sir.' Possett stuck his head apprehensively around the door again.

'Tell them to come back later.'

'I would, sir, but you said to let you know immediately when this one arrived.'

He gave her an apologetic look. 'Who is it?'

'He says his name is Armstrong.'

'Armstrong?' He jerked his head around. 'He's here now?'

'The man you saved from prison?' Abigail turned as well, looking towards the door with interest.

'The very same. Also the man with the world's worst timing.' Theo cleared his throat. 'All right, Possett, you'd better send him in. Where's Kitchen?'

'In the, ah, kitchen, sir.'

'You'd better call him, too.'

'Is there going to be another celebration?' She lifted an eyebrow inquisitively as Possett disappeared again.

'It's a distinct possibility. I don't suppose you'd care to join us?'

'Three old soldiers reminis-isi-ising?' She smiled, relieved that the tension in the room had dissipated before they did something foolish. 'I think I'll take some work up to my room, but you enjoy yourselves.'

'That may be wise. Abigail…' He caught at her hand as she made to go past him. 'If you see Sabrina, don't mention anything about Mr Jones just yet. I wouldn't want to get her hopes up.'

'My lips are sealed.' She tugged her hand away gently. 'Enjoy your celebration.'


'It's good to see you a free man again.' Theo patted the new arrival on the back.

'Thanks to you, sir.' Despite being welcomed with open arms, Armstrong was looking distinctly sheepish.

'Don't forget Kitchen. He practically camped on the magistrate's doorstep.'

'I'm grateful to you both, for taking care of my family while I was locked up, as well. I know I was stupid, but I won't be again.' He looked down at his hands. 'I'm only sorry it's taken me so long to visit. The fact is, I was too ashamed before.'

'There was no need to be.' Theo led him towards an armchair. 'I just wish you'd told us how bad a situation you were in.'

'I didn't want to be a burden, sir, even though I know I've made things ten times worse now. I just wish there was some way I could repay your kindness.'

'Actually, there is.' Theo folded his arms over his chest. 'I want you to run a business for me. A coaching inn, to be precise. I've found one for sale, just outside of London, as it happens. It'll be hard work, but it's yours if you want it.'

'A coaching inn?' Armstrong's face lit up with excitement swiftly followed by disbelief. 'But how?'

'I'll buy the business, you'll run it for me and we'll divide the profits. How does that sound?'

'Too generous, sir.'

'Not at all. It's a sound business arrangement. Discuss it with your wife and let me know.'

'I will.' Armstrong's gaze slid towards the door. 'If you don't mind, could I go and ask her now?'

'By all means.'

'I'll be as quick as I can!'

'We won't move from these chairs,' Kitchen declared, depositing himself by the fireplace.

'I'll be back before you know it, sir.'

'So that's that.' The valet clapped his hands together as Armstrong practically sprinted out of the room. 'That accounts for all of the men.'

'I believe that you're right.' Theo took a seat opposite.

'All settled and correct. Although, just out of interest, how much does a coaching inn cost?'

'Why? Would you like one?'

'And leave you? Never. I just hope that you're saving enough money for yourself. You might want to set up your own household before long.'

'Indeed? And what makes you think I'd want to do that?'

'Just a hunch, sir.'

'Oh, really?'

'Anything's possible.' There was a momentary pause. 'You and Miss Lemon seem very friendly these days.'

'Do we?'

'Yes, sir, you do. She's a fine young lady.'

'She is.' Theo tugged at his cuffs. She was more than fine. She was intelligent and witty and beautiful and exceedingly kissable, everything he would ever have wanted in a woman if he'd ever allowed himself to think about it. 'She's a very competent secretary.'

*'Competent.'* Kitchen gave a snort. 'Seems like a funny word for a woman you can't take your eyes off.'

'Since when?'

'Since the night she told us about her broken engagement.'

'That's ridiculous.'

'If you say so, sir.'

'I'm perfectly capable of taking my eyes off her.'

'You mean like this morning?'

Theo stiffened. 'What about this morning?'

'There aren't many secrets downstairs, sir.' Kitchen smirked. 'One of the maids saw her coming out of here in the early hours.'

'We were having a nightcap after the ball, that's all.'

'Right you are, sir. Still, it's funny how people can change, isn't it?' Kitchen rested his feet on a footstool. 'Just look at the marchioness. Only a month ago, she was a screaming mess, saying how she'd never set foot outside this house ever again, and now look at her. It just goes to show, you can have a fixed idea about something and then change your mind later.'

'I presume there's a subtext to this conversation?'

'I've no idea what you mean, sir.'

'No?' Theo narrowed his eyes. 'So you're not suggesting that a man who, say, swore off marriage years ago might one day feel inclined to change his mind?'

'Well, now that you mention it...'

'Once and for all, Kitchen, I've no desire for a wife.'

'Because you'd make a bad husband, sir?'

'Precisely. And even if that wasn't the case, Miss Lemon has expressed an extreme aversion to marriage herself.'

'Because she doesn't trust men, sir?'

'Exactly.'

'Even though we both know that she could trust you?' Kitchen cleared his throat and stared at a point in mid-air. 'I'm just saying that marriage might be the right thing to do. Considering.'

'Considering what?'

'Considering the amount of time that you've been spending alone together, for starters.'

'Because she's my secretary.'

'I'm not talking about that, sir. As you well know. And it's not right, if you ask me.'

Theo lifted his eyebrows, surprised by his valet's uncharacteristically chiding tone. 'Are you scolding me, Kitchen?'

'Begging your pardon, sir, but, yes, I am. She's a well-brought-up young lady.'

'She's also an independent person with her own mind who can make her own decisions.'

'She still might not realise what she's getting into and she deserves better than a dalliance. What if you get her with child?'

'I won't.'

'If I had a penny for every time I'd heard that, sir, I'd be a very rich man.'

'So would I, but in this case, it's the truth. I admit that I find Miss Lemon very attractive, but I've no intention of dishonouring her. We're friends, that's all.'

'So there's nothing else going on?'

He shifted in his chair. 'I wouldn't say *nothing*.'

'I knew it!'

'But not *that*.'

'Right.' A range of conflicting emotions crossed over the valet's face. 'So what *is* going on, sir?'

'That, Kitchen, comes under the category of none of your damn business.'

'Fair enough. As long as there's no debauchery going on, I'm happy.'

'I'm glad you approve.'

*She deserves better than a dalliance.*

Theo leaned back in his chair, glaring into the fire as the words repeated themselves in his head. That much was definitely true. It was the reason he'd intended to propose to Abigail that morning, only she'd stopped him before he'd had the chance, which meant that it was over, this thing between them, whatever it was, less than twenty-four hours after it had begun.

Oddly enough, he still couldn't bring himself to feel relieved about it, as if, despite his family history, despite the fact that she was obviously better off without him, a part of him had actually wanted her to say yes. So much so that the thought of *never* holding her in his arms again made him feel curiously bereft.

It was the strangest, most unexpected feeling, as if his peace of mind were permanently and irrevocably shattered. His attraction to her had grown so subtly and stealthily that he had a feeling there was no turning back. Even worse, he had the sneaking suspicion that he might actually go mad if he had to work alongside her every day and *not* touch her.

That meant that the decent thing to do would be to find her a new job elsewhere, only the thought of her leaving made him feel wretched, as if…his thoughts stuttered…as if he truly cared for her…no, more than that, truly loved her…as if he wanted more than a dalliance…as if he genuinely *wanted* to marry her.

His sight dimmed and every muscle in his body seized up simultaneously. How could he of all people possibly be contemplating marriage? He'd been against it for as long as he could remember. It was impossible. Insane. Unless…

A chink of light broke through the darkness clouding his vision. The deal with Jones meant that he would soon be free to go in search of Fitzwilliam. And once he found him and dragged him back to London then he would finally be free to get away from this house. And if he could do that, then maybe he'd be free to break his family's pattern of bad marriages, as well…

He looked towards his desk and felt a new and liberating sense of detachment, as if it were just any old desk and not his father's. For the first time in a long time, he felt hopeful. Positive. As if his life were under his own control again. Maybe he didn't *have* to turn into his father or brother. Maybe he could marry Abigail and take her to America with him and they could have a whole new start. Maybe they could have a happy marriage.

Those were several big maybes, but damn it, he was going to try. In the meantime, he simply needed to be strong and keep his hands and eyes to himself. He couldn't declare his feelings until he was certain that he could do the honourable thing and propose to her.

He sensed eyes on him and looked up to find Kitchen with a knowing smirk on his face.

'Not one word.' He glowered. 'Not a single word.'

## Chapter Eighteen

'I need to warn you about something and I need to be quick,' Abigail announced, hurrying into the breakfast room. She'd heard Evelyn talking in her mother's room as she'd passed, which meant that she was probably only a few minutes behind her.

'Good morning.' Theo looked up from his plate of eggs and bacon. 'That sounds serious.'

'It is and it isn't.' She took a seat opposite, trying not to notice how handsome he looked in a powder-blue waistcoat that perfectly complemented his pale eyes, though unfortunately it was impossible to ignore the effect completely. Her heartbeat had already performed a small, decidedly inconvenient skip.

It had been just over a week since their kiss, a week during which both of them had behaved in a superlatively professional, determinedly *un*romantic manner. Admittedly, there had been a couple of occasions where she'd thought he'd been watching her, his eyes following the movement of her fingers as she wrote or boring into the space between her shoulder blades when she'd got up to fetch something, but it was possible that she'd just been imagining things.

In fact, it was likely she had been since he'd been in an uncharacteristically good mood, probably due to his narrow escape when she'd forestalled his proposal. Obviously, that had given him a new, more positive perspective on life. Which was somewhat insulting, albeit still a relief, she reminded herself—exactly what she wanted, in fact. With any luck, soon the attraction between them would pass and everything would go back to the way it had been before.

'I'm intrigued.' He lifted the coffee pot. 'May I?'

'Thank you.' She watched as he poured. 'Just try not to overreact.'

'Now you're worrying me.'

'It's nothing bad exactly, just possibly a bit premature. Remember that Evelyn's only eighteen and young love can be very...' she twirled a hand in the air '... impulsive.'

'Abigail.' He lifted an eyebrow. 'I'm going to need you to tell me what on earth you're talking about.'

'Right.' She took a deep breath. 'Evelyn says that she's chosen a husband.'

'Already?'

'Yes. She met him that first night at the Gaddesby ball and he's called at the house every day since.'

'So she's known him for one week and thinks that's long enough to decide to spend the rest of her life with him?' He put the coffee pot down to lift a hand to his forehead instead. 'I knew I'd regret allowing her a Season. Is she actually going to wait for a proposal or has she already ordered a trousseau?'

'There appears to be some kind of understanding between them. She seems quite definite.'

'Dare I ask the identity of the lucky man?'

'Viscount Everly.'

'I have no idea who that is.'

'He seems nice. Young, but very pleasant.'

'How young?'

'Twenty.'

'And what's so special about him?'

'Actually, he seems quite normal, certainly not a lothario.'

'Maybe that's the appeal. What does Sabrina think?'

'She doesn't appear to have any objections. In fact…' She took another deep breath and braced herself. 'She wants to throw a dinner party for him and his family.'

'Oh, bloody hell. And she expects me to be there, too, I suppose?

'I'm afraid so.' She reached for a hot roll and some butter. 'I just wanted to give you a little warning before Sabrina mentions the dinner.'

'Good. Thank you. In that case, my answer is no. It's much too soon and I refuse to condone such impetuous behaviour.'

'I see what you mean…' she cut her roll in half, trying to sound casual '…but if I could just offer some advice?'

There was a suspicious-sounding pause. 'Go on.'

'If you put obstacles in the way, then Evelyn will probably dig her heels in on principle. I admit, it all seems rather fast, but engagements don't necessarily lead to marriage, as we well know. There'll still be plenty of time for her to change her mind if she wants to, but the more she's thwarted, the more likely she is to rebel.'

'You seem pretty certain.'

'I am.'

'All right. One dinner.' He scowled, conceding the point. 'On condition that you attend, too.'

'Oh, no.' She shook her head quickly. 'I'm not sure that would be appropriate. Being a companion and chaperon is one thing, but I'm hardly a member of the family.'

'You're an honorary member. I want you there or it's not happening and that's my final answer.'

'Very well, if you insist.' She gave a small cough, touched by the sentiment. 'However, there's one other thing I ought to tell you.'

He held on to her gaze, taking a mouthful of coffee before answering. 'Why do I get the feeling I'm not going to like this either?'

'Because you won't. When Sabrina says soon, she means tomorrow evening.'

*'Tomorrow?'*

'I'm afraid so.'

'And you still think I should agree?'

'I do.'

He groaned and rubbed a hand around the back of his neck. 'All right, as long as Sabrina organises everything.'

'I'm sure she intends to.'

'I never stood a chance, did I?' He harrumphed. 'So what's the plan for today?'

'I believe that we're paying a few calls and then taking a carriage ride in Hyde Park.'

'No ball tonight?'

'No.' She dipped her chin, focusing hard on spreading jam over her roll, the very mention of a ball making goose pimples break out on her arms. 'There seems to be an inexhaustible supply of them, but we're attending the opera tonight.' She peeked up through her lashes. 'I take it you're not coming with us?'

'I'm afraid not.' If she wasn't mistaken, his gaze had just heated somewhat, too. 'I need to read Jones's contract one more time.'

'You ought to take an evening off occasionally.'

'I did last week, remember?'

'That wasn't to relax.'

'I don't know about that. Some of it was very relaxing.'

She shifted in her seat, aware of the air between them beginning to thrum and pulse with tension again. Suddenly she felt very aware of his proximity and the fact that they were alone together. If she stretched her legs out beneath the table, she could probably touch his... 'I suppose some of it was.'

'Don't wear blue tonight.'

'Pardon?' She blinked. 'Why not?'

'Because you look too pretty in blue. I don't want anyone else looking at you. Save it for the dinner party tomorrow.'

'Oh.' She caught her bottom lip between her teeth, trying not to smile. 'I'll think about it.'

Abigail glanced around nervously as she followed the dinner guests into the dining room. After a wonderful night at the opera, she'd been in a good mood all day, but it was becoming increasingly obvious that this evening was a mistake. Thoughtful as it had been for Theo to include her, she really wished that he hadn't.

Even attired in her new cornflower-blue evening

gown, she felt self-conscious and awkward, like an interloper who didn't belong. She was an employee, not a member of the family, and no doubt Viscount Everly's family were thinking the same thing. Only it was too late now to turn tail and run.

'A toast.' Theo raised his glass as they all took their seats. 'To family and new friendships.'

'Family and new friendships,' she echoed, taking a sip of the wine and feeling a tug in her chest at the words. Evelyn and the young viscount were sitting side by side, gazing intently into each other's eyes, the very picture of young love, the way she and Henry had probably looked during the early days of their courtship. She only hoped that their story had a happier ending.

She heaved a sigh and returned her glass to the table. She was seated at the far end, a long way from Theo, although it made a good vantage point to watch everyone. The viscount appeared to have taken the words 'family dinner' to heart, bringing a significant number of his own. Aside from his mother and sister, there were three cousins, an aunt and two uncles. None the less, the evening seemed to be going well, largely thanks to Theo.

Despite his objections, he appeared to be on his best behaviour, seeming completely at ease as he conversed politely with the viscount's mother and clearly not about military strategy either. The viscountess looked utterly charmed, even fanning her face and batting her lashes flirtatiously. As Abigail watched, surprised and faintly alarmed to feel a stab of jealousy, Theo seemed to sense her scrutiny, turning his face and smiling as if he were trying to convey some secret message. Somehow the sight made her toes curl.

'So you're Lady Salway's companion?' the gentleman on her left addressed her at that moment.

'Mmm? Oh, yes, for just over a month now.' She smiled politely, picking up her spoon for the soup course. 'And you're the viscount's cousin, I understand?'

'For my sins.' He tipped his head in acknowledgement. 'Barnabas Pembroke. An honour to meet you, Miss—?'

'Lemon. Miss Abigail Lemon.'

'This is all rather a whirlwind, isn't it?' He waved a hand towards Evelyn and the viscount.

'It certainly is, but they seem very happy.'

'Indeed.' He sounded doubtful. 'Although some might say the whole thing's happened rather too fast.'

'Might they?'

'Given the circumstances.' He nudged his seat closer. 'But perhaps you might be able to tell me a little more about those? I'm sure you know all the gossip, Miss Lemon. About the marquess, that is.'

'I'm sure I don't know what you're talking about.'

'No? The rumour is, he ran off with the governess.'

She stiffened. True or not, it seemed in poor form to mention it at the table. 'Surely you know better than to listen to rumours, sir?'

'Ah, family loyalty.' He tapped the side of his nose. 'I understand. Although, before that, there was an opera singer, if I recall correctly.'

'I wouldn't know.' She shot a quick look towards Sabrina, sitting a couple of seats away on the opposite side. If she wasn't mistaken, her posture had just become several degrees straighter. Theo was looking in their direction now, too, she noticed, a definite frown notched between his brows.

'Aurora Rossi, that was her name. She was in great demand, but completely out of my league, unfortunately. She preferred men with titles, as I recall.'

'Sir—'

'Then there was an actress—

'Mr Pembroke.' Abigail twisted in her chair, speaking firmly. 'This is hardly polite conversation.'

'Quite right.' He winked. 'Consider me properly chastened, but you have to admit, this is a strange situation. Who would have thought the marchioness would still bring her daughter out this year after everything that's happened? You can't help but admire her nerve.'

'I admire a lot of things about her.'

'But then I suppose she simply decided to get on with her life, especially if it's true what everyone's saying, that her husband's not coming back.' His gaze sharpened. 'What do *you* say, Miss Lemon?'

'I'd say—*again*—that I have no idea.'

'Oh, come now. You live here. You must know how the land lies.' He lowered his voice. 'Between you and me, my aunt isn't particularly thrilled by recent developments.'

'What?' She glanced anxiously up the table towards Evelyn and the viscount. 'You mean, she doesn't approve?'

'She'd like to know what's going on with the marquess before she decides whether or not to approve. She doesn't care for the possibility of more scandal.'

'There's always the possibility of that with anyone.'

'Naturally, she can't stop her son from doing what he wants, but she could make his life difficult. No man wants to disobey his mother directly.' His voice sounded a lot less friendly all of a sudden. 'Look, let's not dance around the subject, shall we? My aunt wants to know if there's really a dowry. Considering the wreck the marquess made of his finances, how do we know there's enough money left over for one?'

'Because Colonel Marshall is a man of his word and if he says there's a dowry, then you can be sure it will be paid.'

'But does he have the authority to say so? What if the marquess returns and decides otherwise?'

'I'm sure that he's thought of that.' Abigail held onto his gaze stonily. 'These are very blunt questions, sir.'

'Why do you think my aunt brought me?' Mr Pembroke sat back in his chair with a shrug. 'Unlike my cousin, I'm a realist. Love is all very well, but there are other, more practical considerations.'

She snorted derisively. 'You sound like a man I once knew.'

'Indeed?' His eyes glinted in a way that made her immediately regret the words. 'That sounds like an interesting story.'

'But not one I care to share for amusement.' She shifted her seat away. 'I'm only glad for Evelyn's sake that your cousin is more romantic.'

'He's young, foolish and smitten. He'd probably marry her with nothing.'

'Good.' She turned her attention to her now-cold soup. 'Because true love is priceless.'

'True love is…' He stared at her incredulously for a few seconds before bursting into mocking laughter.

'You seem to be enjoying yourselves down there.' Theo's voice resonated down the table.

'Indeed we are.' Mr Pembroke looked in danger of falling off his chair with amusement. 'Miss Lemon has just made the most droll statement.'

'It wasn't intended as such.' She shot him a dagger glare. 'I simply suggested that true love was more important than money.'

'A somewhat idealised perspective, wouldn't you agree, colonel?'

'On the contrary, what would life be without love?'

'What would it be without money?'

'Can we not enjoy both?' Evelyn sounded uncomfortable.

'But if it came to a choice…' Mr Pembroke was persistent. 'Which would you choose, colonel?'

'Personally—' Theo's gaze flickered towards her '—I would say there's no contest.'

'What was all that about?' Theo marched straight to Abigail's side as she stood by the window after dinner. He'd grown increasingly worried throughout each of the interminable six courses, the desire to talk to her becoming so great that he'd allowed the men only ten minutes to drink port and smoke cigars before joining the ladies in the drawing room.

She didn't pretend not to know what he was talking about, throwing a swift look around the room and fixing a pretend smile on her face as if they were simply discussing the weather before answering. 'It seems the viscount's mother has some concerns regarding Evelyn's dowry. She brought her odious nephew along to ask questions.'

'Which he couldn't ask me directly?' Theo glared across the room, tempted to grab the man by the collar and throw him out on to the pavement. 'Did he insult you? Because if he did—'

'Not me personally, no.' She put a restraining hand on his sleeve. 'He just made some rather indiscreet comments about your brother and his…liaisons. I'm afraid that Sabrina might have overheard.'

'Judging by her expression during dinner, I'm certain she did.' He clenched his jaw. 'Though at least Evelyn was far enough away not to.' He studied her face for a few seconds. 'Are you certain you're not upset?'

'Perfectly.' She removed her hand from his arm and placed it over her forehead. 'The meal was just more trying than I'd anticipated. I might retire early, if you don't mind?'

'Not at all.' He battled the urge to pull her into his arms. 'Frankly, the sooner we get this evening over with, the better.'

'Marshall!'

They both jumped, stepping apart as one of the viscount's uncles came lurching towards them, a glass in one hand and looking decidedly the worse for wear. His footsteps were veering so wildly from side to side, it was frankly a wonder he was still upright.

'An honour to shake your hand, sir.' He seized hold of Theo. 'Two medals for bravery at Waterloo, wasn't it? Put the rest of us to shame, eh?'

'Nothing of the sort.' Theo inclined his head politely. 'I was only doing my duty.'

'And now you have to take over from your brother and sort out a wedding to boot? It's a strange situation, eh?'

'So everyone keeps saying,' Abigail murmured.

'But she's a fine-looking girl.' The old man swung an arm towards Evelyn. 'Somebody might need to throw a bucket of cold water over my nephew before long. Of course, when I was twenty, a man only got married if he had to, if you know what I mean?'

'Indeed.'

'Still, I've told my sister that we can rely on you for the dowry. Marshall's a man of honour, I told her. Nothing like his brother.'

'I appreciate the sentiment.' Theo smiled tightly, feeling his temper begin to wear thin.

'Not *entirely* honourable though, eh?' The uncle nudged him with an elbow. 'I see that you've allowed yourself a few perks of the job.' He looked pointedly in Abigail's direction and waggled his eyebrows. 'I can't say I blame you.'

Theo stiffened, outraged both by the insinuation and the small grain of truth behind it. He had never, *would* never, think of Abigail as a 'perk' of his position and yet, to an outside observer, he couldn't deny the way they'd been standing together might have looked somewhat incriminating. He only hoped that nobody else had noticed. 'I've no idea what you mean.'

'Oh, come now...'

'Colonel Marshall is the soul of propriety.' Abigail stepped between them, two slashes of red burning across her cheekbones. 'As I am a respectable lady, and I resent any implication to the contrary. Now, if you'll excuse me, I believe I've had enough conversation for one evening.'

'Sorry about that.' The uncle shrugged as she swept past him, chin held high. 'Didn't mean to offend...'

'Quite.' Theo clenched his jaw, watching as she marched across the room to the door. Following her would make things even worse, but he was having to dig his feet into the floor to stop himself. Damn it all, the sooner he found Fitz, the better.

## Chapter Nineteen

As performers went, the Forsythe sisters were sublime, Abigail thought, closing her eyes and feeling her soul soar along with the music. They'd started with instruments—a piano and harp respectively—then moved on to singing, their voices in perfect, mellifluous harmony. It was almost as good as being at the opera again.

It was just what she'd needed, too, a relaxing escape from Salway House. Despite both her and Theo's best efforts to act normally, she'd been feeling more and more uncomfortable since the night—and comments—of the dinner party, as if those words had tainted everything.

'It's as though they're determined to show the rest of us debutantes up,' Evelyn muttered petulantly as the singing drew to a close and the audience burst into rapturous applause. 'That last part was just showing off.'

'I thought they were wonderful.' Abigail carried on clapping. 'Exquisite.'

'*This* is why I'm always telling you to practise your pianoforte.' Sabrina leaned across to tap her daughter on the knee with her fan.

'I could practise for a hundred years and never sound like that.'

'You could still practise occasionally.'

'We all have our own unique talents,' Abigail reassured her.

'Really?' Evelyn sounded downhearted. 'Then I wish I knew what mine were.'

'Mine was singing, too.' Sabrina looked smug. 'Fitzwilliam said he was smitten the first time he heard me.'

'Then why do *I* sound like a horse?'

'Because you inherited my hair and his voice. Now, I'm parched. Let's go over to the refreshment table, shall we?'

'We can practise the pianoforte tomorrow, if you like?' Abigail linked arms with Evelyn as Sabrina swept away without them.

'I appreciate the offer, but I'm afraid it's already too late.' Evelyn craned her neck, looking around the room. 'I'm just relieved William's not here tonight. He says that he adores me just the way I am, but I'm sure every other man here is in love with the Forsythe sisters by now.'

'William?' Abigail lifted an eyebrow.

'Viscount Everly.'

'You're using his first name?'

'Yes. I said that he could use mine, too. When you meet the right person, it seems so natural.' She sighed happily. 'The past two weeks have been the most wonderful of my life and it's mainly thanks to you.'

'I'm only a chaperon.' Abigail smiled. 'Your uncle's the one to thank, not that he wants you to, of course.'

'But I know you were the one who persuaded him to

allow me a Season and he's been in a much better mood recently.' Evelyn's expression turned sly. '*Much* better.'

'He's under a lot less pressure now that the Chelsea project has been sold.' Abigail felt her cheeks flush guiltily.

'That's not the only reason.' Evelyn moved her head closer. 'Mama hasn't noticed yet, but I've seen the way he looks at you.'

'Now you're imagining things.'

'No, I'm not.' Evelyn giggled. 'I saw you waltzing together at the Gaddesby ball, too. He's really quite handsome, don't you think? I mean, I know he's my uncle and I'm biased, but you never know, it might turn out to be a good thing your fiancé let you down...'

'It's not like—' Abigail stopped mid-sentence as somebody stepped in front of them, blocking the way. Surprised, she looked up and felt her jaw drop at the sight of the man Evelyn had just been talking about, as if her words had somehow conjured him up.

'Henry?'

Her stomach dropped so violently it took a few seconds for her to be able to close her mouth again, let alone remember to breathe. After two weeks of not seeing him at any *ton* events, she'd started to think she was safe, but there he was, standing right in front of her, looking like himself and yet different, too. His face was thinner than she remembered and his eyes were shadowed, as if he hadn't been eating or sleeping properly.

'Miss Lemon. I hoped you'd be here.' He bowed first to her and then Evelyn. 'My apologies for interrupting your conversation, but might I have a word?'

'It's not a good time.' She had no idea how she managed to get the words out when her jaw still didn't seem to be working properly.

'Please. There's something I need to tell you. It's important.'

She hesitated. Not even a tiny part of her wanted to talk to him, but if she didn't then she'd only wonder about it later. Still…

'Do you know what day it is?' His voice softened.

She sucked in a breath. Yes, she knew what day it was. It had been the first thought in her head when she'd woken that morning. It was the thirtieth of April, what would have been their wedding day.

'Five minutes, but that's all.' She turned towards Evelyn. 'Why don't you go to your mother? I'll find you again in a few moments.'

'Are you certain?' Evelyn regarded Henry suspiciously. 'I won't leave if you don't want me to.'

'There's no need to worry. Mr Quinnell here is an old friend.'

'All right, but I won't go far.'

'Over here. It's quieter.' Henry gestured towards a window sconce as Evelyn moved reluctantly away, throwing several dubious looks over her shoulder. It was the opposite end of the room to the refreshment table and draped with heavy damask curtains.

'Very well.' She kept well away from the curtains. 'Now what is it you want to tell me?'

'That I can't stop thinking about you.'

'What?' She gave a small, involuntary jerk.

'Ever since that day you came to the house and accused me of behaving dishonourably. You were right. It was monstrous of me. I don't know what I was thinking.' He raked a hand though his hair. 'I must have been mad.'

'Henry.' She retreated a step. There was something alarming about his expression. It looked unbalanced somehow. Desperate. 'It's over. We're over. It's all in the past.'

'No!' His expression turned anguished. 'It doesn't have to be. Abbie, I came here to tell you that I love you and I was wrong to let you go. I should have married you no matter what my parents thought.' A hand shot out, grabbing hold of one of hers. 'I know that I've treated you shamefully, but let me make it up to you now. Marry me.'

For a fraction of a moment, her heart lifted at the idea. If she wanted, she could still have the life she'd dreamed of only a couple of months ago. She could marry Henry, have a house of her own, children maybe...

Only when she tried to picture a future with him, she couldn't. Instead, she could only imagine a man with blond hair and a scar across one eyebrow, a man who would never back down from a promise or spread false rumours about her, a man she respected as well as loved. Her breath snagged at the realisation.

'It's not too late for us.' Henry moved closer. 'We can still put things right. We can go back to the way things were.'

'You mean another long engagement?' She looked up at him, surprised by how little his proximity affected her now. 'Until we wear your parents down like last time?'

'No.' His eyes glittered. 'We'll get married straight away.'

'Against their wishes?'

'Yes. We'll go to Gretna Green. They won't need to know anything about it. We'll be married in secret and when we return, I'll find somewhere for you to live, somewhere respectable. And then, one day, after I inherit, *then* we can tell everyone.'

She laughed aloud. It was a high-pitched, faintly hysterical sound, but she couldn't help it. Her love for him had been like a banner, she realised, one weathered and torn by the elements, but still hanging by a single, sentimental thread. Until now. Now it seemed ludicrous that she could ever have cared for him. She could almost see the tattered remnants of her love floating up into the air and drifting away.

'Abbie?' He looked confused.

'I was just thinking about how romantic that sounded. You'll marry me and then hide me away like some dirty little secret.'

'It probably won't be for long. My father is old.'

'Henry!'

'All I'm saying is—'

'No! Stop this.' She twisted her hand out of his grasp. 'Henry, it's over. It was over the moment you abandoned me in the park that day. You can't put something like that right.'

A muscle in his jaw flexed and then hardened. 'It's because of him, isn't it? That man, that colonel.'

'His name is Colonel Lord Theodore Marshall and, no—' she jerked her chin up '—this has nothing to do with him. I'm the marchioness's companion, nothing more.'

'I saw the way he defended you.' His features turned ugly. 'Maybe my parents were right. Maybe you *are* a social climber, after all.' He shoved his face closer. 'But he won't marry you, no matter what you think. His brother is a marquess. *He* might be a marquess some day. A man like that has to marry someone of his own class, not the daughter of some bankrupt.'

'I don't have to listen to this.' She turned her back on him. 'This conversation is over.'

'Wait!' He stepped around her, blocking the way again. 'I'm sorry. I didn't mean that. I just don't want you to get hurt.'

'Hypocrite! *You're* the one who hurt me!' She clenched her fists to stop herself from slapping his face. 'Henry, I waited three years for you! I thought that I could rely on you, but you abandoned me to starve on the streets.'

'I would have come back to my senses eventually.'

'Eventually isn't good enough!' Her head was starting to buzz with tension now. 'And if I ever decide to marry, it will be to a man I can trust and respect, a man who would choose *me* over a fortune.' She paused as an image of Theo flitted through her mind. 'So let me make this easy for you. I won't marry you, not under any circumstances. Now I suggest that you go and find yourself an heiress and make your parents happy. Goodbye.'

Shaking, she swung on her heel and strode determinedly back across the room.

'The fiancé you mentioned?' Sabrina gave her a pointed look as she arrived at her side.

'Yes.' She swallowed. 'If you don't mind…'

'I'll call for the carriage. You can send it back again to collect Evelyn and me.'

'Thank you.'

'He's rather handsome, isn't he?' Sabrina looked Henry up and down thoughtfully. 'It's funny, but he actually reminds me of Fitz.'

# *Chapter Twenty*

Abigail sprinted up the staircase the moment she got back, not even glancing in the direction of Theo's study. The pressure in her head was building, as if there were a steel band around her temples, tightening with every breath. More than anything, she wanted the oblivion of sleep, but she was afraid that if she went to bed, she'd only lie on her mattress in the dark, staring hard at the ceiling, thoughts and memories buzzing around her head like a swarm of angry bees.

She stopped on the landing and turned her steps in the direction of the drawing room instead. As she'd expected, the room was swathed in darkness, with only the faint glowing remains of a fire, but it was enough for her to find her way towards one of the sofas, curling herself up in a ball and wrapping her arms around her knees for comfort.

She was in love with Theo. Ironically, she'd realised it at the very moment that Henry had declared himself. She'd felt disappointed because it had seemed like the wrong man saying the words. It had been both a shock and a moment of inspiration. She'd thought that she would never, *could* never, fall in love again, that her heart was untouchable, and yet, without even knowing it, she already had. So much for relying on herself! She'd been an even worse judge of character than she'd thought, misjudging and deluding *herself*, thinking that she could explore her curiosity and attraction to him without consequences. And now her experiment had backfired in her face.

She had no idea how he felt about her, but it didn't make any difference. She might have made the mistake of falling in love again, but this time she knew better than to believe that love conquered all. Their relationship could never go anywhere—anywhere respectable anyway—not for the reasons that Henry had said, although they were valid, too, but because Theo didn't want to marry anyone. The only way it would happen would be if he felt honour-bound to propose again and that was the last thing she wanted.

She clamped her hands to her head, wrenching her fingers through her hair and scattering pins in every direction. Unlike Henry, she couldn't even blame Theo for the heartache she was feeling now. He'd been completely honest with her from the start, just as she'd been honest with him, or so she'd thought. Which meant that the only thing she could do now was leave. If she stayed then she'd make herself even more miserable.

The only thing worse than being hopelessly in love with him would be for him to find out about it, and she had little to no confidence in her acting abilities. Sooner or later, she'd give her feelings away and then he'd be mortified. He'd probably apologise and start talking about dishonour again.

She took a deep breath and then blew it out again,

her long hair now hanging in a tangled mess around her shoulders. Yes, she had to leave. The only question was where to go. Heartache notwithstanding, at least she wasn't in *such* dire straits now as she'd been when she'd first arrived. She had a little money saved, enough to last a few months anyway, and Theo had promised to repay her some of the funds her father had lost.

Sabrina would write her a reference, too, if she asked. She could probably get another position as a companion or governess and there was always her mother's cottage. It had been ten years since she'd last visited. She really ought to go and see what kind of state it was in before she decided on anything else...

She tipped her head back against the chair and then yelped as she caught sight of a silhouette in the open doorway.

'Theo!' She pressed a hand to her chest, recognising his shape. 'You startled me.'

'My apologies.' His voice sounded deeper than usual. 'What are you doing sitting in the dark?'

'Thinking. *Don't.*' She put a hand out as he went to light a candle. 'I like it like this.'

'As you wish. Where are Sabrina and Evelyn?'

'Still at the musical soirée. I came back early.'

'Did something happen?'

'No. I have a headache, that's all,' she lied, her pulse accelerating as he advanced slowly towards her. In the semi-darkness, his blue eyes looked like coals, glowing so intensely they seemed to heat the space between them. Every step he took lifted her body temperature by another degree. By the time he stopped and crouched down in front of her, her entire body was flaming.

'You look upset.' His brow creased with concern.

'It's only a headache.' She caught her top lip between her teeth, watching the firelight flicker across his features. His gaze was too penetrating, his voice too tender. The combination was dangerous, making her feel even warmer right when she needed to be cold.

'Here.' He lifted his hands to either side of her head, gently massaging her temples with his thumbs. 'Does this feel better?'

'Yes.' She closed her eyes and moaned softly. She wanted to say no, to tell him to stop, but it felt too blissfully good. For a few seconds, all of her worries seemed to recede, leaving only feeling.

'You should go to bed.' His thumbs kept kneading.

'Soon.'

'I'll bring you another hot chocolate if you like?'

'No.' She shook her head gently. 'It wouldn't be appropriate.'

'Trying to make you feel better isn't appropriate?' He sounded amused.

'Did you ever take your soldiers hot chocolate in bed?'

'Um—no. Brandy, sometimes, if they were wounded, but never chocolate.'

'That proves my point. It's not appropriate.' She was horribly aware of how prim the words sounded. 'We need to maintain a professional working relationship.'

'Ah.' He trailed his thumbs down the side of her face until he was cupping her chin between his hands. 'What happened tonight, Abigail?'

'I already answered that.' She opened her eyes again to frown at him. 'Why must something have happened?'

'Because I know you. I know you always bite your lip when you're lying.'

'Maybe you don't know me as well as you think you do.'

'Or maybe you just don't want to tell me?'

'Henry.' The name was out before she could stop it. 'Henry happened.'

'What do you mean?' He went very still.

'He was at the soirée this evening and asked to speak to me.' She lifted a shoulder. 'I said no at first, but he was insistent.'

'Did he touch you?' His fingers twitched against her chin.

'No, it wasn't that.'

'What was it like?'

'He took my hands, that's all, and…he reminded me of the date.'

'Today's date?'

'Yes.' She met his gaze briefly before looking away again. 'This would have been our wedding day.'

'I see.' His voice sounded leaden. 'So was that *all* he wanted? To reminisce?'

She twisted aside, forcing him to release her as she stood up and moved away. 'That's between me and him. You've no right to ask.'

'I know.' He followed her, coming to stand so close that she could feel the warmth of his chest against her breasts. 'I know. I just…'

'He proposed. Again.' Even though it wouldn't change anything, she felt a sudden base desire to make him jealous. 'He said that he still loves me.'

'And what did you say?'

'What do you *think* I said?' She shoved her hands against his chest, offended. 'What do you take me for? Do you think I could ever go back to a man who betrayed me? A man I could never trust? Do you think so very little of me?' She gritted her teeth and then shook her head. 'It wasn't like that anyway. He wanted a secret wedding, one that his father would never find out about so he could still keep his inheritance.'

'Forgive me.' To his credit, Theo looked genuinely shamefaced. 'I shouldn't have asked. I just remember what you said when you first came here, about how much you loved him.'

'I did.'

'And now?'

'Now?' She blinked, surprised by the abrupt change in his voice. It sounded different, hopeful. There was an expectant gleam in his eye, too, unless she was simply seeing what she wanted to see, which was undoubtedly the case. 'Now I'm tired and I have a headache.' She was aware of a stinging pressure behind her eyes and scrunched her face up to stop it. 'Honestly, I think the only reason he asked me to marry him was because of you. Because he was jealous. But don't worry, I told him he was imagining things. That I was only a companion.'

'You're not *only* anything.'

'Then what am I?'

She regretted the question the very second it was out. It sounded too much like an appeal, a plea for something he could never give her.

'Abigail, you're…'

'I'm leaving.' She interrupted, wrenching her shoulders back before she could hear how much he valued her as a secretary.

'What?' He sounded stunned.

'I'm leaving.' she repeated. 'I have to. I thought that

we could put what happened behind us, but I've come to realise that we can't work together any more.'

'Yes, we can.' A look of something like panic flitted over his face. 'Look, I'm sorry I asked you about him. You're right, it's none of my business.'

'It's not just because of that. Things are awkward already. Look at what Viscount Everly's uncle thought about us.'

'He was a drunken old fool.'

'But if he noticed something, then other people might, too. You were right when you warned me about my reputation. I should have listened. If I stay, then things can only get worse. I ought to leave. I *want* to leave.'

'Maybe we should talk about this in the morning when you're feeling better?'

'No. I've made up my mind and it's a good time to leave anyway. The Chelsea project has been sold and Evelyn's practically engaged. You don't need me to help with your work or to chaperon her any more.' She nodded firmly, feigning a determination she didn't feel. 'I'll give you two weeks' notice, but then I'm leaving.'

Theo stood absolutely still, staring into the darkness for ten full minutes after Abigail had left, waiting for a pernicious combination of jealousy and anguish to subside. He hadn't thought that emotions could change so quickly, but his had, from joy and relief at the knowledge she'd turned down Henry's proposal to panic and despair when she'd told him she wanted to leave. The words had felt like a knife in his gut.

It had been on the tip of his tongue to tell her how he felt, to sweep her into his arms and ask her to marry him instead, but it would have been no better than Henry asking her to marry him in secret. How could he propose until he knew whether or not he was free? And now...now it didn't matter anyway because she wanted to leave.

*If I stay, things can only get worse.*

He'd thought that she felt something for him, too, but obviously it had been wishful thinking. Their night together had meant nothing more than what she'd said at the time—companionship and curiosity.

He turned around finally and walked slowly out of the room, dragging limbs that felt cold and heavy. Maybe she was right and it was for the best. The chances of him actually finding Fitz had been slim at best, but the knife in his gut was still twisting, penetrating right to his core. She was leaving just when he'd started to believe that maybe, just maybe, he could have made a decent husband after all.

## Chapter Twenty-One

'It's Viscount Everly!' Evelyn dropped the curtain and leapt into the air, squealing with excitement. 'His carriage has just arrived. He's here!'

'Then get away from the window before he sees you!' Sabrina jumped up, too.

'This is it. I know it is.' Evelyn clasped her hands over her heart. 'Last night, he said he had a special question to ask me and it's too early for visiting hours!'

'Not very original, but, yes, it does sound like it might be a formal proposal. Just in case he has trouble getting to the point, however…' Sabrina turned towards Abigail '…perhaps you could hide in the next room and summon me in ten—no, *five* minutes?' She lifted a finger. 'Actually, it might be best if you just wait outside the door once he arrives. I'll cough when we need you.'

'I'll do my best.' Abigail put her embroidery aside and lifted an eyebrow at Evelyn. 'Are you certain about this?'

'More than I've ever been about anything in my whole life! He's everything I want in a husband.'

'Well, in that case…' She exchanged a knowing smile with Sabrina. 'Good luck.'

She hurried out into the hallway and up the staircase, hiding out of sight until she heard the viscount's steps cross the hallway. Then she crept carefully down again, pressing her ear against the door to listen.

'Abigail?'

She gave a start at the sound of her name, looking around to find Theo standing a few feet away, sleeves rolled up to his elbows, regarding her with a quizzical expression.

'Hush.' She put a finger to her lips, trying to ignore the unwanted flicker of excitement in her stomach. Even her decision to leave had done nothing to diminish her attraction to him.

'What's going on?' He came to stand beside her, lowering his voice to a whisper.

'Viscount Everly is about to propose to Evelyn. Or at least we think he is. Sabrina wants me to go in and summon her away when she coughs.'

'I see.' He rested a shoulder against the wall. 'Abigail, we need to talk.'

'What about?'

'You know what about.'

'We've already discussed it.' She threw him a sidelong glance and hardened her heart. 'There's nothing more to say.'

'Yes, there is. I don't want you to think I don't care about you.'

'I don't think that.'

'You don't?' He sounded surprised. 'Then what about you?'

'What about me?'

'Do you care about me?'

'Theo, this isn't the time or place to discuss this.'

'Then come to my office afterwards.'

'Viscount Everly will want to speak with you. He'll probably want to—' She froze at the sound of a cough. 'There it is. I have to go.'

'Ah, Miss Lemon.' Sabrina looked up as she entered. 'I was just about to call for tea.'

'That sounds delightful, my lady.' She curtsied in the direction of the viscount. 'However, there's a small issue with Florence, if you wouldn't mind coming up to the nursery for a few minutes? It won't take long.'

'How intriguing.' Sabrina swept to her feet. 'My lord, I'm sure I can trust you to behave as a man of honour while I'm gone?'

'I promise, my lady.'

'So…?' Abigail clasped her hands excitedly as soon as they were back out in the hall, leaving the door slightly ajar for propriety's sake. 'Do you really think he's about to ask her?'

'I'm certain of it!' Sabrina squeezed her arm and then stopped at the sight of Theo sitting on the stair-case, forearms draped across his knees. 'What are you doing there?'

'Waiting to find out what you want me to say if he asks to speak with me.' He spread his hands out. 'She's your daughter. Do you want me to give permission or not?'

'Of course I do! He's a charming young man.'

'Young being the operative word.'

'So is Evelyn.'

'So they're both equally naive?'

'Better that than for one of them to be a duplicitous rake. At least this way they stand a chance of happi-ness, even if it doesn't last.'

'Sabrina…'

'I know, I know, I'm old and jaded. I'm not saying it

*won't* work. I'm just saying that she's determined and he's a decent man. They stand as good a chance as anyone. Aside from which, he has estates in Leicestershire and Wiltshire, fifteen thousand a year and an agreeable face. He'll do very nicely.'

'Wiltshire?' Abigail repeated the name thoughtfully. The place seemed to keep cropping up in conversation. It was the location of the marquess's favourite hunting lodge, the one Theo *wasn't* selling, but for some reason it seemed to have another, deeper significance, although she had no idea what that might be.

'Yes. Some smaller properties in the north, too, I believe...' Sabrina gave her a curious look. 'Are you all right?'

'Yes, it's just... I feel like there's something...' She drew her brows together. 'Will you excuse me? There's something I need to look up...' Then she turned and headed towards the study, walking so fast she eventually broke into a run.

Abigail sat cross-legged on her bed, rifling through the bundle of papers spread out in front of her. She'd already pored over them in her office all afternoon, listening with half an ear as Theo discussed the marital settlement with Viscount Everly, and most of the evening as well, looking for...*something,* some pattern her unconscious mind had picked up, but hadn't yet managed to articulate.

The family had been invited to a celebratory meal at the Everlys' town house, but she'd demurred, not wanting a repeat of the last 'family' occasion, retiring to her own chamber early instead. She'd heard them return, too, which meant that it was long past her bedtime, but she couldn't stop searching. The answer was there some-where, she knew it. She just had to find it.

At last, she conceded defeat, gathering the scattered papers and parchments into a neat pile, ready to try again in the morning. As she put them aside, however, the top one, a letter, caught her eye. She felt a jolt as realisation suddenly dawned. It wasn't a pattern at all! It was a change in an earlier pattern! She read the let-ter over a couple of times, making sure she was right before springing off the bed, dragging a shawl around her shoulders and racing towards the door. Knowing Theo, he would be back in his study after the celebration dinner and she couldn't wait until morning to tell him.

She raced barefoot down the corridor, the letter clutched to her chest, almost skidding to a halt at the top of the staircase. There was a thin line of light em-anating from beneath Theo's bedchamber door on the opposite side of the landing. For once, it seemed, he'd actually retired to bed. Which meant that she really ought to turn around immediately and go back to hers. Her news would just have to wait. To do anything else would be utter madness. *Again.* Only knowing that and stopping herself seemed to be two completely differ-ent things.

Theo read the same sentence five times before toss-ing his book aside. Frankly, he wondered why he'd bothered coming to bed at all when his brain was pre-occupied with torturing itself, trying to think of ways to persuade Abigail to stay, even though doing so would only prolong his own misery.

'Come in,' he called out at the sound of a faint scratch-ing on his door, heaving himself upright against the bedpost. It wasn't like Kitchen to knock but, given the fact that it was the middle of the night, perhaps he was finally starting to learn some discretion.

'Theo?' A female face appeared around the edge of the door. 'Are you awake?'

'Abigail?' He almost fell off the edge of the bed in shock. 'What are you doing here?'

'I know, I shouldn't be.' She threw a quick glance over her shoulder before darting in and closing the door behind her. 'But I had to show you something.'

He felt his mouth turn dry as she approached the bed. Her body was wrapped in a white-silk nightgown partially covered by a pink-lace shawl, while her long hair was twisted into a single plait tied with a blue ribbon, draped over one shoulder. It looked tantalisingly easy to unravel. It occurred to him that he really ought to order her back to her room, but speech seemed impossible. Every word he'd ever learnt stalled in his throat. Whatever it was she wanted to show him, he was more than happy to see it.

'Look at this.' She thrust a piece of parchment towards him, her eyes bright with excitement. 'It's the last letter you received from the hunting lodge in Wiltshire.'

'Wiltshire?' He had to concentrate very hard on the words to understand them. She was moving closer and closer to the bed while he simply sat there, unable to move since he was, in fact, completely naked beneath the sheets.

'Yes. Do you notice anything strange about it?'

'No.' He gave the letter a cursory look. 'Why exactly are we discussing this now?'

'Because it's only just occurred to me now. When Sabrina mentioned Wiltshire earlier, I knew it was significant somehow, but I couldn't put my finger on it. It's taken me all afternoon and evening to work out why.' She laughed. 'I can't believe I didn't see it before.'

'What?'

'The date, for a start. *Look!*' She leaned forward, pressing a finger against the letter. 'It's from over two months ago. Before that, the letters were just like the ones sent in from all the other properties, usually asking for money. Then this. The steward says that he's let some staff go as requested and made the "necessary arrangements".'

'So Fitz asked him to save money on staff?'

'I thought that was all it was, too, at first, but none of the other stewards wrote to confirm anything similar. So why make an exception? Why cut staff in one property and not all the others? And why did the letters suddenly stop afterwards? Why stop writing two months ago unless…?'

She lifted her eyebrows, obviously expecting him to fill in the blank, which to be fair he might have stood a chance of doing if she hadn't been standing close enough for him to smell the seductive citrusy scent of her hair. Damn it, she was practically leaning over the bed. *His* bed!

'I don't know.' His voice sounded strangled.

'Theo…' She tossed the parchment aside and braced both of her hands on the mattress. 'He must be there!'

'Where? Who?'

'Your brother! Think about it. What if he never left the country? What if he sent that message from Bristol just to make you *think* that he had? Sabrina said this hunting lodge was his favourite property, didn't she?'

'Yes, but…' He stared down at the parchment, trying to focus. 'You mean, all this time, he's been hiding only a couple of days' ride from here?'

'Yes!'

He'd stopped breathing, Theo realised, forcing himself to start again. It sounded plausible. More than that, it sounded *likely*. Fitz had always been lazy. Hiding somewhere close to home sounded like exactly the sort of thing he might do. More than that, it *was* what he would do! Suspicion crystallised into certainty.

'Do you know what this means?' He sat up straighter, seized with a burst of excitement. If it hadn't been for the fact that he was naked, he would have flung the sheet aside and started dressing at that very moment. 'I don't have to hunt for him. I can just go and fetch him!'

'I know!' She nodded emphatically, looking as excited as he felt. 'I couldn't wait until the morning to tell you!'

'Thank you!' He only just resisted the urge to fling his arms around her. 'I'll leave first thing in the morning.'

'So soon?'

'The sooner he's back here, the sooner I can escape. Then I won't have to follow in my father's footsteps, not for a long time anyway. Marry me.'

'What?' She dropped down on to the mattress, her expression stunned.

'I know it sounds crazy, but if I can get away from this house then maybe I can break the pattern of bad marriages. I mean, I don't know if I can, but I'll try. I'll do everything in my power to be a good husband, I swear.'

'Theo...' She leaned forward. 'You don't have to propose to me. I told you the other week, whatever's happened between us, I don't want you to do the honourable thing.'

'I'm not. It was the reason at first, I admit, but when you stopped me proposing, I felt something I never expected to feel. Disappointed. Abigail, since I came back to this house, all I've wanted to do is leave again, but the thought of actually doing it, of walking away and being free of this place, doesn't mean a thing any more if it's not with you. I can't imagine it now without you by my side. I love you.'

'You love me?' Her jaw dropped.

'Yes, I've known it for weeks, only I couldn't propose again until I knew I was free to be a good husband.' He reached for her hands, folding his own around them. 'I probably shouldn't ask you yet either, not until Fitz is officially back, but I can't help myself.'

'I don't understand. We've never spoken about feelings before. I mean, I know we talked about companionship, but...'

'But that's a good start, isn't it?' He tipped his head towards hers. 'I know you've been hurt before, but I swear I'll never do anything to hurt you. Even if you don't feel the same way about me now, just give me a chance. Trust me.'

'Who says I don't feel the same way about you?' Her gaze looked arrested.

'You did. You said you wanted to leave.'

'*Because* I care about you, not because I don't! I thought that you were relieved when I stopped you proposing!' Her face broke into a smile before turning serious again. 'But, Theo, what if your brother never has a son? You'll have to take your father's place then. You'll become the next marquess.'

'Hopefully by that point I'll have learnt how to be a decent husband, but it'll probably be a long time, *years*, before I inherit anything. And I could always refuse the title. Unless you have a burning desire to be a marchioness, that is?'

'None at all, but my parents...'

'Your parents are good enough for me.' He let go of her hands to slide his fingers through her hair. It felt like silk through his fingertips. 'They were happy and they loved each other. That's more than my parents could have said.'

'What if *we* were to have a son?'

He hesitated, disconcerted by the question, before shaking his head. 'Then we'll let him make his own choice about what he wants to do. There are too many what-ifs to worry about. What matters right now is that we have a chance to get away from here, to build a new life together.'

'You mean, America?'

'Why not?'

'What about Lady?'

'She can come with us. As long as she doesn't have to walk anywhere, she'll be happy.'

'You haven't asked me if I love you, too.'

'I know. I don't want to push my luck.'

'But I do.' She placed her forehead against his, a smile almost splitting her face in half. 'I love you.'

'Is that a yes?'

'It's a yes.'

'Abigail...' He seized hold of her lips, pulling her down on to the bed until she was sprawled on top of him, unravelling her shawl so that he could slide his hands over the silk of her nightgown, over the gorgeous curves of her breasts and hips… 'It's been torture, living in the same house, not being able to touch you.'

'I know.' Her voice turned accusing. 'And you've been so cheerful!'

'I was trying to court you.'

'Oh.' She sounded surprised and then pleased. 'Oh, well in that case…'

'Four days.' He moaned, brushing his lips against hers again. 'Two to get there, two to get back, but that's as long as I can wait. I'll arrange a Special Licence so we can be married as soon as possible.'

'Four days.' She laid her cheek against his chest. 'It sounds like an eternity.'

'It's going to feel like one, too.'

'Does this mean I have to go back to my room or can I just lie here?' She nuzzled closer. 'This feels nice.'

'It's still torture.'

'Oh.'

'That doesn't mean you should go.' He clamped an arm around her waist when she tried to pull away. 'I'd rather be tortured than have you leave. Stay.'

Sleep was a funny thing, Theo reflected. He'd spent countless nights over the years struggling to find it, but despite all his expectations, he'd drifted off almost at once with Abigail in his arms. Which meant that by the time he awoke, roused by the sound of thunder outside his chamber window, it was almost dawn, the time when Armstrong usually burst in.

*The time when Armstrong usually burst in…*

He frowned, aware of footsteps already coming down the corridor. He must have woken at the usual time by instinct. Meanwhile, Abigail was still fast asleep, curled up like a cat with her back pressed up against his stomach. Briefly, he thought about hiding her under the covers, before rejecting the idea as pointless. It wasn't as if Kitchen would simply turn around and leave if he told him to and he wasn't stupid either. There was no choice but to brazen it out.

'Abigail.' He put a hand on her shoulder, shaking her gently.

'Mmm?' She rolled on to her back, peering up at him through half-open eyelids. 'Is it morning?'

'Yes. You need to brace yourself.'

'Brace myself?' Her eyes widened just in time for the door to burst open.

'Morning, sir! Raining today—Oh.' For the first time in his life, Kitchen appeared lost for words.

'Morning, Kitchen.' Theo propped himself up on one elbow.

'I…um… Pardon me.' The valet took a step backwards. 'I'll just leave your coffee over here by the door.'

'Thank you, Kitchen. We'll discuss this later, shall we?'

'Very good, sir.'

'Oh dear.' Abigail pulled herself upright when he'd gone, clutching the sheet to her chest despite the fact that she was still wearing a nightgown. 'What if he tells anyone?'

'He won't. He'll just give me a stern lecture.' Theo laughed at her dismayed expression. 'He recently accused me of debauching you. He'll be delighted when he learns the truth.'

'Really?' She looked sceptical.

'Yes. He's been trying to marry me off for years.'

'Well then, I'm glad he's failed until now.' She kissed

his nose before turning her face towards the window. 'Was that thunder?'

'Uh-huh.' He caught her lips again. 'For some reason, you seem extra-kissable in the mornings.'

'The rain sounds heavy.'

'It's not that bad. We should probably keep kissing until the storm passes.'

'Or I should get back to my own room.' She laughed and wriggled away, wrapping her shawl back around her shoulders. 'The maids will be up soon.'

'You're probably right. Just give me a moment.' He willed his body to cool down before swinging his legs over the side of the bed and striding towards the door, opening it and looking up and down the corridor before nodding. 'It's clear.'

'Um… Theo?'

'What's the matter?' He looked around to find Abigail staring at him, her cheeks a vivid shade of scarlet.

'I… You… I mean…'

'Ah.' Belatedly, it occurred to him that he was still naked. 'Wait a moment.' He pulled on a robe. 'Sorry about that.'

'Not at all. It was very…' her eyes sparked '…informative.'

'*Educational*?' He wrapped his arms around her again, bending his head and kissing her even more deeply than before, until they were both breathless.

'Will you come and say goodbye before you go?' She paused in the doorway.

'I promise.' He couldn't resist one last kiss. 'Four days, remember?'

'Four days,' she repeated. 'I can't wait.'

## Chapter Twenty-Two

It was two hours before Abigail heard a knock on her bedroom door and practically flung herself across the room to open it.

'Did I wake you?' Theo stood on the threshold, dressed in a greatcoat and tall boots, which frankly didn't remotely compare to the view she'd had of him earlier. An image of his naked body was scorched into her mind, so much that she was half-tempted to drag him into her room and start undressing him again.

'No. I couldn't sleep anyway.' She slid her arms around his neck, ardently hoping he couldn't read her thoughts on her face. 'The rain seems to be getting worse. Maybe you should delay travelling for a couple of days? The roads will be a mess.'

'Wiltshire's not so far and I'll be careful.' He pressed his hands against the small of her back. 'I'll be back before you know it. There's just something I need to do first.'

'What?'

'This.' He drew her closer, lowering his face and kissing her so deeply she thought that her mind might actually be spinning. 'And this.' He broke the kiss finally, reaching into the pocket of his greatcoat and drawing out a folded piece of parchment. 'I need you to keep it safe for me.'

'Of course. What is it?'

'A Special Licence.'

She gaped up at him. 'How did you get one so quickly?'

'There are some advantages to being the heir of a marquess. I want to marry you the same day I get back.' He tightened his arms around her and then slid his hands lower, over her hips. 'Unlike some people, I don't believe in long engagements.'

'Me neither. I'll be ready.' She paused. 'I've been thinking—what about Sabrina? Should I tell her what we've discovered?'

'No. I've thought about it, too, but if we tell her now then she'll only have four days of waiting and tension. Fitz can do the explaining when he gets back.' A worried expression passed over his face before it cleared again. 'Then once Fitz is home, there'll be no reason for us to stay. We'll be free to go wherever we choose.'

'In that case, there's somewhere I'd like to visit before we go to America.' She put her hands on his shoulders and rubbed her nose against his. 'Somewhere I'd like to show you.'

'Really? Enlighten me.'

'I'd rather surprise you. It's not very grand and I haven't seen it in ten years, but it's a place I love.'

'Then I can't wait to see it, wherever it is.' He lifted an eyebrow. 'Look after Lady for me?'

'I'll give her extra belly rubs, every hour, on the hour. Just promise me you'll ride safely.'

'Don't worry about that. Kitchen insists on coming with me. He sends heartfelt congratulations, by the way.'

She smiled sheepishly. 'I'm glad that he's accompanying you, but he does know he's not invited on our honeymoon, doesn't he?'

'I'll have a word on the journey.'

'Good.' She felt her blood heat at the very idea of a honeymoon. 'Because I want you all to myself from now on.'

It was raining again. Abigail rolled her shoulders as she looked out of the window of her study at the garden outside. The city had been plagued by showers recently, but today, the weather was particularly relentless. The apple and cherry trees that had looked so beautiful only a few days before were being slowly destroyed, crushed beneath the weight of so much water. Blossoms were falling before they were ready, turning the paths into sodden pink walkways. The sight struck her as beautiful and melancholy at the same time. She only hoped the weather was better wherever Theo was now...

At last she tore her gaze away from the view and back to her work. Her eyes were getting tired, but she wanted to make certain that everything was in perfect order for when Theo and the marquess returned. After a month of sorting and filing, she was proud to say that all of her paperwork was exactly where it ought to be. Though she said it herself, she'd done an excellent job. She was so engrossed that it was a few moments before it dawned on her she wasn't alone. The marchioness was standing on the threshold of the study, candlestick in hand.

'Sabrina?' She put her quill down and smiled. 'I didn't hear you come in. Is everything all right?'

'I'm not sure.' The marchioness advanced slowly into the room, closing the door and turning the key in the lock behind her.

'My lady?' Abigail stood up in surprise. There was something different about the marchioness that evening, a strange, almost feverish glint in her eye, not to mention an unsteadiness about her gait, almost as if she'd been drinking.

'We need to talk.' Even her voice sounded different. Brittle and flinty.

'Of course, if you wish, but—' Abigail flicked a glance towards the door '—why lock us in?'

'Because I don't want to be disturbed.' Sabrina moved closer, trailing a hand across the front of the desk. 'Theo sent a note to me early this morning. It said he was going away for a few days on business.'

'Yes, my lady.' She threw another glance towards the door, feeling increasingly unsettled. 'Perhaps we should go to the drawing room?'

'No. I want answers and you're not going anywhere until I get them.'

'Answers? Sabrina, I don't understand.'

'Of course, Theo often rises early,' the marchioness went on. 'But then, so does Florence and she had some *very* interesting things to tell me when I went to visit her in the nursery this afternoon. For example, about how you were talking to my brother-in-law in the corridor outside your bedchamber in the early hours…something about him going to fetch her father?'

'Oh…yes.' Abigail dropped her gaze guiltily. 'The truth is that we think the marquess is still in England. I

know we should have told you, but we thought it would
be better to wait.'

'I don't give a damn about that part.'

She started. 'You don't?'

'No. I'm far more interested in what happened afterwards. Because according to Florence, it looked like
the two of you were kissing.'

'Oh.'

'There was even some talk of a Special Licence, I
believe?' Sabrina took another step closer, bearing an
uncanny resemblance to a snake about to strike, her
eyes narrowed so menacingly that Abigail had to steel
herself not to back away. 'So tell me, Miss Lemon, how
long has this been going on?'

'Not long, my lady.'

'Well, I can't say I'm not impressed. It's very clever
of you really. What better way to get revenge on my
family?'

'Revenge?' She tensed. 'What do you mean?'

'I mean that my husband lost your family's fortune,
so you came here to inveigle your way into ours…
what's left of it anyway.' Her nostrils flared. 'My husband abandoned me and you saw it as an opportunity!
Or did you simply see a chance to better yourself? It's
quite a leap from impoverished gentleman's daughter
to future marchioness.'

'No!'

Sabrina tapped a fingernail against her chin. 'I remember what you said about your former fiancé's
family, about how they accused you of being a fortune
hunter. Maybe I should have paid more attention.'

Abigail gasped, stung by the words. 'That's unfair.'

'Of course you were cunning at first, dressing like

a mouse, being oh-so-useful to everyone, all the while plotting to take my place.'

'That's not true! Nobody wants to take your place. That's why Theo's gone to find your husband. So that he can bring him back and the two of you can be reconciled.'

'Reconciled?' Sabrina tipped her head back and screeched with laughter. 'Don't be absurd.'

'But you could still have an heir.'

'How? My husband hasn't shared my bed since nine months before Florence was born. The only thing we share now is contempt. Believe me, there won't be any more children. And Fitz won't be back either.'

'How do you know?'

'Because I know my husband.' Sabrina bared her teeth, her lip curling with derision. 'He always takes the easy path and coming back, facing the scandal, confronting me, isn't that. He doesn't have the stomach for it.'

'But Theo thinks—'

'Theo doesn't know him like I do! He hasn't even seen him in ten years! What does he know about Fitz?'

'But then…' Abigail sank down into the chair behind her desk. 'Theo's trapped.'

Sabrina ignored her, pursuing her own train of thought. 'You know, after the shock of Fitz's departure had passed, I was actually quite happy with our situation here. Theo had no intention of marrying, which meant that I got to keep my place as the marchioness without the bother of a husband. And then *you* had to ruin it.'

Abigail shook her head, only half-listening. If there was no chance of a reconciliation between Sabrina and the marquess, then there was also no way for her and Theo to escape and start a new life together... She wrapped her arms around her waist, feeling sick to her stomach as the vision of the future she'd glimpsed that morning collapsed around her. There would be no getting married in four days and going to America now. Theo would be stuck at Salway House, being the marquess in practice if not in name, in a role he despised and resented. And love could triumph over many things, but surely not feelings that ran so deep. He'd go through with the wedding because he was a man of honour and he'd already proposed, but he'd be miserable.

'I'm only thirty-six.' Sabrina's voice cracked, becoming high pitched as she swayed from side to side. 'Too young to be sent to the country to moulder away! Out of sight, out of mind, as if I never even existed, while you get to live *my* life!'

'What? No one's going to send you anywhere.'

'Really?' Her expression turned hopeful. 'Do you really mean that?'

'Of course. You might know the marquess, but I know Theo and—Look out!' Abigail reached a hand out, but it was too late. Sabrina's candlestick had already tumbled out of her hand and on to the piles of paper on the desk. There was a momentary stillness, followed by a sudden roar before the whole surface was ablaze.

'Get back!' Abigail jumped up and sprang around the desk, grabbing the marchioness by the waist and hauling her out of the way as she stood, seemingly transfixed by the sight.

'What happened?' Sabrina sounded confused, like a small child.

'It doesn't matter. We have to get out of here. The key!'

'What?'

'The key to the door! Where is it?'

'My pocket.' She fumbled around in her dress. 'Oh. I thought…'

'Possett!' Abigail flung her fists against the door, bellowing as loudly as she could.

'Ah, here it is!' Sabrina thrust the key into the air triumphantly, then screamed as a lick of flame caught the hem of her skirts.

'Get down on the floor!' Abigail rushed back towards her, grabbing the edge of a rug and flinging it over her legs, batting at the flames to muffle them.

'Miss Lemon?' Possett's voice came from outside the door.

'There's a fire! Fetch some water!' She wrestled the key out of Sabrina's clenched fist and then dragged her back to her feet. 'Come on!'

'There's so much smoke!' Sabrina was sobbing now. 'I can't see.'

'And you won't be able to until we get out of here.' Abigail rammed the key into the lock, willing it not to jam. Mercifully, it turned without effort, sending the door swinging open and both of them tumbling headlong out of the room.

'Oh, no!' She looked back over her shoulder in horror. The whole of her study was ablaze now, all of the papers she'd spent so many hours reading and organising curling up into black coils before going up in smoke. The fire was spreading, too, catching hold of the curtains and racing up the walls.

'Your ladyship, Miss Lemon!' Possett and a footman gripped them both under the arms, hauling them away from the scene.

'My daughters!' Sabrina screamed. 'Where are they?'

'We're getting everyone out of the house now!'

Abigail kept looking over her shoulder, riveted by the sight of the flames as the footman pulled on her arm, dragging her out of the room, through the hallway and on to the street.

'Mama! Abigail!' Florence and Evelyn came rushing to greet them, Lady at their heels. For once, the old dog was actually running.

'We need a doctor!' Abigail called over their heads to Possett before hastening to reassure them. 'It's for your mama's leg, but she'll be all right.'

'I'm sorry.' Sabrina clutched hold of her hand as they were both bombarded with questions. 'I'm so sorry.'

'I know.' Abigail ducked as the windows of the study shattered abruptly, sending fragments of glass and clouds of smoke billowing out on to the street. 'I know.'

'How's your leg?' Abigail stood in the Countess of Gaddesby's pastel-pink sitting room. As news of the fire had spread, one of the countess's footmen had arrived with a carriage, offering the use of her house as a temporary refuge for the marchioness and her daughters.

'It's still throbbing.' Sabrina looked up from her *chaise longue* and winced. 'But I deserve it.'

'No, you don't.'

'I don't know what I was thinking.' Her expression turned anguished. 'When Florence told me about you and Theo I just panicked. It felt like Fitz leaving me all over again. I was so afraid that you'd send me away and then forget all about me.' She laid her head back. 'I knew even as I was saying it that I was wrong, but I've been humiliated so much already and my temper has never been very good. I lashed out.'

'I understand.'

'I'm not very good at apologising, but…'

'It's all right, Sabrina. Truly.'

'How bad is the damage to the house?'

'It could be worse. The study and the rooms above it are a mess, but the other side of the building is relatively undamaged. I managed to sneak up and get my things.' She smiled ruefully. 'Possett wasn't too happy with me.'

'I'll ask the countess to prepare a room for you, too.'

'No.' Abigail shook her head quickly. 'I have to go.'

'What? Go where?'

'That doesn't matter. I just have to leave before Theo returns.'

'But—'

'There's no future for us, not if the marquess isn't coming back.' She hurried on before Sabrina could interrupt. 'I never wanted to take your place, no more than Theo ever wanted to be the marquess. We were going to go away and start a new life, but if he has to stay here and take care of all this then the last thing he'll want to do is get married. He'll be too afraid of turning into his father. And I don't want to be in the position of having another man change his mind about marrying me.'

'Theo would never go back on his word. If he's asked you to marry him, then he'll marry you.'

'I know.' Her voice caught. 'I trust him to do the right thing, but I think that might actually be worse. Either way, I don't want to see his face when he comes back and tells me what's happened. I don't want to see him regret our attachment. I've been through that before and I can't go through it again.' She pressed her lips together tight. 'Sometimes love isn't enough, I know that better than anyone, but if I leave now then we can remember each other the way we want to. I'm doing this for both of us.'

There was a long pause before Sabrina nodded. 'Will you be all right?'

'Yes.' She bent and kissed the marchioness's cheek. 'I've left Lady with the girls. Tell them goodbye from me.'

## Chapter Twenty-Three

The room was about ten degrees too hot, the fire in the hearth blazing as if it were the very depths of winter, not early summer, and resembled a poorly kept pigsty. Theo looked around in disgust. There were empty bottles scattered all over the floor and every available surface was piled high with discarded plates containing the mouldy remnants of half-eaten meals. He didn't even want to know what the smell was. In the midst of the chaos, there was only one occupant, a man slumped in a chair by the fireplace, snoring loudly with a crystal tumbler clutched in one hand across his chest.

Theo stood and stared for almost a full minute, wondering if he'd made a mistake. Admittedly he hadn't seen his brother in ten years, but the man in front of him looked nothing remotely like the Fitz he'd left behind. He was several sizes larger for a start and his startling good looks had been replaced by a florid complexion, low-hanging jowls and a nose that glowed like a beacon in the candlelight.

He took a few steps forward, stretched a foot out and nudged the sleeping figure awake.

'Eh? What is it?' A single bleary eye opened and glared at him. That expression at least was familiar.

'Fitzwilliam.' Theo lifted his chin. 'It's good to see you again, brother.'

'Theo?' The voice that emerged from the depths of the chair sounded more like a growl. 'What the hell are you doing here?'

'Looking for you.'

'Huh.' His brother lifted the tumbler, drained the last few dregs and then heaved himself up with a show of reluctance. 'You look all grown up. How have you been?'

'Fighting Napoleon. You might have heard there's been a war?'

'Now that you mention it, I do remember the newspapers mentioning something about that.' He chuckled. 'How did you find me?'

'I didn't.' Theo pulled off his greatcoat. 'My secretary did.'

'Your secretary?'

'Yes. Her name's Miss Lemon.' He removed a heap of clothes from an armchair, muttering an oath as a mouse jumped out from between the folds. 'And that's all the explanation you're going to get. I came here to get answers, not to give them.'

'If you've found me, then you already know most of the answers.'

'Some, not all.' He sat down, half-expecting to hear squeaks of protest beneath him. 'I like what you've done with the place.'

'Very funny.'

'It may have been a mistake, sacking most of your staff.'

'I didn't want people reporting on my whereabouts.'

'What about your friend?'

'Who?'

'The governess. Miss Calder.'

'Oh, her.' Fitz opened his jaw so wide he looked like a bear yawning. 'She left a month ago. Apparently a hunting lodge wasn't quite the splendour she expected.'

'Hard to believe.'

'You didn't come all this way to ask about a governess.' Fitz rubbed a hand over his face. 'Come on, little brother. If you have questions, then hurry up and ask them. I'm tired.'

'All right.' Theo leaned back cautiously. 'Why did you want everyone to think you'd left the country?'

'You know that answer.'

'So I'd sort your mess out for you?'

'Exactly. You were always so good with responsibility. So much better than I ever could be.'

'That doesn't mean I enjoy it.'

'But you've done it, haven't you?' Fitz smirked. 'No doubt the whole estate is in perfect working order by now. I wouldn't even be surprised if you've finished the Chelsea scheme.'

'Actually I've sold the project on to another builder. You made a little money, not as much as you probably hoped, but it's saved you from ruin.'

'There you go!' Fitz spread his hands out. 'It's all worked out for the best.'

'Not for the people you ruined.'

'It was an investment. Some investments fail. They knew the risks.'

'A man of honour would still attempt to make some kind of restitution.'

'Restitution.' Fitz rolled his eyes scornfully. 'You know, father used to wonder how it was possible we were both his sons.'

'I remember.'

'Then what do you think he would have said to *that* little suggestion?'

'I don't care what he would have said about anything. If I was a disappointment to him, then he was more of one to me.' Theo put his hands on his knees and pushed himself back to his feet. 'Now I'm going to find a bed and get some rest. It's been a long journey and I want an early start back to London tomorrow. I suggest that you start packing.'

'Why?'

'Because I'm taking you back with me.'

'To be reunited with my loving wife?' Fitz laughed. 'How *is* Sabrina, by the way? Has she sent some message of love for me?'

'No. She doesn't know anything about me coming here today.'

'Ah.' Fitz knitted his hands together and stretched his arms out until the knuckles cracked. 'Then tell me, how many minutes do you think it would take for her to start throwing things if I went back?'

'I'll talk to her beforehand, prepare her for the surprise.'

'Very admirable. Unfortunately, you're ignoring one small point.' Fitz fixed him with a hard stare. 'I'm not going back.'

'Oh, yes, you are.' Theo felt the hairs on the back of his neck start to prickle. 'You can't just abandon your responsibilities.'

'I already have. As for Sabrina, she doesn't want me and I certainly don't want her.'

'You have a family together.'

*'Daughters.'*

'Yes, daughters.' Theo sat down again angrily. 'Two of them. One of whom wants to get married.'

'Really?' For the first time, his brother looked interested. 'Who to?'

'Viscount Everly.'

'Everly.' Fitz nodded thoughtfully. 'Fair enough. You may give them my blessing.'

'She needs a dowry.'

'You'll think of something.'

'Fitz.' Theo was aware of a growing sense of panic. This meeting wasn't going at all like he'd planned. 'Don't push me. If I have to knock you unconscious to get you back to London, then I'll do it.'

'And then what? Lock me in a room for the rest of my life?' Fitz's eyes narrowed. 'You can't force me to do anything and, if you try, I'll make a whole new mess for you to sort out. I'll make Sabrina's life a misery, too, just for fun.'

He folded his arms behind his head. 'I prefer it here. Life is so much easier. I have everything I need and no wife to berate me. So what I propose is this. You leave me alone and pay my bills and, in return, you can do whatever you like. I'll sign something to say that you have my permission. You can even sell some properties to make your restitution if you want, but not this one. Or the one in Aberdeenshire. I'm rather fond of that.'

'Fitz…' Theo swallowed, beginning to feel desperate. 'You can still reconcile with Sabrina. You've done it before.'

'Too many times.'

'It's not too late to have a son.'

'Ah.' A flicker of amusement appeared in his brother's eyes. 'That's what this is really about, isn't it? You just don't want to be the marquess. It's funny, most men would give their little finger to inherit a title and fortune, but not you. You hate the thought of ending up in the same position as our father.'

'This isn't a joke.' Theo reached down, grabbing his brother by his lapels and hauling him to his feet, red-hot anger scorching through him.

'The problem for you is that you can't escape it.' Fitz's florid countenance twisted into a sneer. 'Like it or not, you're the heir, the next in line.'

'It's still your responsibility for now.'

'But I don't want it any more. Which is why you'll be going back to London alone.'

Theo unclenched his fists, letting his brother fall back into his chair with an audible thud. He needed to get away before he did something violent. As much as he hated to admit it, Fitz was right. Even if he dragged him back to London, he could hardly make him behave properly. He couldn't stop him from making the lives of everyone around him a misery either.

He took a few steps away, wrenching his hands through his hair, disgust and rage warring inside him. Ten years ago, his father had forced him into the army and now his brother was forcing him into another position he didn't want.

If Fitz was determined not to face up to his responsibilities as the marquess, then *he* had to. To all intents and purposes, he was the new marquess already. He was trapped all over again, which meant that all of the plans he and Abigail had made were ruined. He should never have asked her to marry him.

Or…

He unclenched his fists, feeling his anger peak and

then wash away like a wave breaking on a shore. All of a sudden, the thought of returning to Salway House didn't strike him as so bad any more. He might not want the position itself, but the thought of returning to Abigail made his heart sing.

It occurred to him that as long as she was there, the rest was bearable. And maybe she was right, maybe he didn't have to let the past define his future. Maybe he didn't have to turn into his father. Maybe he could be a good husband despite his family, if he wanted it and worked hard enough.

There was no maybe about it. He would be. He would define his own future.

'As you wish.' He picked up his coat and strode to the door.

'Is that it?' Fitz sounded surprised.

'Yes.' He turned around briefly in the doorway. 'I'm going to bed. If that's your final answer then I'll arrange for a legal document to be drawn up and sent here for you to sign. Goodnight, brother, and goodbye.'


'Almost home, sir.' Kitchen stifled a yawn as he and Theo rode side by side through Mayfair. It was getting dark and after four consecutive days of riding, they were both exhausted.

'I suppose we are.' Theo nodded. '*Home*. That'll take some getting used to.'

'I have to admit, I'm a little disappointed, sir. I would like to have seen America.'

'You could still go.'

'And leave you?' Kitchen sounded offended. 'What kind of a second-in-command would I be if I did that?'

'The kind who's left the army?' Theo grinned.

'Speaking of seconds-in-command, however, there is one important job you could do for me.'

'Anything, sir, as long as it's not riding anywhere else for a day or two.'

'I'll be needing a best man in the morning. Unless you have any objections?'

There was a momentary pause followed by a suspicious-sounding sniff. 'I'd be honoured, sir. I'll gather the men, too, arrange a guard of honour.'

'It might be a little short notice, but—' Theo stopped mid-sentence as they turned the corner of the square, wide awake again suddenly. The lower left side of Salway House was a shell, the windows blown out and black. 'What the hell?'

'It looks like there's been a fire.'

*'Abigail?'* Theo charged ahead, throwing himself off his horse and racing through the front door.

'Theo?' It was Sabrina who answered. She was sitting, curiously enough, on her own on the staircase, a lamp by her side.

'Sabrina?' He crouched down beside her at once. 'What are you doing?'

'Waiting for you. We expected you back tonight.' She gave a wan smile. 'Don't worry, I'm not alone. Possett's around here somewhere and he insisted on leaving some footmen to guard the place, but I wanted to be here when you arrived.'

'What happened?'

'There was an accident. I dropped a candle.' She gestured towards his office. 'Through there.'

'Was anyone...?' He could hardly get the question out.

'No.'

'Thank goodness.' He hung his head in relief. 'Where's—?'

'How's Fitzwilliam?' she interrupted before he could finish the question.

He jerked his head back up. 'You know?'

'Florence overheard you the other morning.' Her lips twisted. 'Don't tell me, he refused to come back?'

'Yes. I got it all wrong. I thought that if I spoke to him...'

'Then he'd do the decent thing?' She smiled sadly. 'You really don't know him very well, do you?'

'I'm sorry, Sabrina.'

'I'm not. I'm only sorry for you. I know you never wanted to come back here.'

'That's true,' he acknowledged. 'Only, funnily enough, this place is growing on me.' He turned his head towards the blackened study. 'Or it *was*, anyway. We may need to redecorate.'

She didn't laugh. 'Because of Abigail?'

'Because of all of you.' He smiled and then tipped his head to one side. 'But especially Abigail. Where—?'

'Gone.' She looked nervous again suddenly. 'She's gone.'

'What?' He felt as if he'd just been punched in the throat. 'What do you mean?'

'I mean that I've ruined everything. She left just after the fire.'

'Why?'

'Because I called her a fortune hunter.'

'You *what*?'

She winced. 'And because I told her that Fitz wouldn't come back.'

'Oh, no.' He sank down on to the step below, his legs giving way beneath him. If Abigail had thought that Fitz wouldn't be returning, then she'd probably assumed he'd change his mind about marriage. Which he *had,* but only for half a second.

'I'm sorry.' Sabrina was weeping now. 'I apologised, but she said she had to leave before you came back. She didn't want you to feel obligated.'

'Obligated?' He swore under his breath. 'Did she say where she was going?'

'No.'

'What about the girls? Do they know?'

'No, I've already asked. Theo?' Sabrina looked up in alarm as he started up the staircase. 'You can't go up there. It might not be safe!'

'I won't be long!' He charged across the landing, then up the second staircase towards Abigail's bedroom. A quick rifle through her drawers and cupboards revealed that all her belongings were gone. All her clothes, all her trinkets, all her… His gaze fell onto the table beside the bed. She'd kept a small painting there, he remembered. Of a cottage. He'd only glimpsed it briefly, but from what he remembered there had been stone walls and a thatched roof… And she'd mentioned a cottage to him once, hadn't she? One evening when they'd been working late and he'd asked about her childhood. It had been something to do with her mother, some long-abandoned property she'd inherited, although foolishly, he hadn't asked her where it was. Why the hell hadn't he asked? And there was only one person he could think of who might know.

He only hoped she was still where he'd last seen her.

'Yes, she came to say goodbye.' Mrs Jessop folded her arms over her bosom. 'But that was three days ago.'

'Do you know where she's gone?' Theo stood on the

back doorstep of Abigail's old house on Cavendish Lane, trying not to sound as if he were begging.

'Yes.'

'Will you tell me?'

'I don't know.' The cook regarded him suspiciously. 'It seems to me she would have told you herself if she'd wanted you to know.'

'I know. It's a complicated story, but the long and short of it is that she thinks I don't want to marry her, but I do. Honestly, at this moment, it's just about the only thing I *do* want. Please, Mrs Jessop, I need to find her.'

'She swore off marriage.'

'So did I! That's what makes us perfect for each other!' He spread his hands out imploringly. 'Look, I think she's gone to her mother's old cottage, but I don't know where that is so if you could just give me a clue, I'll be indebted to you for ever.'

The cook pursed her lips, tapping her foot for a few seconds before unfolding her arms. 'All right, but I'm doing this for her, not you. It's in Cambridgeshire, a village called Market Compton.'

'Thank you!' He was tempted to kiss her.

'If she says yes, come back and tell me, and mind you take good care of her.'

'I will and I will, I promise!'


Oh, no… Abigail put down her bags and stared in horror at the swathe of greenery where her mother's cottage had once stood. In the almost eleven years since she'd last visited with her father, nature had taken over with a vengeance. Ivy and honeysuckle had crept over what were presumably walls and a roof, while the garden was an inhospitable jungle of tall grass, blackberry bushes and nettles.

To be fair, the building hadn't disappeared completely. She couldn't see a single window, let alone the front door, but if she peered very closely, she could just make out a few patches of brickwork. The structure was obviously still there, but any hope she'd had of it being remotely inhabitable had just evaporated. It wasn't entirely hopeless, but it was pretty close. Mr Adams had been right. She ought to have sold it. She still could.

She looked down at the key she'd optimistically removed from her bag, sucked in a deep breath and turned around, directing her steps back in the direction of the village. The coach had dropped her outside a respectable-looking hostelry, the Boar's Head.

Perhaps she could speak to the owner, let them know that she was prepared to sell the land at a reasonable price if anyone was interested. If she looked particularly pitiful, perhaps someone would take pity on her and buy it outright. In the meantime, she'd take a room for the night and decide what to do and where to go next. It was time to put on another brave face and move on.

The one thing she wouldn't do was think about everything and everyone she'd left behind.

## Chapter Twenty-Four

'That's it?' Theo stared at the mass of foliage and then back at the farmer who'd offered, for a fee, to show him the place. 'Are you certain?'

'Absolutely. No one's lived there for years, mind.'

'So nobody's come to reclaim it recently?'

'Not that I know of.'

'I see. Thank you.' He handed over a few coins. 'You've been very helpful, but I'll find my own way back.'

He waited until the man had gone before climbing over the garden wall and pushing his way through waist-high undergrowth—he got the impression it had once been a lawn—to the huge clump of greenery ahead.

If he hadn't been so gut-wrenchingly disappointed, he might have been impressed. There was a building there somewhere, but nature definitely had the upper hand. Slowly, he moved towards the centre of what presumably was a wall, towards the spot where there might plausibly be a door, and pushed his hand through the ivy. Yes, there was a handle, a ring he could turn, if only he had a knife to force his way through. Damn it.

He took a step back just as a family of sparrows burst indignantly out of the foliage. If Abigail had come here, she would doubtless have taken one look at the place and moved on. The house would take more money to restore than it was worth.

He was just turning away when he heard a woman's voice. Surprisingly, it seemed to be coming from inside the structure. Even more surprisingly, it was singing. His stomach clenched at the sound.

'Abigail?'

The singing stopped.

'Abigail?' he called out again, making his way around the edge of the building, pushing at the walls in case there was some secret way in. Had he imagined the voice? His mind didn't usually play tricks on him, but given everything that had happened over the past week, maybe it had decided to start.

'Abigail?' He tried a third time.

'Theo?' There was a scuffling sound from inside. This time he was sure of it.

'Where are you?'

'In the kitchen. Come around to the back.'

In the kitchen? He raced around the corner to find that some of the ivy had been cut away, recently by the look of it, to reveal another door. And there, standing in the doorway, smudges of dirt on her face and with her mouth open wide in amazement, was Abigail.

'Am I dreaming?' She shook her head, dislodging several stray twigs from her hair. 'What are you doing here?'

'Looking for you.' He didn't hesitate, closing the distance between them and pulling her into his arms. Half of his insides felt as if they were jumping for joy while the other half were slumping with relief.

'Why?' She stiffened, though she didn't push him away.

'Because…' All of a sudden, he didn't know where to start. 'Because you ran away without saying goodbye.' He took a step back though he kept hold of her, sliding his hands from her shoulders down to her wrists. 'Did you clear all this?' He nodded his head towards the door.

'Yes, but not by myself.' She blinked a few times, as if she still couldn't quite believe her eyes. 'I almost gave up on the place, but then I went to the local inn and told the innkeeper's wife my story. It turned out that she remembered my mother and her family so when I asked if I could borrow some gardening tools, she volunteered a few of the local men to come and help me get in. This took us a whole morning.'

'Is it safe?'

'Come in and see for yourself.' She turned and led the way down a long corridor, opening her arms wide as they entered a surprisingly clean and tidy-looking kitchen. Despite being overrun on the outside, the house appeared to have done a surprisingly good job of keeping nature out. There was a table and chairs, a sink, two workbenches and a stove in one corner.

'It's dark and smells a bit musty, I know, but I've cleaned up most of the dust and cobwebs. My next job is to clear the windows and let some air and light in.'

'I'm impressed. This is…' Theo paused, trying to find the right word.

'Other than not being able to light a fire, it's quite habitable.' She shrugged her shoulders. 'Well, reasonably habitable anyway.'

'Surely you're not actually living here?'

'Not yet. I took a room at the local inn.' She paused and folded her hands in front of her. 'So…how did you know where I was?'

'I remembered you mentioning your mother's cottage, so I went to ask your old cook.'

'Mrs Jessop told you?' She sounded surprised.

'Yes. She didn't want to at first, but then I explained how much I wanted to marry you and she gave me the name of the village.'

'Theo.' Her chin jerked at the mention of marriage. 'You didn't have to come. You don't have to marry me. Sabrina told me it was unlikely the marquess would come back with you.'

'She was right. He's staying in Wiltshire.'

'So that means you're trapped.'

'Yes.' He smiled. 'It does.'

'So I won't marry you. I know that it's not what you want and I'd rather have no husband than a reluctant one.'

'Actually, marrying you is exactly what I want.'

'What?'

His heart turned over at the look of bewilderment on her face. 'I want to marry you.'

'But…what about repeating a bad cycle?'

'I've no intention of doing that.'

'You don't?' Her voice wavered.

'No.'

'How do you know?'

'Because *I* decide how I act, isn't that what you said to me once?' He took a step towards her. 'And because I realised something when I saw my brother again, when he told me that he wasn't coming back. I had a few seconds of panic and then… I honestly didn't mind. I realised that my family aren't the same family I left behind ten years ago. Salway House isn't the same house either. It's different. I don't hate the idea of living there any more, especially now that Sabrina's taken care of the study for me. *I've* been the one keeping the past alive. Worse, I've been letting it damage my present.'

He reached out and put his hands around her waist. 'I'm not letting my father or brother dictate any more of my life. They can force me into the army and into acting as the marquess, but they can't force me to be alone. And I don't want to be alone any more.'

Her eyes flickered. 'How do I know you're not just saying all this to be honourable?'

'Because you can trust me.'

'I know.' She licked her lips. 'Even when I left, I knew that.'

'So?'

She didn't answer at first. Instead she twisted her face away, reaching a hand out to the table beside her and trailing her fingertips along the surface. 'You know, I almost gave up on this place. I was halfway back to the village before I realised something, too.'

'What?'

'That if I left then you wouldn't have any way to find me.' She turned back to him again, eyes bright. 'Deep down, I think I knew that you would.'

'Thank goodness for Mrs Jessop.'

'I knew that you'd think of her. If you wanted to, that is.' A guilty blush stole over her cheeks. 'So when I said goodbye, I told her only to tell you if it seemed like you really wanted to know.'

'I *really* wanted to know.'

'Otherwise I was going to restore this place. I was going to be properly independent.'

'You still can. Restore it, that is. We can even make our home here if you want. I don't care where I am any more, Abigail, as long as it's with you.'

'Really?' Her eyes welled with tears. 'You'd live here?'

'Why not? I'm not the marquess yet and now that most of Fitz's business affairs are in order, Sabrina can manage the household perfectly well without me. All I know is that I can't live without you.'

'Stop it.' She pressed the palms of her hands against her eyes. 'Or I'm going to cry and you hate that.'

'I could never hate anything about you.' He lifted a finger, brushing a stray tear from her cheek. 'But I do need you to tell me one thing.'

'That I love you?'

'Even more pertinent than that. Remember that Special Licence I gave you? Please tell me it wasn't in the study when it burnt down.'

'You mean *that* Special Licence?' She pointed towards a piece of paper propped up on one of the work benches. 'No, it wasn't in the study.'

There was curiosity, Abigail reflected, and then there was rampant, mind-consuming, body-weakening curiosity. By the time she and Theo returned to the coaching inn as man and wife, hers was a raging torrent.

'I can't believe we're actually married.' Her breath was coming in short bursts as they stumbled towards the bed in a tangle of limbs, shedding garments as they went. The room was so small that the floor was covered in a matter of seconds and it was only a few steps before they fell, sideways, on top of the bed, which gave a loud crack, followed by a splintering sound, sending them both rolling straight into the middle of an extremely saggy mattress.

'Oof!' Abigail's head promptly collided with Theo's shoulder. 'Maybe we would have been safer in the cottage.'

'I always thought that marriage was a dangerous business.' He grabbed hold of her waist, rolling her on to her back. 'Although thankfully this is the kind of danger I enjoy.' He grinned. 'And we're only just getting started.'

'Is that so?' She drew the tip of her tongue across her lips, looking up at him coyly. 'You know, you never fully explained "physical companionship". You haven't told me what to expect.'

'You're right.' His expression clouded over abruptly, his eyes filling with concern. 'I forgot. We should talk first.'

'I'm teasing.' She laughed. 'I got a pretty good idea in your study that first night and as for the rest...' she pushed her body up against his '... I think I can work it out.'

He groaned. 'I've thought about that night at least once every minute since.'

'So have I.'

'But I don't want to rush you either.' He touched his forehead to hers, his eyes bright with desire and love. 'If you're not ready, then I can wait, for as long as you need.'

'Can you?' She laid a hand against his chest, spreading her fingers out over the place where his heart was beating a heavy tattoo. 'Because I can't.'

'Neither can I.' He laughed. 'I mean, I could, but…'

'But you don't have to.' She smiled softly. 'I think that we've waited long enough.'

She stretched out beneath him, completely naked now, relishing the silky warmth of his body against hers. It was perfectly scandalous how *un*self-conscious she felt with him, how much she wanted him, too. His torso was hard and lean and muscular where hers was soft and yielding. She wanted to rub her hands over all of it, to touch and caress every contour, to reassure herself that he was real. Part of her mind could still hardly believe that he was really there, that he'd come after her, that he'd still wanted to marry her despite everything.

'So tell me…' his lips seemed to be everywhere all of a sudden, touching her throat before trailing downwards, across her collarbone and down over her breasts '…just how curious are you feeling?'

She rolled her eyes with a laugh. 'You're never going to let me forget that, are you?'

'Unlikely, but then I'm curious, too.'

'Oh, really?' She wrapped her arms around him, pulling him closer and burying her face in his shoulder.

'*Extremely* curious.' He winked and then shifted his weight off her suddenly, sliding to the end of the bed.

'Theo?' She lifted her head in surprise, worried that she'd done something wrong.

'I said I wanted to kiss every inch, remember?'

She lay back again, almost purring with pleasure as he lifted her leg and placed her foot down flat on the bed, then pressed his lips to her ankle, her calf, the back of her knee, the inside of her thigh… She gasped and tipped her head back, her breathing increasingly ragged as his lips moved against her, aware of an urgent, tightening sensation building low in her abdomen and spreading outwards until she felt wet and tense and filled with a nervous energy that she needed to do something with before she went crazy.

At last he held himself over her again, nudging her legs apart and settling himself between them.

'You know, I would never do anything to hurt you,' he murmured between kisses. 'But it might be painful at first.'

'I don't care.' She took his head in her hands, holding on to his gaze and her breath as he slid inside her, pushing slowly but firmly until their hips met and they were completely joined.

He was right. It *was* painful at first, but only for a few moments, until sensation took over and he began to move, gently and tenderly at first, then harder and faster, in a steady rhythm that made her skin tingle and her body throb with pulses of feeling. And then she started to move, too, mirroring every push and thrust, writhing and bucking beneath him, completely lost in sensation.

Panting, she wrapped her legs around his waist, drawing him closer and deeper until she had no idea where her body ended and his began, until finally another burst of sensation, stronger than all the others, erupted inside her, forcing her hips off the bed and wrenching a cry from her throat. Two seconds later and Theo cried out, too, finding his own release as she fell back on to the mattress and lay shuddering beneath him.

'Abigail?' He was shuddering, too, she realised, his lips pressed against her hair.

'Mmm?' She couldn't have formed a more coherent answer if she'd tried. She had the feeling that her mind was floating somewhere above the room while her body continued to shiver with aftershocks.

'Promise me you'll never run away again.'

'I promise,' she mumbled, smiling happily before tumbling headlong into sleep.


'Will you marry me?'

'Um…' Abigail lifted herself up on one elbow, peering down at Theo anxiously. She didn't know how long they'd been dozing, but suddenly she felt very awake. 'Should I worry about your memory?'

'I mean *again*.' He grinned. 'It's just occurred to me that a few people are going to be very upset if we return to London and present our marriage as a *fait accompli.*'

'You might be right.' She knitted her brows. 'I'm sure that Florence would like to be a bridesmaid.'

'Not to mention Kitchen. Not the bridesmaid part, obviously, but I asked him to be my best man. He said something about a guard of honour, too.'

'I wouldn't mind seeing that.' She draped her body over his with a contented sigh. 'So, colonel, how does it feel to be married?'

'Like I never want to leave this bed, but I should be the one asking you that question.' He lifted a hand, cradling her cheek. 'How do *you* feel?'

'A little sore, but…' she smiled wickedly '…quite satisfied.'

'I'm glad to hear it. I believe I may have previously underestimated the benefits of married life.'

'So what exactly are you suggesting about our wedding?'

'Well, it might sound odd…' he wrapped his other arm around her waist '…but it occurred to me that we could keep today to ourselves and have another, official wedding when we get back to London. Nobody else need ever know we're already married.'

'So today would be like a secret ceremony?' She rested her chin on his chest, a conspiratorial gleam in her eye. 'That sounds quite fitting. For us. Then we'll have two anniversaries every year.'

'I like the sound of that.' He started to smile and then froze. 'Actually, no, I don't.'

'What? Why not?'

'Because if we go back and *don't* tell them about today then they'll want to plan a big wedding and we won't be able to share a bed again for days. Weeks, possibly. I'll have to keep my hands off you.' He shook his head vehemently. 'Forget I spoke. It's not worth it.'

'Not necessarily. You know where my bedroom is.'

'Kitchen will scold me. He's surprisingly protective of you.'

'Really? I'm touched.' She pushed herself up again, drawing a circle on his chest with her fingertip. 'In that case, we'll just have to get all of our curiosity out of our systems now. There's no rush to get back to London, is there?'

'There's all the mess from the fire to sort out.' He looked thoughtful. 'Although Sabrina told me to take as long as I needed and she has Kitchen to help her.'

'There you go. We'll send a message saying that we're going to be slightly delayed...' She dipped her head, nuzzling her lips against his as her hands strayed lower. 'In the meantime, I have a few more questions for you...'

# Chapter Twenty-Five

Mayfair on a wet day was charming, Theo thought, slowing his horse to a sedate walk. The earlier rain had kept most of the crowds and carriages at home, but now that the weather had finally cleared, the air felt clean and fresh. Or was that just him? One month of marriage, albeit a secret one, and he felt like a whole new man, brimming with hope and positivity.

Perhaps that was why he'd woken up in the early hours, seized with a sudden and profound sense of purpose. He'd taken care not to wake Abigail, kissing her shoulder before sneaking out of her bedchamber and along to his own, dressing swiftly and then stealing out of the house to visit Armstrong and his family.

They were, he'd been thrilled to discover, happy and busy in their new coaching inn, providing him with a hearty breakfast, overwhelming him with congratulations about his 'upcoming' nuptials and sending him on his way feeling as though a weight had finally been lifted from his shoulders. It felt liberating to know that all of his former soldiers were settled, himself included, even if he and Abigail were the only ones who knew it.

\* \* \*

It was early afternoon by the time he arrived back at Salway House, whistling cheerfully to himself as he climbed up the front steps.

'Ah, there you are, Sir.' Possett opened the door, his expression ominous.

'Here I am,' he agreed, pulling off his gloves. 'Why? What's happened?'

'It's the marchioness, sir. I'm afraid that she's rather upset.'

'Again?' He felt his spirits plummet. 'Good grief. What has Fitz done now? Has there been another letter?'

'Ah…no, sir. It's not the marquess this time. It's… ah…you.'

'*Me?* What have I done?'

'You were supposed to be here an hour ago, sir.' Possett inclined his head in the direction of the drawing room. 'For the portrait sitting.'

'Oh, bloody hell.' Theo clamped a hand to his head and groaned. 'I completely forgot. Is she breaking things?'

'Thankfully, no. Miss Lemon managed to calm her down. It took a while, but they eventually decided to make a start without you.'

'Right.' He squared his shoulders. 'I suppose I'd better go and apologise'

'That would probably be wise, sir.'

'I don't suppose you'd summon a few footmen for my protection?'

'I would, sir, but they're all afraid of her ladyship.' Possett leaned closer. 'However, I did take the precaution of hiding all the pokers.'

'Good man. Wish me luck.' Theo tugged on the hem of his waistcoat, took a deep breath and then made his way reluctantly towards the drawing room, bracing himself for a torrent of recrimination. To his surprise, however, the scene that greeted him was one of calm tranquillity.

'So you've decided to show your face at last?' Sabrina looked at him contemptuously out of the corner of her eye, though she didn't move her head, maintaining her pose with a self-control he'd never imagined her capable of.

'Yes. I'm sorry. I—'

'Forgot? Evidently. Even after I reminded you at dinner last night? *Twice.*'

'Um…yes.'

'Just like a man. You're fortunate that Abigail was here.'

'Indeed.' He threw an inquisitive glance towards his so-called fiancée. She was sitting on a sofa between Sabrina and Evelyn, also unmoving, though if he wasn't mistaken, her lips were twitching with amusement.

'I apologise for my tardiness.' He turned to the artist, still confused by his reception. 'I hope that I haven't caused too much trouble?'

'Not at all, sir.' The artist shook his head quickly. 'We thought that you might stand behind the sofa.'

'Banished to the fringes, where you belong.' Sabrina went so far as to arch an eyebrow.

'Personally, I don't blame you for being late, uncle Theo.' Evelyn squirmed in her seat as he took up his position. '*I* would have been late if I could have. I never knew that having your portrait painted could be so boring. Parts of me are starting to go numb.'

'We're all bored and numb, darling.' Sabrina sounded as if she were speaking through gritted teeth. 'But since

I commissioned this family portrait as a *wedding present* for your uncle and Miss Lemon, we're all going to sit still and behave with decorum. Even if only one of them appreciates the gesture. Now stop slouching.'

'But why do we all need to be here at once? Can't Mr Hardacre just paint us one by one?'

'Yes, and he will, but he needs some preliminary sketches to work from. This won't be necessary most of the time.'

'Thank goodness.'

'It must be such a terrible trial to you, darling, having to spend so much time with a mother like me. Fortunately, you'll be free soon enough. There's only three months until your own wedding, after all.'

'But I don't want to be free of you.' Evelyn's voice sobered. 'I was only teasing. I *like* spending time with you.'

There was a moment of heavy silence. 'You do?'

'Yes. I know we argue a lot, but I love you. Very much. Very, very much actually. I know that *you'd* never run away and abandon me.'

'Well, I love you, too, and of course I wouldn't.'

'You see!' Evelyn turned her head towards Abigail, earning herself a disapproving squeak from the beleaguered artist. 'We'll manage perfectly well on our own once you and uncle Theo retreat to the country next week, although I still don't see why you have to leave so soon after your wedding.'

'Because we have a lot of work to do on the house. I doubt the roof will last another winter and there's a *lot* of gardening to be done, but don't worry, we'll come back and visit often.' Abigail smiled. 'Since we happen to love you, too.'

'Good gracious.' Sabrina gave a loud sniff. 'If we're not careful, people will start to think we're a real family.'

'But we *are* a real family, aren't we?' Florence, sitting on the floor with Lady's head in her lap, twisted around, her small face a picture of confusion.

'All done,' the artist announced, surrendering to the inevitable. 'I think that's all I need for today.'

'Thank you.' Theo inclined his head. 'I apologise for all the declarations of love.'

'Not at all. It made a refreshing change.'

'Speaking of declarations of love…' Abigail murmured, sliding her arms around Theo's waist as they made their way to the door. 'I haven't had one yet today.'

'Really? How remiss of me.' He bent to kiss the tip of her nose. 'I'm sure I thought it several times, but for the avoidance of doubt, I love you, too.'

'Honestly.' Sabrina dabbed at her eyes. 'You'll give Evelyn false ideas about marriage.'

'Actually, I've found their relationship very instructive.' Evelyn chirped up again. 'I tested William and I'm pleased to report that he passed.'

'Tested him? What on earth do you mean?'

'I told him my dowry was all gone.'

'Evelyn!'

'I said that uncle Theo needed the money to pay off father's debts after all and that he was free to break our engagement if he chose, but he *still* wanted to marry me. He said I was priceless.' She smiled dreamily. 'I'm calling it the Lemon test.'

'That's not a bad idea.' Theo nodded approvingly. 'Well done, Evelyn.'

'*Please* tell me you've told him the truth now?'

'Oh, yes. He was very relieved.'

'I'm beginning to think that you may be a bad influence, *Miss* Lemon.' Sabrina commented on her way through the door, a knowing smile on her face.

'Why did she say "Miss" like that?' Abigail took hold of Theo's arm, drawing him back. 'Does she know the truth about us?'

'It's possible. She's been talking to Kitchen a lot recently.'

'How does Kitchen know?'

'Kitchen knows everything. Especially when I'm not telling him something.'

'I didn't think he and Sabrina were so close.'

'They weren't, only it seems they struck up an alliance of sorts dealing with the aftermath of the fire. I believe he may have found himself a new commanding officer now that he's decided I don't need him any more.' Theo chuckled. 'It's funny, but all that time I spent making sure my men were settled, I had no idea he was doing the same thing for me.'

'So now he can let you go?' Abigail beamed. 'I'm honoured he trusts me so much.'

'It's not official, but I'm pretty sure he'll be staying in London when we leave. And woe betide anyone who snubs Sabrina from now on.' He rubbed his nose against hers. 'So tell me, how exactly did you calm her down earlier?'

'Oh, I just agreed with everything she said, that all men are irresponsible and feckless and can't be trusted.'

'I see.' He clenched his brow. 'Now, I don't know whether to thank you or not.'

'In fact, I agreed so vehemently that she grew quite concerned about causing a rift between us. And since

she's rather fond of you, she calmed down considerably.'
She lifted a shoulder. 'You're welcome.'

'Very devious.' He moved his lips towards her ear.
'So, will it be your bedroom or mine tonight, *Miss*
Lemon? Or the study again?'

'The fireside rug *was* surprisingly comfortable, but
we'd better make it my room, especially if Sabrina's
suspicious.'

'One more week and we won't have to resort to sub-
terfuge any more. We can be completely alone.'

'In our run-down, close-to-collapse, filthy old cottage?'

'Yes, but most importantly, alone. Except for Lady, of
course, provided that she travels by carriage and doesn't
have to do anything except sleep when we get there.'

'I think we can manage that. We'll make a lovely
home for her. If we can save an estate from collapse
then we can make an overgrown cottage look beautiful again. We make a good team, after all.'

'The best.'

'Who would have thought it?' She tipped her head
against his shoulder. 'Remember that first day I came
here? Jilted, dripping wet and penniless?'

'While I was overworked and depressed?'

'And just look at us now.'

'Just look at us now,' he echoed. 'I wouldn't have it
any other way.'

# *Epilogue*

'What on earth are you doing?' Abigail stood in the doorway of the second guest bedroom, watching her husband wave his hands wildly over his head. After a year of marriage, her stomach still quivered at the sight of him, even now when he appeared to be fighting a losing battle with thin air.

'Shut the door! He's got in again!' Theo ducked as a blur of grey feathers swept past him, accompanied by the sound of flapping wings.

'Who? Gerald?' She looked up to the rafters.

'I really wish you hadn't given the little wretch a name.'

'He's not a wretch.' She shifted her hands to her hips disapprovingly. 'You have to look at the situation from his point of view. He still thinks of this as his home. He probably lived here all his life until we came along with a new roof and new windows and fresh paint. Now he doesn't know where he belongs any more.'

'I can tell him where he belongs.' Theo muttered darkly. 'Every time I open the window as much as a crack, he finds a way in and starts nesting. What if he lays eggs? Gerald could be Geraldine. How do you tell with pigeons? Then we'll never be rid of him. Or her.'

'Maybe I should fetch some bread? Then we could throw it out of the window and see if he follows?'

'Anything's worth a try.'

'Or maybe I could make a model of an eagle? Out of pottery perhaps? Or I could sew something?' She tapped a finger against her chin thoughtfully. 'The shape might be enough to scare him away.'

'That'll take too long. What we need is a cat.'

'That's just cruel! You can't hurt him. Besides, what would Lady say?'

*'Go away, cat, I'm sleeping?'*

'Well, yes, probably, but she'd also be heartbroken if you brought another animal into the house. She'd think that you'd replaced her in your affections.'

'If she wants affection, she ought to be in here behaving like a real dog, chasing and biting and dripping blood from her fangs.' He leapt towards the window suddenly, slamming it shut as Gerald whooshed through. 'I don't believe it, he's gone of his own free will.'

'I'm not surprised after all those threats.' She went to stand beside him. 'Poor Gerald.'

'Poor Gerald, nothing. He hasn't even gone far. Look.' He pointed at a nearby tree. 'There he is, waiting and plotting.'

'You know, I'm not entirely sure the countryside is good for you.' Abigail turned around, perching on the window seat. 'When a grown man has a pigeon for an arch enemy, maybe life just isn't exciting enough.'

'Oh, I wouldn't say that.' Theo placed a hand on either side of her, leaning forward to press his lips against the side of her neck and then nuzzle her earlobe with his teeth. 'Some parts of country life are very exciting. There are things we can do in the garden here that we'd never get away with in London.'

'Well, that's true, although if you recall, I got stung by a nettle last time. In a particularly delicate area, as I recall.'

'And didn't I kiss it better?' He grinned. 'Which is something I'm more than happy to do again, by the way.'

'Maybe later. Right now, I have news. A letter from Evelyn.'

'Oh, no.' He held his hands up again. 'I refuse to hear another word about the many virtues of Viscount Everly. Some details should be kept private.' He leaned in again, kissing her shoulder this time. 'Can't it wait an hour or two? Maybe three?'

'She's having a baby.'

'Ah.' He went very still.

'What's the matter? It's good news.'

'Yes.' His expression sobered. 'It is and I'm happy for her. I just…'

'Don't want me to be upset?' She placed a hand on her flat stomach and smiled. 'I'm not. If it happens for us, then it happens, but if it doesn't then I'm still a very lucky, and happy, woman. I'm thrilled for Evelyn, truly.'

'Then so am I.' He arched an eyebrow. 'I wonder how Sabrina feels about being a grandmother?'

'I'm sure she's full of helpful advice they can argue about.' Abigail laughed. 'We'd better go and visit soon.'

'Again? It's only been a few weeks.'

'It's been three months and if we leave it much longer, Kitchen will be coming out here to check on you. He only trusts me so far.'

'One year alone with my wife.' Theo adopted a hang-dog expression. 'Is that too much to ask? Just one year of complete solitude with no interruptions?'

'We have plenty of time alone together.' Abigail pushed herself up off the window seat. 'But I also have an eagle to make.'

'Can I at least gaze lovingly at you while you do it?'

'While there's still the bottom half of the garden to clear?'

'There's a reason I keep putting that off.' He followed her to the door. 'The entire Chelsea project was nothing compared to this cottage.'

'But it's the prettiest cottage in the county, so everyone keeps telling me.'

'It does look rather good, I admit.'

'Besides, the honeymoon can't last for ever, can it?' She stepped out on to the landing. 'We have to settle down into an old married couple some time.'

'That's defeatist talk.'

'You're right.' She stopped at the top of the staircase. 'Oh, very well, one hour, but after that…'

'After that, back to work.' He grabbed her hand enthusiastically, pulling her towards the front of the house and their bedroom. 'Do you know what I've always admired the most about you?'

'I have no idea.' She ran after him, laughing.

'Your work ethic!'

\* \* \* \* \*

*If you enjoyed this story, be sure to read
Jenni Fletcher's Regency Belles of Bath miniseries*

An Unconventional Countess
Unexpectedly Wed to the Officer
The Duke's Runaway Bride
The Shopgirl's Forbidden Love

The Highlander's Tactical Marriage
in The Highland Alliances
Snow Kissed Proposals
"The Christmas Runaway"
A Marriage Made in Secret

# Get 3 FREE REWARDS!
## We'll send you 2 FREE Books plus a FREE Mystery Gift.

**FREE**
Value Over
**$20**

Both the **Harlequin®** **Historical** and **Harlequin®** **Romance** series feature
compelling novels filled with emotion and simmering romance.

# HARLEQUIN
## PLUS

Try the best multimedia subscription service for romance readers like you!

---

## Read, Watch and Play.

Experience the easiest way to get the romance content you crave.

Start your **FREE TRIAL** at
www.harlequinplus.com/freetrial.